Outstanding praise for Genie Davis and
The Model Man

"A terrific writer with a wonderfully wry sense of humor and a visual style." —Bestselling author Jane Heller

"Marvelously conceived and finely executed . . . from a very talented new author. Genie Davis has crafted wonderful characters who come alive and entice the reader into their story immediately." —*Affaire de Coeur*

"A delightful story of secrets, murder and love [from] a promising author." —*Romantic Times*

"Truly a find . . . well-crafted [and] as entertaining as one of Stephen J. Cannell's television shows." —*Booklist*

"One fine writer who puts you through an emotional wringer . . . wow." —The Belles and Beaux of Romance (on *Dreamtown*)

"The intense underlying emotions of two people so in tune with each other's bodies was beautiful to imagine . . . I will definitely place Nikki Alton on my must-have list. She is a sure thing with a screaming orgasm on top!" —*Fallen Angels Reviews* on "Rodeo Man" in *The Cowboy* (Genie Davis writing as Nikki Alton)

Also by the Author

The Model Man

"Rodeo Man" in *The Cowboy*
(Genie Davis writing as Nikki Alton)

To my children

Chapter One

"L.A. is melting," I said, as I shook the water out of my hair.

In spite of the rain and taking the bus north up the coast from my Playa Vista duplex to the edge of Santa Monica, I was only about fifteen minutes late for my shift as afternoon on-air personality, otherwise known as a DJ, at KCAS-FM, indie rock 101.3.

Still, Theodore the Underground Rock Explorer was pretty irritated about covering for me.

"Jessie, you're late at least twice a week. Whether it's been raining in apocalyptic quantities or not."

I ignored him. He was in a bad mood. Theo was almost always in a bad mood because his wife was riding with an all-chicks motorcycle club instead of working, and his teenage son had two silver rings in both eyebrows and a D- in History and French.

I rummaged through a stack of CDs on a shelf labeled appropriately JESSIE'S SHELF. It didn't mean that the other jocks couldn't take the stuff on my shelf and play it, it just meant they had to put it back on the shelf when they were done, which of course they hardly ever did.

I found "MacArthur Park" easily enough. Nobody else but me would play that. About two weeks ago, when the rains first started, I spun the tune Internet voters tabbed "worst song ever" for a one-time joke that morphed into a listener-requested habit. As the heaviest rainfall in L.A. since 1897 deluged down, if I didn't play it first thing, people called me up and yelled at me.

I leaned over Theo and plopped the CD in the player. Sometimes I played the Donna Summer disco version, but today it was Richard Harris warbling about MacArthur Park melting, conjuring up images of tie-dyed shirts and beaded headbands.

Theo got up and handed me his headphones. "This stupid song is just one sign of it."

"The apocalypse?" I asked.

"Turning the big 3-0. You're getting more and more maudlin. You need a steady relationship, improve your mood."

"Having a steady relationship hasn't done that much for yours," I countered.

Theodore looked at me closely. I made an effort to smooth my normally straight light brown hair, which was, due to the rain, all frizzed up now like I was doing an imitation of Bette Midler imitating Janis Joplin in *The Rose*.

"Still seeing that drummer?" Theo asked.

"He played guitar," I said. "Drummer was two years ago." Followed by six months of abject celibacy, a record I feared I was now destined to top.

"Played guitar, past tense?"

I kept my eyes, hazel, but sometimes in romantic moments, described as "golden," averted from Theo's inquisitive gaze. I really should learn not to tell anybody I knew that I ever dated anybody.

Richard Harris was building to a raging musical crescendo. ". . . Someone left the cake out in the rain . . . all the sweet, green icing flowing down . . ."

Of course it wasn't cake icing, it was mud and water oozing away this February, causing road closures, collapsed roofs, cracked foundations, and flooding down the banks of the Hollywood Hills and the Pacific Palisades in terrible waves no surfer would want to ride. Compared to problems like that, breaking up with a guy I hadn't so much as kissed since Thanksgiving seemed pretty trivial.

My gaze finally met Theo's. "Yeah," I admitted, "I'm officially single again."

Theo patted my shoulder. "You ought to front a band. Call it the Ex's," Theo said. "Am I right? There was lead singer guy, that was before you came to work here, but you were still mooning over him when you started. There was flute guy, then drummer guy, and now guitar guy. You need to hook up with a bass player next, and a roadie, and you'll be all set."

I laughed as appreciatively as I could. Theo circumvented the bucket our roof was steadily leaking into and left me alone in the sound booth.

It was just a week ago that the guitar guy, otherwise known as Jack, and I were standing out in the rain by my car that wouldn't start, and I'd still, more or less, emphasis on less, considered us a couple.

Jack was holding the umbrella. He wasn't even wet, not one little bit. The water was beading up on his nicely rainproofed cowboy boots, his jeans weren't damp, his stylish fur-trimmed ski parka was zipped up to his neck. The rain was soaking my leather jacket, never intended as a raincoat, and running down inside my T-shirt and splashing on my jeans.

To be fair, he'd started out holding the umbrella over me, while we tried to figure out what was wrong with my car—wires just damp, battery dead, alternator shot, whatever. I didn't have a clue, and even though it was his idea to look under the hood, it turned out he didn't either.

It was then that he blurted out, "Jessie, I really care about you."

And I, stupid sap that I was, looked up at him under the big black umbrella, looked into his dewy blue eyes, at the smooth, sunken cheekbones framed by long blond hair, and I just pushed aside all the doubts I'd been having while he was off touring with his band the last four months.

He was so artistic and haunted and had a beautiful way of playing a twelve-string guitar while looking into my eyes, the same soulful way he was doing then. I'd almost forgotten, that was all, because we'd been apart so long, mostly just leaving voice mail messages on each other's cell phones every night.

I said, "I know. I care about you, too—and—"

"Wait." His fingers were on my arm, pressing firm enough to silence me.

"I care about you *but.*" His voice got all choked up. "I met this girl the other night, at the bar I was playing up in SLO—look, I was attracted, okay? Really, really attracted. And it hit me, it hit me hard you don't feel like that, like I felt, if you love somebody. So even though I still care, I just don't think I love you. Anymore I mean."

That was when I stepped out from under the umbrella.

"Jessie, please—" He slammed the hood of my car and trailed me down the street to the bus stop.

I was only having doubts about this guy? I should've dumped him before he went off on tour with his completely unoriginal eighties tribute bar band, and before I'd lent him five hundred bucks that I realized then I would never see again.

"Come on. Don't go off all mad. I'm just trying to be honest here," he pleaded.

The bus pulled up with a belch and, oh so satisfyingly, one tire skidded in the overflowing gutter and there went Jack's neatly pressed jeans. Not just wet, but muddy, too. There was even a gum wrapper clinging to his drenched thighs.

I laughed. I actually laughed. Every once in a while, the universe slipped into balance. Just a little bit, anyway.

Today, I allowed myself one last sigh for what might've been but probably never was, and then I turned to the task of drawing up my typically eclectic playlist of alt-country, jazz, blues, whatever constitutes rock these days, and old Joni Mitchell.

We don't follow a set playlist at KCAS, we play what we like, not something somebody pays us to like. This kind of free choice is just about unheard of anymore in a major market.

People who don't know me very well and hear what I do for a living always tell me what a dream job I have. Some people who don't know me at *all* even tell me what a dream life I have.

The truth is, even when my third-hand car is running, the studio roof isn't leaking, the room I'm working in doesn't smell like dirty socks because of the mildewed carpet, and I think I'm in love with a guy because a year ago he put my name in a song he wrote, I don't have a dream life. And being a disc jockey, even working a good gig like this one, isn't the dream job everybody thinks it is.

Out of 158 FM stations in the greater Los Angeles basin, we are number 156 in market share. At any moment, the corporation that owns us could turn us into an automated easy-listening station, or a syndicated all talk, as they've threatened off and on for as long as I've worked here.

Even if we continue to be our independent selves, there's still no job security, because with everybody thinking being a DJ is all fun, all the time, a dream job, there's a million people in line waiting to take your job—people who know the names of bands you haven't even heard of yet, and can also make smart-ass jokes into a microphone and push a CD into a player or a tape into a tape deck just as well as you can.

Also, as is true of many dream jobs, unless you make it to the very top of the dream job heap, it doesn't pay very well. I've made more money waitressing and as a scheduler at a recording studio, which was where I met the record producer who was also the part-time program director here at KCAS at the time. He told me I not only had beautiful eyes and incredibly long legs, but that I had such a great, sexy voice, I should be on the radio. I was hoping he meant my self-produced garage band record should be on the radio, but he meant I should come to work as a jock. We only went on two depressingly chaste dates, then he left and got a better paying job as a computer programmer, but I've been at the station four years.

Some people, mainly my cousins in Cleveland with the stock brokerage, are always asking me why

I don't get a real job, or have a real relationship.
Like it's that easy.

Right, I turned thirty, so now I need to settle
down. Okay, let me just go on down to the nearest
7-Eleven and pick up a package of chips, a Coca-
Cola Slurpee, a well-paying, normal job with a
future, a husband, and oh yeah, a six-pack of kids
to go.

It's not that easy, of course, and anyway maybe I'm
still too restless to settle down, or give up, whatever
you want to call it. I'm still drawn, I guess, to the romance of lost causes, whether it's the career I never
really had as a writer and performer of love songs
whose melodies and rhythm elude genre so well no
one knows what market niche I'd fit into—so far that
niche is "un-signable"—or the lost cause of love with
other semi-unemployed, self-involved musicians.

But now, as I turned on the mike, I got the same
little thrill I always did seeing the "ON AIR" light
snap on.

I started my usual rap. "You're listening to KCAS,
101.3 FM *Lost* Angeles, and you're tuned into Jessie
on this rainy afternoon."

And once again, the universe slipped into balance. Maybe this job isn't exactly a hotshot musical career, and it doesn't offer a solid future like
stockbroking, and there're no guarantees when it
comes to love, but sometimes you just have to roll
with it, rock and roll with it, and trust everything
will turn out all right anyway, in the end.

My bus inched its way through rush-hour traffic
down Santa Monica Boulevard, past store windows
filled with ludicrously overpriced shoes and street

people outside those windows holding plastic garbage bags over their heads. It swung down Lincoln where the botanicas and bodegas sit side by side with yoga salons and oxygen bars. It pulled to the curb to switch drivers where Lincoln morphs into Sepulveda Boulevard at the airport. The jets came in low through the clouds, zipping over the ethereal, pastel columns of glowing light that serve as a gateway to LAX, and look like a discarded digitalization from the last *Star Wars* prequel.

At last Sepulveda's office towers and industrial parks disappeared and the street renamed itself again, this time as Pacific Coast Highway, affording steep downhill views of the ocean and a confluence of dry cleaners and fast-food restaurants and up-market take-out spots and surf shops through the rain-lashed windows. And then we were in Playa Vista and just down the street from my friend Lisa's club, The Sea Shack, its lights already blazing through the rainy twilight.

Getting off the bus, I could hear TONIGHT'S BAND—THE BEACH BRAHS, according to the marquee over the door, faintly warming up, and I felt like I was coming home.

And of course in a way, I was. I always just walk in after work to hear some music, drink some white jasmine tea. I pore over talent tapes and help her with bookings, emcee many weekends, and yeah, sometimes I get up on stage myself, the unscheduled warm-up act.

In other words, The Shack, like Lisa herself, is an important part of my life. A home away from my nearby apartment with its view of the electric power plant blocking the ocean; one of the last ungentrified apartments on one of the last ungentrified

streets in the South Bay, the soft sand crescent of
Santa Monica Bay south of the International Airport and north of the Port of Los Angeles that includes Playa Vista.

I opened the scarred wooden door to The Shack,
and slipped inside. Once just a big old freestanding
garage that housed a fleet of taxicabs, it now had
rows of theater-style seats against two walls near the
stage, mismatched tables from various auctions and
garage sales in the middle of the room, a boxy stage
at one end, signed band posters and framed photo-
graphs from a variety of eras on the walls, and a long,
scarred bar against the back wall opposite the stage.

"Hey," I called out. Lisa was rifling distractedly
through a stack of papers at a table in the back.

"Hey there," she said. I slipped into a chair across
from her and only then did she stop the rifling and
look up at me.

When she did, despite the dim light, I could tell
she'd been crying.

I took her hand and squeezed it. "What's wrong?"
I asked.

Lisa is only three years older than me but thirty
times wiser, a former nurse who cared first for her
ailing father who founded this club, and then her
husband, after a construction accident. She weath-
ered their infirmities and their passing from this
mortal coil, and through it all, kept a smile on her
face for her friends. Some of the musicians who
played the club regularly called her Mona Lisa,
some Mama Lisa. She was nurturing and slightly
mysterious at the same time.

But naturally, sometimes she needed comforting too, and even if I publicly played the part of the
zany kid sister she never had, as well as the host of

open-mike night, I usually gave as good as I got on the comfort and nurture scale. We were very different people, sure, but we both really, genuinely cared about and took care of each other.

"Come on. Tell me what's wrong," I said, releasing her hand.

"I dunno." Lisa swiped at her eyes. "Maybe this whole club thing, maybe it's not such a good idea anymore." Her voice grew thick.

I looked at her carefully. She loved the club.

"Why would you say something like that?" I asked.

"They're going to close me down anyway," she said very quietly. "Sooner or later. Sooner, now."

"What? Who's gonna do that?"

"The city. And I just finished fixing it up. The new bathroom. The handicapped ramp I was supposed to provide. New electrical outlets up to the fire code. Reinforced beams, up to the earthquake code. I've complied with everything the city asked for. I guess I should've seen this coming. First one thing, then another, but I really thought I was home free now. Instead, they're gonna take it away."

"Whoa, whoa, whoa," I said. "Why would the city try to close you down?"

She still wasn't listening. "Took away our liquor license when Dad died. And yet I still get complaints that there's drunks peeing in the bushes. They're certainly not drinking here."

"Coffee can go right through you," I tried to joke, but Lisa was having none of it.

She cut me off with a wave of her hand. "I've got acoustic tile all around this place, and they still say when the door opens, people coming and going, the tile doesn't protect the public."

"Protect them from what?"

"From me!" Lisa said. She drummed her fingers on the table. "They don't want me here anymore. This has always been a mixed residential-commercial neighborhood. And now they're saying this district is going to be rezoned for residential only."

"Going to be?"

"I know it's a political bag job, but so what? Once it's considered, it's voted upon by the council. It's a quirk in the system, it doesn't go to public vote. If the council unanimously concurs on rezoning, the mayor just has to approve. And trust me, he's dying to approve."

"Why?"

"Because real-estate values will be higher. In comparison to all the new town homes they can jam in around here, along with the bloated McMansions, this club and the other mom-and-pop businesses in this neighborhood, are not considered an asset to the community despite their sales tax revenues."

"Not an asset! Why, this club, it's the best, it's the only live music venue in the entire South Bay." I sounded just like the radio commercial I sometimes ran for her place.

"My dad started in 1946. I figured we'd be here a hundred years for sure, that this place would belong to my grandchildren, if I ever have them. But that'll never happen. The rezoning was supposed to come to a vote this week! I'm doomed, Jessie."

"Don't talk like that."

"It's too hard. Everything's just been delayed a couple of months because of what happened, that's all."

"Delayed? By what? What else happened?"

Lisa sighed. She twisted her curly red hair in her fingers.

"Do you know anything about Playa Vista politics?" she asked me.

"Sure. We're an incorporated town, not a part of the city of Los Angeles. We have our own mayor, Haldon, no Hayden, that's right. He came to my door last year and gave me a key ring, which I used for the apartment key I gave to Jack." I stopped short, realizing that son of a bitch didn't give me back my key, but I decided this wasn't the time to discuss it.

"Are you aware there are three members of the city council representing each district in town, and they get voted into office, too?"

"Sure. Kind of. I've seen pictures in the paper. All three of them look like they are a hundred years old."

"Not anymore."

"Why? They had collagen injections?"

"No." Lisa sighed again.

I have a kitten that sighs when you won't play with him or you tell him he cannot swing on the curtains and rip them down, and you clap your hands like you mean it. He gets a pitiful put-upon look in his eyes, very similar to the look Lisa had in hers.

"*Our* district's councilman resigned this past weekend. He actually supported me. He thought the club provided a community service, an alternative to, and I quote, 'alcohol-soaked venues and strip clubs.'"

"Wow, that's high praise indeed," I said.

"But now he's gone. Supposedly for 'family health reasons.' And the two councilmen still seated are most decidedly not in favor of me keeping this club.

Their supporters' money is in housing development. Not this place. And you just can't fight city hall. Haven't you heard that expression?"

"Look," I said. "You *can* fight this. We can. Together. Trust me."

She looked at me as if she was longing to trust somebody, anyway. So I plunged on. "After all, you've got time on your side now. They had to put off the vote because—"

I wasn't sure why. I really didn't know anything about local politics. I was just trying to be plucky and supportive.

"Because you have to have an unanimous vote of all *three* councilmen and then the approval of the mayor to change zoning in this town. So before they can vote, we have to hold a special election to elect a new councilman from our district."

"Well, see! So all you need is a third guy to come in and not agree with the other two."

"That won't happen. The push is on for redevelopment. If whoever gets elected wants to get anything done, even if he or she loves the club, even if he comes here every night of the week, he'll give in on this."

"I wouldn't give in," I said.

"You're not running for city council," Lisa said.

A dim little lightbulb went off in my head. "I could."

Lisa blinked at me. "*You'd* run for city council?"

"How hard can it be? I talk for a living anyway. That's all most politicians do—they talk."

"But why would you even want to run?"

"To help you out."

"I'm a lost cause, sweetie."

"Look at my life. I like lost causes. I liked Jack,

for example, and he was a lost cause for months now. Maybe forever. So maybe I ought to take on such a cause with at least the potential for a positive outcome."

Lisa laughed. It wasn't that funny what I said, but in fact she couldn't stop laughing, and then she was crying. And then I started to cry too. We reached across the table and hugged each other and wiped our eyes, like we'd accomplished something. Then we both sighed, like maybe we hadn't.

"Maybe you *should* run, Jessie. And not just for me, either. Think about it. What's the real difference between being a DJ and a politician?"

"One has integrity," I suggested.

"The politician makes more money," Lisa said.

"How much money does a city councilman—or woman—make?" I asked. Making money at something I was looking at as a goodwill gesture had never occurred to me. Of course running for city council in the first place had only occurred to me five minutes earlier.

"In this town, city council members make thirty-three thousand dollars a year. It's the highest-paid city council salary for a town under fifty thousand residents in California."

"Why do they pay so well?"

"My dad said our town was rife with politicians lining their own pockets."

"Wow," I said. "I might as well take advantage of that."

Thirty-three thousand? I made twenty at the station, and the only graft I ever got now was free CDs.

Suddenly becoming a city council member seemed like not just an "Okay, I'll jump in and try to do the right thing to help my friend" kind of idea, but a really lucrative idea, too.

"I'm your councilwoman," I decided.

"Well, first you have to get elected," Lisa reminded me.

"Oh, right," I said. My euphoria was short-lived. I'd kind of forgotten that part. "I guess I'll need signs. And posters and stuff. Maybe even key rings?"

"I'll hook you up with the company that does the club's promotions."

"I guess I have to pay for that stuff, too, huh?" I said with some trepidation.

"We can do a couple of fund-raisers right here to raise your money! How many other city council candidates have a club at their disposal?"

"Um. How many other candidates are there?" I asked.

Like the getting-elected part, and the needing-money-to-buy-stuff-that-would-help-me-get-elected part, I'd sort of forgotten about the competition part.

"Seven. But only one or two of them have big bucks and political experience."

"Ah," I said. That sounded like one or two too many to me, but I kept my mouth shut.

"I have a fantastic e-mailing list," Lisa said. "I bet we can pack this place. The Dublin Five is the biggest draw, and they're playing Thursday and Friday already. We'll get everything locked in for Friday night. Oh. You need to open a bank account."

"I have one—" I managed.

"For the campaign, silly. You can't comingle personal funds with donations!"

"Of course not," I agreed. Perish that thought.

Lisa bubbled on about who owed her favors, and

whether I could or should perform at my own fund-raiser, and how we should form a committee to elect Jessie Adams. I joined in with the bright chatter I'd gotten started. I was pleased to see how up and confident Lisa seemed all of a sudden, how the whole mess with the city trying to close her down dissipated, and I was glad it was because of me. But I had to admit a little frisson of doubt was creeping in as to whether I could deliver the kind of salvation I was promising.

I'd had this feeling before, although kind of in reverse, when it struck me that maybe the guys who said how much they adored me didn't really adore me, like Jack who sure was good about leaving phone messages that concluded with "You're the best. I love you to pieces." Yeah, right.

Maybe I was as full of it as Jack was. *I'll help you save your club, Lisa, yes I will. I'll just get elected to city council!* What if I talked well and got key rings to hand out and everything and I still didn't win?

But I decided there was no point in letting Lisa down now. Not tonight, anyway. All the same, I was also beginning to understand how it was that record company execs would tell you they couldn't wait to work with you, and then next day they were "thinking it over," and then you never heard from them again.

But since I wasn't a heartless recording industry executive or a boyfriend about to head for the Hollywood Hills, and since I actually cared about Lisa, I was stuck.

If I'd wanted to think my candidacy over, I guess I should've already thought.

Chapter Two

I woke up the next morning with a vague sense of apprehension, like now I'd done it, all right. For a moment I forgot exactly what it was that I had done, besides lose my lousy nonrelationship with Jack. But then I remembered. I had committed myself to be a candidate for political office.

In another time and place, feeling similarly insecure about my purpose in life, I suppose I might've joined a convent or checked myself into a mental hospital. Surely politics beat those two options.

I got out of bed with great reluctance and headed down the hall and across my living room to my little boxcar kitchen. I fed my cats. I stared in my empty refrigerator. I scooped out the litter box.

I opened the kitchen window just a crack. I could smell the rain, the ocean's algal bloom red tide fishy smell, and bacon and eggs wafting up from Ruby's Diner down in the harbor. I had nothing that resembled food in my apartment, other than cat food, and I wasn't that desperate. Maybe you could get some sustenance from just the smell of breakfast.

At the moment it wasn't raining, although the

rain still dripped like tears off the eaves of my postage-stamp-size front porch and smeared the window. My partial harbor view revealed a chilly gray sea, a faint layer of fog over it, boats and anemic-looking palms rocking fiercely in a stiff wind.

A lot of people think of L.A. as made up of weirdly beautiful red and purple flowers blooming year-round, palms swaying gently in a dazzle of sunlight against a backdrop of warm blue sea until twilight, of course, when the sunsets are spectacular splashes of balmy color. At least that's what I thought about L.A. when I lived in Boston going to music school and couldn't wait to move to the left coast.

Most people who actually *live* in L.A. realize that's how it is in Hawaii. I want to move there someday. I hope when I get there I don't find out that what most people in L.A. think Hawaii is like is really, say what Tahiti is like, and I find myself chasing around in search of a tropical paradise that doesn't even exist.

Anyway, I'd have to chase paradise another day. Today, I had a campaign to begin.

"Maybe this whole election thing will change my life," I said out loud.

My cats were sitting near the window and watching raindrops, but when I spoke, they both turned and looked at me, like, was I talking to them?

My old cat, Sally, a seventeen-year-old matted black Persian with major incontinence issues, jumped down onto the floor and yowled like you'd expect one of the witches' cats in *Macbeth* to yowl, and marked my feet; the kitten, Squeak, the one who sighs like Lisa was sighing last night, at least when he isn't squeaking, chased a Cheerio around on the floor. I should be a better housekeeper, but then the kitten wouldn't have nearly as much fun.

I should be lots of things—a respected musician, a major radio personality with medical benefits and a dental plan, loved and desired—but apparently what I was going to be was a city councilwoman. It was a start, anyway, although exactly what it was a start of, other than say, madness, I wasn't sure.

The kitten killed the Cheerio and ate it. Then he sighed. A Lisa sigh.

His sigh propelled me out of my kitchen, through the living room and safely past the keyboard I could be playing, the CD player I could be listening to, carefully selecting songs for that afternoon's play list, the television I could be watching, the cat-clawed slightly saggy leather sofa I could be napping on.

Instead, I tossed off my Kasey Chambers T-shirt and rummaged through my closet for an outfit appropriate to wear while meeting my election-filing deadline.

That deadline was today, which seemed sort of fast, what with the old councilman only resigned a week and all. But I supposed a special, emergency election required emergency action. The election itself was exactly thirty days after the filing deadline.

That was encouraging news, actually. Things usually went well for me in the short term; as an example, the first month with Jack had been positively dreamy.

It seemed to me neither band-name T-shirts, of which I have a plentiful collection, jeans and cowboy boots nor a faux-fur-collared sweatshirt and black tights were quite right for declaring my candidacy. I reached into the back of my closet and pulled out a sturdy, dated, dull gray skirt from my recording studio scheduling days and a lace-collared semi-sheer silk blouse from the same era. Combined with a discreet camisole beneath the blouse, I thought I was the epitome of electability.

"I have to fill out all this stuff?"

I was still a little out of breath, partly with surprise, because the stack of paperwork now before me would fill one entire filing cabinet; and partly, as my car showed no predilection for running, because I'd just walked down our town's twelve percent incline hill to the city clerk's office. Its steepness has been documented at our annual New Year's Day 10K run, when L.A. TV reporters who otherwise pay no attention to the existence of Playa Vista, interview the obligatory octogenarian who made it down the hill.

It's my opinion that the steep downward slope actually makes it harder to walk than to jog, but jogging in the slingback heels I was now wearing would've been suicidal. So I'd minced down the slippery hill, under the cover of a small, cheap umbrella that afforded only minimal protection for my much-abused leather jacket, which in itself provided only somewhat adequate protection for my nice blouse.

Getting damper by the second, I walked past the upscale grocery store with its wooden floors and fresh herbs, and the chain coffee establishment, whose Mochas were no way in the same class as Lisa's.

Both establishments were emblematic of the new Playa Vista community, increasingly gentrified. I continued on past the fish bait store, surfboard shop, and bail bondsman, which more or less represented the old Playa Vista; and past the fire and police station necessary to both versions of the community, arriving at last at what is euphemistically known as City Hall Plaza. In reality there is no plaza, just a cluster of mid-sixties drab buildings with government-type offices in them, in one of which I now sat.

"All this paperwork must be filled out by twelve noon sharp today. And write a candidate's statement," Susan Birch, city clerk, sniffed. She was wearing a polyester pantsuit she must've bought when she first started working for the city; a service plaque on the wall noted her "Thirty Years of Service."

She took no notice of my attire, and if I'd realized how casual our meeting was going to be, I could've easily gotten away with a sweatshirt and jeans and sneakers and not had damp toes and aching ankles.

"All of the many *other* candidates already e-mailed their statements, or dropped them off on diskette. But given the deadline for filing is less than an hour from now, you can handwrite if you're neat about it. It does make extra work for us, though."

"Sorry. I didn't even know there was going to be an election until yesterday."

She tapped long French-tipped nails against each other. "Some of our candidates have been preparing— in the event of a vacancy—for years. And you just found out yesterday?"

I couldn't tell if her incredulous tone revealed awe or horror. I just kind of shrugged. Then she shrugged.

"Will you be paying by check, cash or credit?"

"Paying? For what?"

"The *fee* for your candidate's statement, distributed in the mail to all registered voters."

"Ah. The fee. Ah. Now there's something I didn't know about until right this *minute*."

She didn't seem amused.

"Credit," I said.

Considering the fact that I obviously had to get my car fixed at some point, I hoped the fee was for say, fifty bucks. Or better yet, twenty-five.

I pulled out my wallet and flicked my Visa between my thumb and my forefinger. I hated to ask, but I did. "How much is this statement fee exactly?"

"One thousand in English, twelve-fifty for English and Spanish."

I swallowed. Now was the time to back out. To tell Lisa it wasn't going to work.

And yet, even as I sat there with my soon-to-be-maxed-out credit card in my hands, and in front of me a mountain of paperwork and a candidate statement to be filed, perversely, comfortably even, the more ridiculous this whole half-baked run for city council thing seemed, the more I wanted to do it.

I could win! For one golden moment, I absolutely knew I could. Of course, not that long ago I just knew Jack was the one for me, too. Still, I drew a deep breath, smiled, and handed my card over to the clerk.

Once the charge cleared, she seemed to like me a little better; at least she quit frowning at me and instead asked me to swear that the forms I was about to fill out would be filled out correctly, the whole truth and nothing but, as if I were in a court of law.

"Sure," I said.

She gave me a funny look again. "I need you to raise your right hand and repeat after me," she said. And very slowly this time, she went on about the whole truth and everything, with me echoing, and managing to restrain myself from rolling my eyes.

Only then did she give me a nod that more or less indicated approval and left me alone with my paperwork and the sound of the rain splattering against the office windows.

The first forms all had to do with identification. I filled in the blanks to the effect that I was one Jessica (Jessie) Marie Adams, born in Boston, Massachusetts, educated at and barely received a B.A. from the Boston School of Music, resident of Los Angeles for ten years, in the South Bay for nine years, in Playa Vista itself for eight, choice of residence due to the fact that my first serious sweetheart on the West Coast liked to surf Rat and El Porto when he wasn't playing his flute like the second coming of Ian Anderson from Jethro Tull. Fortunately, that last part didn't have to go on a form, just the length of residence part.

Next came actual proof that I was who I said I was—if I was pretending to be someone other than myself, why would I pick me, exactly? Still, I had to cough up my social security, driver's license, and phone numbers, just in case I was a terrorist running for city council.

Then came questions like was I married, did I have children, my occupation and source of income. Nope not married yet, but still thinking there was a possibility of same. No kids yet, but if the marriage thing didn't pan out, maybe I'd have a love child, which was apparently perfectly acceptable for more successful musicians than I, without any apologies for being unable to keep a man long enough to be the putative father of the child.

Okay, unmarried, no kids. Moving on to occupation

and source of income. "DJ" had too much of a hip-hop connotation and might give people the idea that Lisa's club attracted gangs or something. Saying musician also connoted instability and bad influences, especially if one added *unsuccessful* musician into the mix. On-air personality had too much of a Bill O'Reilly feel, might turn off some voters. I settled on "professional communicator." Now that had a certain ring.

I then swore I would agree to keep religion out of politics, be responsible for collecting my campaign signs when the election was over, not put campaign flyers into people's mailboxes except via the U.S. Mail, not participate in any electioneering on Federal property, not litter, disclose the source of all campaign funds raised, open a separate bank account for said funds, and agree to a strip search.

Actually the last one was not one of the things I agreed to, but it wouldn't have surprised me. I handed all my forms to Sue, who seemed like she was impatient for them.

She handed me one sheet of paper back with large empty blocks in which to print my name. "That's for your place card," she explained.

"My place card?"

"For the debate this evening."

"There's a debate this evening?"

There was just one thing after another I didn't know.

"Because of the tight time frame for this special election, the League of Women Voters has agreed to hold a debate immediately following the filing deadline. Tonight at seven, in Council Chambers. You don't *have* to speak, of course, if you feel awkward about speaking in public."

I laughed. "Nope, that's the one thing I don't feel awkward about here."

And then came the grand finale, my paid-for one-hundred-words-or-less candidate statement.

"Anything you specially want me to include?" I asked Susan, who was hurriedly scrawling her own signature at the bottom of every piece of paper I'd passed on to her.

"Why anyone should vote for you!" Sounding exasperated, Susan swiveled toward her computer and began to type on the keyboard with frantic haste. "Remember. You have less than an hour to leave your statement with me."

I asked for and received a legal pad and a pen and I thought for a minute and then, with Muzak in the background playing the equivalent of a fingernails-on-the-blackboard rendition of "Girls Just Want To Have Fun," I wrote in my very best, Catholic girl's school, nun-fortified handwriting.

"I'm running for this office because the city council of Playa Vista must be accountable to its residents and work solely for their benefit. We must forge relationships with all members of our diverse and vibrant community."

That was *good*, I thought, and true too, as far as it went. Although I honestly wasn't that sure how diverse or vibrant our community was.

Thanks to the kind of rezoning I was fighting in Lisa's name, pretty soon the only guy not making mid-six figures and above residing in Playa Vista would be the homeless guy who'd migrated south from Santa Monica and kept a tent pitched just above the high tide line under the pier. And maybe me, of course.

I wrote, "Our town needs vision. We need to look

at long-term goals while preserving important area
landmarks, prevent excessive taxation, and budget
without sacrificing quality."

I impressed myself. That part about taxes and the
budget sounded especially good. Wasn't everybody
concerned about budgets and taxes? Being a politician wasn't that hard really, was it?

But I thought about what the city clerk had said,
how I should be telling people in my statement why
they should vote for me. I hadn't addressed that
part yet. And why should they exactly? I was cuter
than the existing city councilmen? Just last week I'd
interviewed The Killers' bass player on air? I'd
emceed for The White Stripes all-acoustic show last
New Year's Eve?

I chewed on my pen for a while and listened to
the Muzak that was now providing a sort of funeral-
home-creepy version of "Bridge Over Troubled
Water" as a soundtrack, and to the rain now virtually attacking the windows. I tried not to get too distracted by the fact that I was going to have to walk
all the way back uphill again to my apartment in
the rain, in heels, with the direction of the wind
such that the rain would be blowing in my face.
Quite a challenge. Challenge. That was it!

"Why choose me as your candidate? I understand, firsthand, the challenges facing Playa Vista.
I live in this community. I've seen it change, often
without enough regard paid to what effects change
can have. As a professional communicator I can
assist with and enhance communication"—duh—
"and clarify issues."

I was really on a roll. "The goal of my candidacy
is simple: to be accountable to everyone in our
community—from senior citizens to children, from

professionals to students, home owners, renters, business owners, historians, and you."

Done. It seemed utterly impossible to get away from using the word *community* more than once. Also, I wasn't sure what I meant by historians, but the word had just popped into my head, and with the word came the wings of an idea.

Maybe the best way to save Lisa's club was to make it a part of history! I thought of it as a musical landmark. Why not a landmark of a building! The place was old, after all. Then people wouldn't think of it as an eyesore out of which issued guys who peed in the bushes; but a proud institution, an asset.

I recopied my statement more neatly. It was not exactly the prose of the ages, but it was good enough, and it was already ten minutes to twelve.

Sue was nowhere to be found; perhaps like Elvis, she'd left the building. And now it was my turn to follow her.

I scribbled on her memo pad, noting the current time and left my statement on her desk. Then, trying to maintain my resolute, can-do, candidate-for-city-council attitude, I marched out of her office, opened my umbrella, and hurried out into the maelstrom.

It was raining so hard now that I could hardly see where I was going, but I pushed myself into a kind of fast-forward momentum and turned right into it, heading uphill.

I'd already been dreading the walk, but apparently I hadn't been dreading it enough. I was surprised at just how much harder uphill in heels in the rain is than downhill in heels in the rain, especially when the rain has hit the torrential mark. It was sluicing down the sidewalk, heavy enough and fast enough that it was like fighting the current of a river.

For a moment I thought about turning around, going back into Sue's cubicle and using her phone to call a cab. But despite my cavalier profligate charging of twelve hundred dollars, I didn't have more than two dollars cash on me, and would not have until tomorrow's paycheck. So ankle deep, I plunged upward, ignoring the cold water slopping in over my shoes. Momentum was everything.

I hunched over to lower my center of gravity and held the umbrella down over my face like a shield, hoping the wind wouldn't turn the thing inside out. I kept my eyes on my soaked shoes and chugged along past the buildings that made up City Hall Plaza. It seemed like it took forever just to get abreast of the police station.

Just a little while longer, I told myself, and I could duck into the surf shop and take a breather.

And then something, or someone, bulldozed right into me.

I mean like, pow, like a football player had tackled me, except I didn't quite fall down. The same player was picking me up before I hit pavement, even as my umbrella was knocked out of my hand and went rolling across the sidewalk, into the street, all the way downhill again.

"Hey!" I said, when a little bit of breath came back into my lungs.

"You okay?" said the guy, who was wearing a trench coat turned up at the collar beneath which were the traces of a cheap navy blue suit and tie, and whose cropped short, curly dark hair was dripping into his face.

"I guess," I gasped. My leather jacket was askew,

exposing my blouse to the rain, and I felt like someone in a very, very wet T-shirt contest.

Self-conscious, I tugged at my jacket, and realized only then that this guy still more or less had me in his arms. In his rather large, muscular arms. And that it felt really surprisingly good being held like that. That it had in fact been a long time since anyone had held me like that, that firmly, that securely, that confidently. Certainly Jack hadn't. He held his *guitar* like this guy was holding me. It was honestly a new and nice feeling to be in a clinch like that. I examined my clincher a little closer.

He had intense green eyes, a square jaw, good full lips, and a sort of dark cast to his cheeks, a kind of patina of five o'clock shadow, as if he'd forgotten to shave when he got up that morning.

He released me abruptly and I felt myself slipping backward again, the rain and the high heels and the being on a hill and everything.

He grabbed me again, more or less clutching me right up against him, and along with the strong arms I felt a broad, strong chest, and the ridiculous urge to pin myself fast against it.

I righted myself, and we stood there glowering at each other in the driving rain.

"I lost my umbrella," I said. "You crashed right into me."

"You crashed into me," he said. "With that umbrella pointed out like some kinda weapon. A deadly weapon. Assault with same."

"Ha-ha," I said. I hugged my arms around my jacket and my chest. It must've been that cold dampness that made me get the shivers all of a sudden.

"You weren't watching where you were going," we both said to each other at once.

He gave a grunt of assent. "Sorry this happened. Glad you're okay."

"You owe me an umbrella," I said. "You can't just walk away."

He sighed. He sighed a deep and terrible sigh and a little vein on the side of his head began to pulse. "Look," he said, "it's a lousy day. Don't hit me up for a cheap umbrella."

"That's exactly why I am hitting you up. It's a lousy day. I'm soaked. I won't feel like getting soaked again later because you walked into me—excuse me, we walked into each other—and you made me drop my umbrella."

"Jesus," he said, rubbing his hand across his forehead.

"Invoking the name of our Lord is not going to save you from forking over twenty bucks or a replacement umbrella."

He shook his head like I was asking for a pot of gold or something. Since we were right by the police station I pushed my advantage. "I could march right in there and file a complaint."

He sighed again. "Do you really want to do that?"

"No. I really want my umbrella back, so I don't have to walk all the way up this hill getting drenched because you bulldozed right into me."

"I don't want to dispute who bulldozed into who but—"

"Good," I said. "We're making progress."

"Where are you walking to?"

"My home."

"I don't have an umbrella to give you, but I could give you a ride," he said. He poked his thumb in the direction of a slightly disreputable-looking tan sedan car parked in a slot along the side of the police station. The slot, like three others, was marked POLICE VEHICLES ONLY.

My mouth parted slowly. "You're a cop?"

He gave a sort of half shrug, neither yes or no, but enough of a yes that I figured the odds of me getting him to give me a new umbrella under the threat of an assault charge were slim.

"I guess I'll just—"

I was going to say "Walk," when I saw a sudden bright flash illuminate the sky over the sea, and the bang of thunder that followed it shook the ground we were standing on. He reached out a hand to steady me again, which was nice of him. He held on after the thunder stopped booming and shaking, leaving behind the shriek of a dozen car alarms.

"I'll just take you up on that ride," I said.

He dropped my arm as if he'd forgotten he was gripping it, and stalked over to his car. He unlocked the passenger door for me, and I slipped inside, dripping a big puddle on the seat.

My assailant shook his head like a dog would and got most of the water off his hair, and then climbed in behind the wheel.

He pulled something out from beneath him— a rubber bone. The dog analogy was getting a little too apt.

He actually smiled. "Jessie," he said. "Funny girl."

I got this weird feeling running up and down my spine. He spoke with such affection. Such intimacy. It freaked me out, and I also sort of strangely liked it, the way I'd strangely liked him holding me in his arms.

But he was staring at the rubber bone in his hand, not at me.

"Um," I said.

He kind of snapped out of it, whatever it was,

threw the bone in the back seat, and stuck his key in the ignition.

"Sorry," he said.

"'Sorry' isn't quite going to cut it," I said. "Do you know me?"

He was backing out of the space, but he slammed on his brakes.

"What do you mean, do I know you? You just walked into me. I just offered you a ride. Of course I know you."

"How do you know my name?" I demanded.

"I don't—" He looked genuinely puzzled.

"You just said, while staring at that—that bone—Jessie. You said—"

"Jessie's my dog." He took his foot off the brake and finished backing up. "That's her favorite toy." He smiled. "So your name's Jessie, too?"

"Yeah."

"You like rubber bones?"

"Not specially."

He gave up and sunk back into his former moroseness until we were out of the parking lot.

"I know you were headed up the hill. But where to once we crest the top?"

"El Dorado Street. Behind the power plant."

He swung the car left, left again, and we sat silent at a traffic signal, the windshield wipers slapping, my jacket dripping onto his seat.

He turned right on El Dorado before he spoke again. "I am sorry about our collision. Normally, I'd be a little more considerate. But it's been—kind of a day."

"I've had those," I said.

"This one of them?"

"Ha," I laughed. "No, actually, I've had a lot worse."

For example, last week, when Jack returned from his tour only to dump me, and my car wouldn't start.

And of course there were other times, other breakups harder on the heart than Jack's defection—the times my music was out of tune with the prevailing winds of enthusiasm in the recording industry, several job firings that resulted in temporary destitution and eternal bill collecting, not to mention when I was twelve and my mom passed away, and when I was sixteen and my dad followed her, and it occurred to me that I was more or less alone in the world.

It was strange that I was thinking these thoughts, as this guy I didn't know, whose name I didn't know, but whose dog's name I did know, was pulling up to and then past my apartment. But stranger still was that I had the urge to tell him exactly what I was thinking. And the feeling that if I did, for some reason this absolute stranger with the good grip would understand.

But that was all too incredibly weird, so instead all I said was "Hey, that's my driveway back there."

He pulled a tight U-turn like he was cornering a criminal or something, brakes squealing on the wet pavement, and pulled up at my doorstep.

"Thanks for the lift," I said.

"You're welcome," he said. "And thank you for—well for kind of taking a little of the gloom off the day."

"I have?"

"Yeah, you have."

And we both looked at each other. There was something in the way that we were both looking at each other that was as downright weird as me wanting to spill my whole life story. Like we knew each other, you know, longer than ten minutes. Like we liked each other. Like he wanted to tell me his life story too. Like we were both wishing there was some plausible reason we could fall into each other's arms all over again. My heart said, "Why not?" My mind said, "Danger, Will Robinson, Danger."

My voice said, "Bye," and I opened the passenger door.

"Stay dry," he said.

"Not much chance of that."

"No, guess not."

"You try and stay dry, too," I suggested.

I was walking up to my building now, observing how the rain had stained the stucco and how the paint, already peeling a little on the railings and doors, was buckling under the peeling places with water.

"I'll tell Jessie you said hi, Jessie," he called out.

I turned back. His car window was open and the rain was splattering in on him.

"Ha," I said. I waved.

Now I was climbing the steps to my second-floor apartment. Each step seemed to take forever. Or maybe I was walking really slowly, like I wasn't entirely sure I wanted to go back into my apartment, alone, at least not while the guy I'd just been exchanging weirdly significant looks with was still staring up at me. I could feel him staring up at me. I could feel his eyes on me as if it were his hands on me, still holding me.

Below me, through the slats in the stairs, I could see the guy who worked for a pizza delivery service and his mother both peering up at me through the edge of their curtains. They always reminded me of Norman Bates and his deceased madre, but since I saw both of them looking up at me now at the same time, I was relatively if not positively sure she wasn't deceased and he wasn't in drag.

I had my key out, and was already gauging how long it would take me to grab a hot shower, walk to the bus stop, actually catch a bus and make it to the station relatively on time for my show. I started wondering if I could get Lisa to drive me to the bus stop and wait until the bus came, since I didn't have an umbrella anymore, and just how evil it would be to my body and soul if I had something like a chocolate macadamia nut sundae from Lemar's Ice Cream Hut right across from the bus stop, assuming, since they knew me there, they'd let me get it on account, when I heard footsteps behind me.

I spun around. There was this guy, this cop guy, or of course, who said he was a cop? Maybe he was a criminal just let out of jail, recklessly stealing a police car, or a criminal who had recklessly parked his car in a police car space. Other than the fact that he had nice green eyes, hair that was too short for my taste, insanely broad shoulders, that faintly disreputable beard, and a dog that he liked who had a toy bone in his car, I knew nothing about him.

But there he was on top of me, practically.

"Yes?" I said as coldly as I possibly could. And I must've been cold, because I was kind of shivering again, from my wet clothes and the nasty weather and all.

The rain was lashing into his face, I could see that his shirt collar was as wet as I was all over, I could also see that he was totally disregarding the rain, and that he was just looking at me, right into my eyes, with this kind of intense "I either like you very much, or I am going to arrest you soon" kind of stare.

He leaned forward and kissed me. I gathered

arrest was not what was on his mind. He just pressed his lips hard against mine, tasting a little of coffee. And I found myself kissing him back. And the kissing was awfully nice and lasted a long time before I pushed him away from me.

He lifted his hands up, no contest. "Felt so good, that's all. When you kind of fell right into my arms."

And I found I was falling right into his arms all over again. We were in fact locked in this ridiculously tight embrace, as if we were both holding each other up to keep from falling off my little porch and back down the stairs and right into the square of sopping grass the pizza guy and his mom cultivated as a vegetable patch but nothing ever grew in.

We stayed like that long enough that it began to feel like an act of insanity, especially with the rain pouring down off the edge of my roof right on top of us, and then he released me, and we were both kind of gasping; maybe we'd inhaled rainwater or something.

"Are you going to ask me in?" he said.

"I shouldn't," I said.

"You have to," he urged me.

My hand was shaking as I unlocked my door. And I never really officially asked him in; he just kind of followed me inside and closed the door behind him.

Chapter Three

Squeak came running over squeaking, and tried to mark my legs with his little face, but they were too wet and he ran away again, still squeaking, over to his now-empty food bowl. Sally just sat on the window ledge in the kitchen peering out into the hall at me and this strange man with a kind of resentful look in her wide green eyes. Then she growled. She growled at everybody and sometimes she peed on their feet. It would kind of spoil the moment if she came over and greeted this guy in that way.

"Oh," he said, "cats. You have cats."

Very observant of him.

"Uh-huh," I said.

Very catchy of me, very clever. Definitely eased the awkwardness of the moment.

I thought of the coffee taste on his lips. "Do you want some coffee?" I offered.

But he shook his head and just pulled me against him again, and when we came up for air that time, he was pulling my jacket off my shoulders and throwing off his own raincoat, and dropping both garments down in the hall.

He moved his lips from my lips and down my neck, and then lifted them back up again to nibble on my ear. I am a total sucker for ear nibbling, and I gave a little moan, which seemed to be all the encouragement he needed to move from ear nibbling down over the smooth, wet fabric of my blouse, which he untucked from my skirt and lifted up, all the while working his hands around the hooks of my bra.

He was having a little trouble with the hooks.

"Tougher than handcuffs—" he muttered, but eventually he got it, and he had my blouse all bunched up and my bra pushed back. He was using that little nibbling thing he'd used on my ears only down all along my collarbone and between my breasts and on my breasts too, where he threw in some gentle licking and stroking, and I was a complete and utter goner then. Everything I'd been missing, everything I'd been wanting, every physical and emotional desire I had apparently been repressing, came spilling out of me in a soft low moan.

Then I was helping him out of his suit jacket, and tugging at his tie and unbuttoning his shirt all at once.

I was no better with ties than he was with bra hooks, I don't think any of the four guys I've serially committed to in the last ten years have even owned a tie, much less worn one.

But we got around that, and he worked off my skirt and I unbuckled his belt, and we were all wet and panting with our clothes falling off right there in the hall, with Squeak coming back chirping at us over and over and twining his tail around our legs.

We kind of got stuck again there, not sure how to proceed, or even if we should, I guess. But he took my hand, lifted it to his lips and kissed each one of my fingers, up and down each digit from fingertip to palm, and I gasped again. He led me by my hand into my bathroom, closing the door behind us to keep Squeak out.

"Thought it was the bedroom," he muttered, but it was too late to turn back then, he was already lowering me to the floor on top of my pink-and-orange fluff throw rug, stripping off my underwear and my sodden stockings, tugging off his own shorts and socks, while our hair dripped onto the fluffy little rug.

"Oh, God," I said when we collided body to body, linked up, rolled and rocked and gasped for a while. "I don't even know your name."

"Chuck," he said, keeping my hand in his, and kissing my fingers again, the inside of my arm, even my elbow, until any further introduction seemed long beside the point.

"What's with all the records and CDs and band posters everywhere?" Chuck asked me.

I'd just taken a shower, and slipped into what I hoped was a sexy silk robe, instead of my usual post-shower attire of a towel or extra-large T-shirt. He wasn't looking at me though, he was looking at my CDs.

"I'm a DJ at KCAS," I said. Then remembering my campaign statement, I threw in "You know, a professional um, communicator." I might as well get used to saying that.

"Huh," he said.

He sure wasn't giving me much to work with.

He moved across my living room to my keyboard. He ran his fingers across it, lightly picking out the scales.

Seeing his fingers moving up and down the keys as they had just so recently been moving up and down my body gave me a little thrill.

I don't think I'd ever felt what I felt with him touching me, our bodies intertwined up against the bathtub. When it was over, we just kind of lay there on the damp rug, like we were both in shock, and he said, "My God," and I echoed that.

Then he kissed my lips, really sweetly, and gallantly helped me up off the floor. I kind of wrapped a towel around me and he slipped his jockeys back on.

"You're—amazing," he said.

"So are you," I said.

And then I shivered yet again, because probably I was still cold and damp and everything, or maybe it was something else. Some new and previously unrecognized form of desire.

"You got a chill?"

"Yeah, I think I need a hot shower," I said.

"Okay, I'll just be, you know, right outside. Getting dressed. Waiting."

The hot water warmed me up, and I tried to be fast, I mean the whole idea of him waiting was both exciting and daunting. What was he waiting for? What came next after a, no pun intended, performance like that?

I guess what came next was him not having much

to say and then touching my keyboard with the same kind of intimacy that played across my skin, and me staring at his hands as if they were still touching me.

"KCAS. Can't say I've ever listened to it."

"We're alternative."

"Ah. Oh, wait, there's a girl does an all-jazz and blues show."

"Yeah. Sunday afternoons. Not me," I added.

We both laughed, like I'd said something funny. We were both nervous, I realized. It wasn't just me.

"I'm a musician, too," I told him. "I mean, not professionally at the moment. But I've, you know, performed and all." How incredibly lame. Why didn't I talk about my eighth grade talent contest, too?

"Sounds good," Chuck said. He seemed distracted.

Considering how perfectly aligned our bodies apparently were, our words were just grazing off each other, near-misses at conversation. We were not exactly winning any awards for witty repartee.

His gaze kept flicking around my living room, across the battered leather sofa, at the Day of the Dead figures from a Tijuana shop, the once-trendy Southwest-style coffee table and bookshelves, bowing in the middle a little from all my CDs and tape cassettes and old vinyl.

"Yeah. It's fun, the music and all," I offered, as his gaze returned, somewhat vacantly, to my face.

"I bet."

"You like your job, too?"

"Yeah. Except for the paperwork. Policing has an awful lot of paperwork. And hoops to jump through sometimes. Lots of hoops. Just got a phone call. Have a few more to jump through today, in fact."

I glanced at the clock in the kitchen. Sometime soon, too soon, I had to be heading to the station. It made me edgy, like I'd better hurry up, we'd better hurry up.

He saw me looking. "Later than I thought," he offered.

"It always is," I tried to joke.

He had his pants and his shirt and shoes and socks on again and his curly hair stood up straight on his head, probably because he kept running his hand through it.

"I fed your cats. Wouldn't let me alone, the little one."

"Oh. Thanks. He wants to be fed five times a day."

"The other one kept growling at me."

"She does that."

He stood regarding me, and I regarded him back.

"So . . ." He rubbed his hands together, like he was trying to conjure up the right words. Evidently, he failed. He dropped his hands to his sides and then he crossed his arms and smiled at me, and I smiled back, and then he said, "So" again, with a little more finality to it this time.

And I felt something shut down in me, like this was as far as either one of us was going to go today, and maybe we had gone quite far enough.

"So, I have to go to work," I said. "In a little over an hour." It sounded ruder than I'd intended.

What I really wanted to say was "So, that was really, really, incredibly, impossibly nice, and soon I have to go to work, so maybe you should leave now but come back later." Or even, "I have to go to work but I don't want to. I want to spend the day with you," and for him to say that he felt the same way too, and for me to say, "Too bad about work, I'll call in sick," and we'd both fall into each other's arms again, and this time, tell each other our entire life stories, and stop with the awkward, prickly, honestly kind of annoying small talk that went nowhere, and really open up, emotionally and intellectually as well as physically, and maybe finish up the evening by say, driving out to Vegas and getting married.

Boy, I really was a good Catholic girl at heart. I sighed. Chuck appeared to have misinterpreted the sigh.

"Oh, of course. You have to get going." He nodded like that explained everything, and what a relief. "Me, too. I have to get back to work. And I have to feed Jes—my dog."

"Okay, then—" I said.

He walked toward me, gave me a quick hug. Very quick, like he was afraid if he made it any longer, something else would happen between us, and as if he no longer wanted anything else to happen, but maybe I still did.

What made him even think I wanted anything to happen? In the first place or ever again. I was just weak and vulnerable, on the rebound from Jack. I was susceptible. That's why I had just maxed my credit card to enter a city council race. That's why I had just made love to a complete stranger who was apparently a cop.

I had never ever made love before in my life to anyone who was not a musician. Really and truly, that was a lot more shocking than the complete stranger part.

"Look," he said, "I didn't mean to—I wanted to—I just—"

"Forget it," I said. "Happens all the time."

Not to me exactly. I've had exactly four serious "relationships" in my dating life, and not only were they all with musicians, they were all with musicians who spent many hours wooing me with their music, playing me their favorite fellow artists, swearing, even if they later recanted, that they loved me, before things progressed very far. I was engaged to two of them before I even slept with them. But here I was telling Chuck that virtually every day of my life I had wild, wicked, crazy relationships like what I'd just had with him.

My cheeks caught fire and I opened my mouth to speak but I sort of thought whatever I was going to say next was only going to make things worse, so I just closed my mouth again.

"Oh," Chuck said, "okay then. Happens all the time."

By attempting to salvage my pride, to make sure he didn't get it stuck in his head that he was really all that, I had now convinced this guy that I was nothing but a slut. And to think that only a few minutes ago I was already contemplating heading off to Vegas with him, this complete and total stranger who now seemed almost embarrassed to look at me. Well, okay, I was almost as embarrassed to look at him.

When I did finally stop contemplating the cat fur on my sofa pillows, I saw him run his hand through his hair one more time and then he rubbed at his chin like he'd never before realized that he had one. "Need a shave," he said.

He had kind of a dazed look on his face. I suppose I had kind of a dazed look on mine as I watched him pick the rest of his stuff off my floor and head for the front door.

"I'll call you," he said.

"You don't have to," I told him, hugging my arms across my chest.

A ghost of a smile played across his lips and drifted away again before it became anything substantial.

"Then it was nice meeting you," he said.

I was dressed and depressed when someone knocked on my door twenty minutes later.

I confess, I ran to answer it, expecting it was him, with a bouquet of flowers or an invitation to dinner or something, maybe just come back to say look, he knew it was awkward for me as well for him, but maybe we could meet for coffee later. Or maybe he'd say "Look, I can't deny it, you can't deny it. Obviously something major just happened between us, so of course I'm going to call you later." Or simply "You never gave me your phone number." Or maybe "Wow, I can't be apart from you, I can't keep my eyes off you, my hands off you, my heart is pounding in my chest—"

But it was Lisa. I must've looked crestfallen. She stepped inside and looked pretty bummed herself.

"Did you do it?" she said.

"Do what?" I asked, guilty.

"File!"

"Oh, yeah, I did, sure." My cheeks burned and years of Catholic school guilt flared up in my heart. I stammered when I spoke, me the professional communicator. "I, uh, filed and I, uh, made the noon . . . the noon, you know, deadline."

Lisa gave me a funny look. "Are you okay?"

"Yeah, sure," I said.

My voice was all shaky. I passed a hand over my feverish face. I'd just made love to a complete stranger. And worse, he didn't feel like a complete stranger. He felt wonderful. He felt fabulous. He made me feel wonderful and fabulous and I'd just shooed him away. Why did I do that? Just because we had these little conversational glitches and maybe absolutely nothing in common except raw physical attraction, no matter how nice I wanted to make it in my head? Still, why when he made me feel the way I was still feeling now, did I just more or less throw him out like that? Of course, he sure gave up quick.

"What's wrong with you?" Lisa was really concerned now.

I drew my hands off my face and tried to pull up a logical reason for being upset.

"Twelve hundred dollars," I managed to get out. "That's what's wrong. It cost twelve hundred dollars to get a campaign statement printed in the election materials the city sends out. Isn't that outrageous? And even more outrageous, even though I paid it, I don't really have twelve hundred dollars."

"Twelve hundred. Ah," she said. "I can see where that would be kind of upsetting."

Still, she sounded dubious, as if she was waiting for the real reason. I wanted to tell her, I honestly did, but first of all it was kind of embarrassing to admit I was apparently so desperate for sex that I'd grabbed some off the street. And second of all, if I described my experience any other way, as what used to be called love at first sight or something, I would sound utterly and absolutely insane. Maybe I was insane. I was so insane that I'd just spoken aloud.

"I'm insane. That has to be why I did it," I said.

"No, no, you're just—impulsive. And you're trying to help me."

"Oh, right, I did it to help you." And my ironic tone baffled Lisa further.

"Twelve hundred, that's nothing," Lisa said, although the expression on her face was such that it kind of looked like she thought it was. "I made phone calls all morning. We're all set for your fundraiser Friday. The lead singer for The Dublin Five, he remembers you from the club and he says he really likes you. He said he'd throw in a hundred bucks from the group! I bet we can get at least twelve people to give a hundred bucks."

"Or twenty-four people to give fifty bucks," I said. I could almost see that happening.

Obviously, Lisa could not.

"Or like fifty people give twenty-five dollars each." She nodded, like she could visualize that. "Or one hundred people—we sometimes get a hundred people in on a night—if they each give twelve dollars, that's nothing!"

"Nothing," I agreed.

"Just don't be glum," she added.

"I'm not glum."

"Yes, you are."

"Well, I'm not glum about that."

"Oh, it's Jack," said Lisa wisely.

"Jack?" I said, having momentarily forgotten who he was. My impulse was to correct her and say Chuck.

She waggled her eyebrows at me like I was an idiot. I felt like an idiot. I couldn't stop thinking about Chuck touching me, kissing me, holding me, undressing me.

Stop thinking about that, I told myself, and was

again surprised to find I'd spoken aloud. Maybe I really was insane.

"Stop thinking about what?" Lisa asked.

"Anything negative," I said super cheerfully, and hoisted myself off my sofa.

"I really appreciate you doing this," Lisa said. "This whole campaign."

"I need a new project, I need something to take my mind off—" I was about to say Chuck. Not Jack, but Chuck. The guy I told not to bother to call. The guy I'd just had extreme, incredible sex with on the bathroom rug.

I just shook my head. "I'm glad I'm doing it," I said. If I wasn't running for office, I would never have even run into Chuck, literally run into him, much less . . . well, much more. Okay, I was nuts. *Just admit it, just move on, just look through your closet for that straitjacket.*

But Lisa had brightened immediately. "I'm glad you're glad. Really—this is a momentous day."

"I guess you could say that," I admitted.

Chapter Four

Every time the request line rang, I imagined it was Chuck, tuned in and turned on; he knew where I worked—surely he could've managed to call Information and get the phone number.

Thinking of him, I played way too much Lucinda Williams, Fiona Apple, and David Gray, sang along way too loudly, mike off, of course, and reveled in the dissolute irony of the Jack White/Loretta Lynn duet of "Portland, Oregon."

Nobody at the station even noticed the dazed and glazed state I was in, or rather they did kinda notice, but they assumed it was because of my rapid induction into the world of politics.

"Good luck," said Theodore, looking utterly stupefied. "I always thought politicians were like the enemy or something, but good luck anyway." Under his breath though, I heard him mutter, "Enemy."

He was mostly drowned out by a loud groan and a couple of thumps from the roof.

"What's that?"

"Sounds like a donkey mated with an elephant, to

continue our political theme," Theo said. "Assuming such a creature would be on the roof with a bucket of tar, attempting to patch the studio leak. In actuality, that's our erstwhile program director, proving he can do more than think up stupid name-that-tune contests, which I really resent, because our average listener is about ten times more intelligent than he is."

We could hear more groaning, so I leaned over the console and pried open the soundproof window. I stuck my head out in to the rain and called to him. "You okay up there, Sandy?"

He grunted something resembling "Fuck you" at me, so I figured he was okay up there above the pigeon-poop-spattered ledge, wearing a plastic Hefty bag billowing around his somewhat large midsection and usual Hawaiian shirt. He was waving around something that looked like a kitchen spatula dripping with black goo.

When he came into the studio an hour later to check on the effects of his difficult handiwork, he had the goo on his trembling hands and splattered in his hair.

"Almost fell down in the middle of Santa Monica Boulevard," he said. "It work?"

I almost hated to tell him that the roof still leaked, so I didn't; after all, he could see for himself the yellowish dripping dirty water still filling up the trash can in the middle of the studio. It seemed like it was filling up slower though.

"It'll never stop raining," he said. "Life sucks."

"Yeah," I agreed. "But not always. I mean sometimes maybe it's possible that it does not suck."

"That why you're doing this election thing I heard about?"

"No. I don't know. Sort of. To prevent it from sucking too badly for Lisa."

"Nice club, always liked it."

"I'm having a fund-raiser there tomorrow night. You should come. Good music. Good cause." He seemed unimpressed. "Free food," I added.

Sandy smiled at the idea of food. He rubbed his belly, which meant he got more black goo on his shirt.

The phone rang in the studio and I jumped and grabbed it. It was just somebody requesting "MacArthur Park," which I had, in my emotional muddle, forgotten to play.

Sandy smiled again, more benevolently. "This whole political process is making you jumpy," he said.

What else could it be? Only I even knew Chuck existed. Maybe I was so totally insane that I'd just imagined he existed. Dreamt he existed, fantasized that we'd done what we'd done. That was almost as likely as what had happened, actually. I could drive myself crazy pretty easily thinking along those lines. Probably along with the old chestnut of "MacArthur Park," I should start regularly playing a slightly younger chestnut, Atlanta Rhythm Section's "Imaginary Lover," as my signature song.

Meanwhile, to keep myself from wigging out entirely, I borrowed our receptionist's laptop and logged on to the Net to brief myself on Playa Vista politics before the night's debate.

I found it tough to concentrate. All the time I was reading up on harbor dredging and tax bases, all the time I was playing mournful love songs, I was waiting for Chuck to call.

Had I scared him away, just because I'd made

him think I was easy? Shouldn't that, short-term anyway, continue to be somewhat of a drawing card?

I was flying without wings here. I was lost in the ozone. I was trying to read a map without understanding the language in which it was written. I was out of my comfort zone. Why didn't he call? Other people called and interrupted my study of archaic small-town zoning laws.

Lisa's poster maker called and agreed to make me 250 posters and 200 signs by Saturday, with the caveat that "If you want 'em that fast, you'll have to use what I have on the press and the paper I got in stock. That would be yellow paper and black ink. And if you're not giving me a credit card now, you have to hand over the payment C.O.D."

I agreed, but then I would've agreed with anything to get him to hang up, so I could take the other call flashing on my phone.

It was the political reporter for our local paper, Brian something from the *Daily Sail,* confirming my candidacy. If he could track me down, why couldn't Chuck?

Then Lisa called from the grocery store to ask if she should make vegetarian or beef chili for my fund-raiser. I said beef, because I like it better, and if no one showed up and I was destitute and hiding from the sign guy, I could at least live on chili for the rest of my life.

"I'm feeling really, really hopeful about all this," Lisa said. "I've called so many people and they're just literally banding together to support me about the club. And your campaign, of course! It's really gratifying."

I'm sure it was gratifying for her and I was glad

she was really hopeful, but as the afternoon dragged on, and Chuck didn't call, and I couldn't even tell anybody the truth about why I felt so keyed up, I realized my entire life was a sham. No wonder I was going into politics.

Of course, maybe it was a good thing that he hadn't called. After all, he was so not my type. So non-poet-laureate. Such short hair. That scratchy, little bit of beard on his cheeks that brushed against the skin of my shoulders and spine and breasts and thighs and—

I liked smooth-faced guys with long blond hair and the kind of touch that could stroke guitar strings as well as my cheek. I bet Chuck couldn't even play a tambourine.

Maybe he just didn't want to seem too eager. Maybe he didn't want to bother me at work. Maybe he had already found out my home phone number—he was a cop; cops could find out things like that—and he'd call me tonight.

The phone buzzed yet again in the studio, and I let out a little yowl, like I was Sally the cat about to pee on the front door.

It wasn't the request line; it was the intercom this time.

Heather the receptionist griped at me. "You ever gonna give me back my laptop? Sandy wants the week's ratings run! Other people have things to do besides you, you know, Polly Political."

"Okay," I said meekly, miserably. He was never, ever going to call.

"Oh," Heather went on, "don't hang up. There's some guy on the office line for you."

"A guy?" I repeated, trying to keep the excitement out of my voice.

"Yeah, sounds like a personal call. I'll put it through, but tell him to use your cell or something. Don't tie up the main number," Heather said.

I hung up the intercom and picked up the studio line when it flashed. "Hi," I said, ultracheerfully. My heart was crawling its way from my chest into my throat. It had to be him this time.

"This Jessie?"

Silly me, imagining Chuck had finally called. This voice was hoarse and gravelly, harder, not Chuck.

"Uh-huh. Who's this?" My heart thudded slower, and I know I reeked of disappointment.

"I'm a big fan. And I found you. That's great. Figured it had to be the same person."

"Same person as what?"

"Running for Playa Vista City Council. Saw your name in this afternoon's paper. Last to file, but boy, judging by the KCAS Web site, nice smile."

For some reason I felt the hairs rise up on the back of my neck. His tone was not that of a really big fan. It was more the tone of someone who disliked me, and now had something else to hold against me.

"How can I help you?" I asked coolly.

"It's more how you can help yourself," he said. "Politics, not for everybody, you know. It's sort of a rough hustle. And small-town politics, they can be the worst."

"Who are you?" I demanded.

But the line had gone dead. I supposed crank calls went with the game. But why did a crank call and not Chuck? Why was I acting like I was all involved with Chuck, like we had a *relationship* instead of an assignation?

I might as well face it. I would never see Chuck again; he didn't want me. Well, he wanted me, he got me, and he was done with me now. Sort of like Jack, except instead of such a revelation taking over a year and a long absence that did not make the heart grow fonder, it happened in under an hour. At least my failed love life was getting more concise.

I shook off what could've been a bad mood. I was not going to be brought down. Not by a crank call or a sexual peccadillo. All things considered, I should forget about both of them and focus on the task at hand: getting elected and saving Lisa's club.

I got off the bus a block early, threw my leather jacket over my head, and went out into the rain to the deli-grocery on my corner. In the ATM there I deposited the paycheck Sandy had advanced me, and withdrew a twenty. My renewed solvency bought a copy of the *Daily Sail*, and the splurge of a single chocolate-glazed grape jelly-filled doughnut.

You could buy a dozen of them instead of just one at a time, but it was a really bad idea in my opinion to keep a dozen of the things in the house. There was only the slightest difference between them and heroin.

While I waited for the guy behind the counter to wake up enough from the nap he'd apparently been taking to ring me up, I opened the paper. Page two of the South Bay News section—there was the election story.

*Debate tonight for City Council Special Election to
be held March 12 . . . to fill council seat left vacant
by . . . many worthy candidates . . . including professional communicator Jessica Adams.*

It was time to start acting like a candidate. I
smiled at the yawning, acne-scarred young guy with
a tattoo on his left arm of a parrot eating an eagle,
which really didn't make a lot of sense. What did
make sense anymore, anyway? I extended my hand,
practicing my firm candidate's handshake.

"You registered to vote?" I asked.

"Yah." He swiped a lock of magenta-tinged black
hair out of his sleepy eyes.

"Well, I hope you'll vote for me! I'm running for
city council. Jessie Adams."

"Please to meet you," he slurred. "I'm running,
too."

He reached across me and jabbed a finger in my
newspaper. "Right there. Tad Ludoviwiski, professional businessman and dyslexia spokesman. Dyslexia
can be a handicap—or not! So like maybe, you vote
for me, I'll vote for you." He winked. "Or maybe we
could go out sometime."

But I was already waving good-bye and was out
the door and up the street. If this was my competition, I had nothing to worry about.

After the jelly doughnut and feeding the cats and
cleaning up the little puddle of pee Sally left right
in front of the door as usual, I cast off jeans and my
"Rollin' with the Homies" Paul Chuck rapping
hamster tank top for an inoffensive pastel blue,
empire-cut cotton shirt, a loose weave gray vest, and

a knee-length black skirt with a ruffle. More of the least dated remnants from my recording studio scheduling days.

There was a knock on my door and Lisa swooped in with a smoked turkey sandwich on rye with thin sliced Swiss cheese, lettuce, mustard, and light mayo. Lisa knew what I liked, all right. Being fed.

"You excited?"

"Mmmf," I said between mouthfuls. Even though I'd scarfed down that doughnut, I was still starving.

"You ready?"

"As I'll ever be." I took a long swallow from a bottle of water. "I spent all afternoon reading up on Playa Vista. I'm an expert on this town and everybody in it!"

"You really sound like a politician."

"Well-informed, huh?"

"Phony," Lisa said affectionately.

I dropped a few pieces of nonmustardy turkey on the floor for Squeak and Sally, who were positively going nuts poking at me and about to ruin my stockings. Stockings. Stockings reminded me now and who knew, possibly forever, of Chuck.

"Why are things always so hard?" I found myself asking.

"You're doing great. I'm just messing with your mind," Lisa assured me.

"I can mess with my own just fine, thank you."

"I wish I could be in the audience, but you know, the club doesn't run itself," Lisa told me. "All you have to do is watch out for Ned Rutkin and you'll be fine."

"Who's Ned Rutkin?"

"Ned is your main competition." Lisa smiled. "And kind of an ass. He has all the money in the world and

the mayor's backing, and the full enthusiasm of two
still-serving city council members, and is completely
against me, and a dithering idiot who thinks maybe
someday he can grow up and be governor and he's
just rich enough that maybe he can."

"And he's only *kind of* an ass? I think he's a full-
blown, most definite one. In the 'kind of' category I'd
put the guy who works at the deli on the corner. Tad
something unpronounceable. He's running, too."

"Tad runs for everything. He's been doing it for
years. He never wins. He never even pays for a candidate's statement."

It never occurred to me that you could run and
not pay for such a statement. Too late now.

"Even without one, he always gets, say, a thousand
votes. His grandfather was mayor or something and
he thinks he's like entitled to win. *Him* you don't
have to worry about. Ned, you do. All those signs
he's got up just this afternoon! Even in front of the
police station!"

In front of the police station . . .

"Don't look so unhappy. Just chuck those blues!
I know it's an uphill battle but—"

Whatever else Lisa said was lost on me after the
words Chuck and uphill.

"Oh, God," I muttered.

"Jessie, you'll be great. Really. Don't worry about
Ned. Don't even think about him."

I forced myself to smile. "Trust me, I'm not."

Chapter Five

"We need a symphony," this guy, fat, maybe thirty-five, looked like a bright pink-faced meat loaf was saying. He thumped his hand on the table, as he already had four times, for emphasis. He was stuffed inside an expensive designer suit that proved for all time that clothes did not make the man, unless the way in which they made the man was to look foolish. I believed he was the sign-happy Ned Rutkin I promised I wouldn't worry about, but I wasn't sure.

We, the candidates, were sitting in folding chairs in front of two long folding tables that wobbled when you leaned on them. We had name cards ostensibly in front of us, but the cards were slightly askew, partly due to the continually wobbling tables, and mostly due to the thumping of the pink guy.

He could be Ned, or Ned could be the guy next to him, who was lean, twenty years older, and wearing a bright red shirt and a dark blue tie with a large white star on it. He had a comb-over and a bulbous nose. The one of them who was not Ned was named Conway Marcus.

There was a third name card jammed in next to

Conway or Ned, that of Ida Pinckney, whom I believed was the soft-faced sixtyish lady next to me, as I knew for certain she was not Jessie Adams, even though that was the name card that had drifted in front of her, because that was definitely me.

Also, I knew that I was not Salome Finch, as it appeared that I was, per the card in front of me, and that she was most likely the tall, exotic-looking woman around my age, or sigh, younger, two seats down. She was stunningly beautiful except for rather wildly flaring nostrils. She had a perfect body, including what had to be a seventeen-inch waist. She was in every way a rival, not just politically speaking. She was the kind of girl who would've dissed me in high school, and stolen my boyfriend if I had one, just to prove she could do it. Not that he was much of a boyfriend, but for all I knew she'd stolen Chuck, and that's why he hadn't called.

The guy right next to me was Tad. He had no name card whatsoever, although there was evidence of a shredded piece of cardboard with which he was building a sort of tepee.

As for the bottom two contestants, oops, candidates, here in what was most assuredly a completely unamazing race, their name cards had spilled off the table and onto the floor. I actually knew who they were though, because both Royal Garritty and Benni Cardell had set upon me with much handshaking the moment I'd walked into the council chambers.

Royal had a weird business card decorated with angels and little puffy clouds and butterflies that identified him as a "Dream Merchant—specializing in foreclosed home sales." Sounded more like the stuff of nightmares than dreams, but Nightmare Merchant didn't have a very good ring to it.

"You're gonna have a hard time going against me," he bragged. "I always get my way. You have to get used to it or get goin'." He laughed like he'd said something funny, but I didn't think he was joking around.

He was one of those guys who looked like someone set a heavy flat rock on top of his head at birth that changed the shape of his skull permanently.

Benni was a big-boned, horse-jawed woman of indeterminate middle age. She was really, really loud and apparently she disagreed with everyone all the time, even if you agreed with her. She wore horn-rimmed glasses and smiled with her wide lips pressed tight together. When she walked up to Royal and I, she said she was pleased to meet me. So naturally, especially since at that moment I viewed her as rescuing me from Royal's bombast, I said, "I'm pleased to meet you, too."

"Are you? Why exactly?" Her voice had a very defensive tone.

"It was nice of you to introduce yourself," I replied, getting the message she was no great improvement over Royal.

"So you're the new girl on the block. Just signed on to the fight. I don't think we should be hostile to each other, do you?"

"Definitely not," I replied.

"Because you know what a wise man once said to me?"

"No idea." I opened my purse and took out my cell phone and pretended to be listening to something on it.

"He said you say one mean word, and it's the

same thing as if you ripped open a pillow and all the feathers flew out. You can no more stuff those feathers back in than you can take back that mean word. Don't you think?"

"Sure."

"So you think you can put feathers back in a pillow once they fly out—everywhere—feathers everywhere?"

"Probably not."

"So probably not! Ha. No mean words then."

I supposed that precluded me telling her to go drop dead. Instead I just slunk off to my seat where Tad was smirking at me like something served me right.

And now, here we were, the assembled candidates debating. We more or less resembled the cast of classic Oscar Mayer hot dog commercials—fat kids, skinny kids, kids who throw, if not climb on rocks. No one appeared to have chicken pox, although Tad's complexion was sort of bad.

For the same reason I'd often imagined myself performing on a stage in a decent-sized concert venue with adoring fans filling the seats, rather than in front of five or six disinterested drunks in the back of a bar, I'd pictured this debate attended by a vast and politically savvy crowd asking intelligent and pointed questions.

Instead, the audience consisted of about ten "concerned citizens," all steamed up about one thing or another, and all wearing weird clothes like Bermuda shorts with rain boots; the better-dressed significant others and campaign supporters of the candidates, who were easy to pick out because of their waving to and kissing the cheeks of the various candidates, all except me of course, since Lisa, my only supporter so far, was at the club; and five to six intensely sullen-looking students observing from seats marked with yet another hand-lettered sign as belonging to the YOUTH COMMISSION, whatever that was. It had a kind of ominous Cold War Soviet ring to it, but it was probably something a lot more benign.

There was also a sallow-skinned guy with hair in a ponytail and a threadbare turtleneck who was videotaping this so-called event for its dynamic cable access broadcast. So far he'd knocked into the camera at least three times, repeatedly pitching the lens toward the floor for shots of our shoes, then righting it so the lens pointed up at the flourescent lights blazing in the ceiling.

The shrill-voiced moderator who identified herself as "Mrs. Morris" added to the generally dismal ambiance, tapping her fingers and cracking her knuckles by turn, as she presented the rules prior to the debate's commencement. We had three minutes to answer individual questions, one to a candidate, plus time for a candidate closing statement; one minute each for rebuttals to everyone else's question.

We drew lots to decide who received the first question, and Ned or Conway, smirking happily, sunk his capacious jaws into "How would you improve life in Playa Vista?" suggesting we add a symphony to our community.

"Take it back!" screamed an old lady in the audience. "We already have a symphony!"

Ned or Conway looked fairly nonplussed. "N-no," he stammered, "Santa Monica has a symphony. L.A. has a symphony. Palos Verdes has a symphony. Playa

Vista should have one, too. All we have is a high school band. That's different."

"There's no difference!" she shrieked.

"Strings," I ventured, even though pink meat loaf didn't deserve any help from me. He'd spent what had to have been well over his three minutes up until the symphony comment going on about the importance of requiring twenty-first century Pacific Rim language fluency of everyone in the Playa Vista government to stimulate international trade and shipping. Even I knew we had no international shipping center, no harbor capable of holding any boat larger than a catamaran, no reason to compete with San Pedro's massive shipping channels. And even if we did compete, what exactly would we trade and ship, anyway? Lattes? Bikinis?

I didn't like the guy's smug, sleek self-assurance, or his fancy suit. I couldn't believe the moderator was beaming at him like he was the greatest pink meat loaf she'd ever seen, time limit be damned. He gave me the same feeling I get about rattlesnakes or black widow spiders or Kiss tribute bands, like I just wanted to get out of range fast.

The woman who was so sure we already had a symphony now made her way out of her folding chair and leaned over pink-faced meat-loaf guy, wrestling the microphone out of his hands and shrieking, "You don't know what you're getting into!"

The same could've been said of me, I supposed.

Next to me, Ida Pinckney shook her head disapprovingly. "Utterly no manners."

Finally, the moderator said, "Order, please! The other candidates need to respond to Mr. Rutkin."

Okay, Ned *was* the meat loaf.

The woman stomped back to her seat and

Conway Marcus stroked his comb-over lovingly, as if it were a pet he was keeping on his head.

"What can we do to improve life here in bey-oooooteeeful Playa Vista? Well, I don't know how life can get any better, you want to know the truth. But I think we need to really tax the bejunipers out of people building the big palaces. You know what I mean. The Tudor doors and the cupolas. Condominium developers, with their plans for high-density hokkum, they get charged too. Kinda a Robin Hood tax. Steal from the rich, feed the poor. And show videos. Big-screen projected videos on the beach. The old ones, like *From Here to Eternity*, stuff like that. You know that great scene where they're rolling around in the surf? Yeah, that was a movie. Free popcorn, free movies, free dinners, too. We got a few of those fast-food places here in town. Let 'em give it away, they make enough burgers out of our sweat and blood."

Not an attractive combination of words, but I got his point, and I could basically even agree with what he was saying. Maybe he was a little eccentric, but he didn't give me the bad vibes I got from smarmy Ned.

"I'm a social reformer kind of guy. An environmentalist. I think we should fill in the boat harbor, and make it a swamp. Used to be a swamp. To swamp it shall return. Just throw in a bunch of dirt and see what happens. Gators come, let 'em come. Be like another Everglades, only on the West Coast—"

Conway was losing me there. A certain restive quality came over the audience, such as it was, and I imagined I was not alone.

"Time," said the moderator, and Conway cleared his throat, petted his hair and shut up.

"We'll improve Playa Vista by *thinking*," Ida said briskly. "All of us think too little now days, and that includes our political leaders. We need to take a step back, become informed and educated before we make any rash decisions about new languages or international trade or swamp land or taxation or re-zoning, for that matter. That's how we'll improve life in our community. By using our minds." She nodded wisely and stopped before she was called.

I liked Ida. She was a little bit like my fourth grade teacher, but I still liked her. Royal Garritty snorted. The antisymphony lady let out a theatrical yawn. Most everyone else was just staring at her as if she'd spoken ancient Greek.

My turn. *Keep it simple. Be brief, be brilliant, be gone.* "I'm Jessie Adams and I'm happy to be here." There. That was brief. And I'd managed to introduce myself, too, get some name recognition going. Very cool.

"I'm just a resident like most of you. Political office is not something I would've ever considered being involved in, until I discovered an historical landmark and a true asset to our community, The Sea Shack, was in danger of being closed because of the rampant building spree soon to be condoned by new zoning laws. Those laws reach far beyond their effect on a landmark institution. They won't improve our community, they'll destroy it. And that's why I'm here tonight. To prevent that destruction, to improve rather than *destroy* Playa Vista."

The moderator opened her mouth and I closed mine, a little out of breath. If I wasn't exactly brilliant, at least I had a nice dramatic hook, me being against the zoning laws that will destroy us.

Tad folded his arms across his chest and began with a low-key chuckle. "Me, I'm not a chicken-little-the-sky-is-falling ordinary resident like Jessie, here. No offense meant of course. Me, I'm Tad Ludoviwiski, the only person with the name recognition to be a leader. My grandfather, he was mayor in 1936. And you know what he always said? He said, 'Vote for me!' And I can only echo that. Wanna improve Playa Vista? Vote for me—for me, for me, for me. Get it? I'm echoing."

He handed the mike to Salome, who widened her nostrils farther than they were already dilated. "I am a purveyor of holistic health supplements with a background in the arts. I am proud to be here. Proud of all of us here in this room for taking the interest of our community so to heart. So to heart that it is beating, beating, beating with a new sound."

She'd apparently liked Tad's echo effect and appropriated it. Tad didn't seem to mind. He was staring at her, a thin line of drool creeping, creeping, creeping from the corner of his mouth.

"Beat—beat—beat. People, that's the sound of caring and love. The two things that improve all life, not just life in Playa Vista. If you care and if you love, I hope you'll vote for me, Salome Finch on March 12."

Royal wiped his sweaty forehead with the back of his hand and smiled a really cheesy smile. "Many of you in this room and out there in TV land know that like my fellow candidate, Mr. Ludoviwiski, I've lived in your community my entire life and so has my family."

There were lots of whoops and cheers from the audience. People liked this sweaty flat-headed guy?

"And you know what Royal Garritty is all about. You say how do we improve, I say *I* am improvement!

I take distressed properties and I make them—not
distressed! I can do the same thing for this entire
city. I can de-stress everything. Take stuff that might
be a little shabby—one of you mentioned a neighborhood bar—"

"It's not a bar," I said, annoyed, and the moderator shook her head at me and a low, loud "Shhhh"
swam from her lips.

"Whatever it is, I can fix 'er up. We can make a
mountain into a molehill and a molehill into a
beautiful gated community. That's been my entire
life's message and it remains so now."

There was more applause and he sat back in his
chair oh so very satisfied. I felt little hot prickles
erupt on my neck. Okay, I liked him even less than
Ned. Ned was emblematic of all the fatuous things
wrong with government, the recording industry,
and probably my life. But Royal directly got in my
face. I wanted to walk outside and pluck up one of
Ned's signs and slam Royal over the head with it. Repeatedly. Or as Tad and Salome would say, repeatedly, repeatedly, repeatedly. Of course then I'd get
arrested. Maybe by Chuck, who'd pretend he didn't
even know me. Maybe he wouldn't have to pretend.
Maybe he'd already forgotten I even existed.

Benni pushed her chair back, stood up, and
asked in a loud commanding voice, "Does anyone
here like pie?"

Several people in the audience responded with
affirmative enthusiasm, as if they were in a revival
meeting. The cheers Royal evinced paled in comparison to this. I noticed one of the most vocal
Benni supporters was the anti-symphony woman.

"That's right, that's right! Pie." Benni nodded
vigorously. "That's what we've got here. A pie of a

city. You can cut it up or slice it up any way you want vis à vis these so-called zoning issues, but it's still a pie. A really good, well-baked pie. What we need is to improve the filling. The filling!"

There were more cheers, and I swear I heard an "Amen!" coming from the Youth Commission.

"Here's what I mean," she said. "We want a good pie, we want the choicest ingredients. We don't want crab apples or windfall pears or nightclubs"—with a scathing look at me—"or uneducated degenerates"—with a glance at Tad—"or elitist idealists." She smirked at Ida, who flushed indignantly beneath her powder. "We don't need the developers or the politically well connected, either," she said, her eyes flashing first toward Royal and then toward Ned.

"We don't want any properties getting distressed, or people either! We don't need big boats coming into our pretty little swimming beaches, trading us foreign junk for our pie! No, sir. The deal here is to bring *our* values up, not just real estate values, but the values of our *lives*, people! Make this the best of all possible pies—then everyone will want to buy!" She blushed with enthusiasm, pleased with her rhyme. "It's all so simple, really. Everyone, even Mr. Rutkin, with *all* his political experience, keeps complicating a very easy recipe—a recipe for success."

I tried to suppress a groan but I think it was audible. At least Mr. Video swung his camera, previously hovering around Salome's boobs, back toward me.

The rest of the evening proceeded rather smoothly if not exactly scintillatingly. I rebutted competently and tried not to roll my eyes at the other candidates or let any more groans escape my lips.

As to my own individual question, I got to answer if I believed in the distribution of free condoms to promote safe sex. Wow! Thank you, audience member, for thinking up that one. And thank you, moderator, for giving it to me.

"I do not believe that one's personal behavior should be controlled by the government," I said, while a few of Benni's supporters tittered in the audience, Tad grinned at me salaciously, and Salome, for whatever reason, flared her nostrils excessively.

"If, for public health reasons, such a distribution was considered essential, then I'd support it. I don't think that this question is very pertinent to the current election, in which the issues are clearly how is this city to be zoned that will provide for the best lifestyle of our residents, and what we can do to assure the best financial resources for our community. I will say that our government, regardless of the issue, needs to consider the well-being of the many, and respond appropriately."

Even I was surprised at how much like a politician I sounded. I didn't really answer the stupid question, and I sounded both benevolent and boring, a comfortingly familiar pattern I'd observed in so many candidates for public office. Tad even stopped grinning.

"Very good, dear," Ida whispered to me.

Several of the candidates—Ida, Ned, and Royal—declined to respond to my response; Salome said it was all about love and goodwill, which was her basic response to every question; Tad said that without sex he wouldn't be with us today and that was the sort of overall moral question he promised to consider constantly; Conway said that condoms and the Kama Sutra should be distributed to all, free of charge; the irrepressible Benni suggested that a wholesome community with the right kind of sugar in its coffee would never have to make such a decision.

Finally, everyone had a turn to sum up, the moderator thanked us, the camera guy yawned and stretched, and it was over. I escaped as swiftly as possible into the lobby.

There I got to see thuggy, sweaty Royal embrace Conway Marcus. They were standing close, their arms about each other's waists in a tight cinch. I was briefly sure they were lovers. Then Conway yelped, and it was not a yelp of say, ecstacy.

"Chuckle head. Let go of my arm," he said.

"Why? Am I twisting it, the way you twist my words and try and steal my votes, you old—"

"Hey," I said.

They both looked up at me and they both looked as guilty as if they *had* been lovers caught in a kiss. They pulled apart. They both straightened their shirts.

"We always joke around like this," said Royal. "Conway would never want to be thought of as a weak victim or anything like that."

"Right," said Conway. "And it would be wrong and insulting to characterize our beloved developer of dreams here as a bungling bully."

"He's an alcoholic asshole," said Royal with a sneer.

"Royal wants an introduction to a friend whose house he hoped to purchase on the cheap, and I have defied and vilified him as he deserves."

"More information than I needed," I said. "About your interpersonal carnage. Just didn't want to see anyone get hurt."

So of course they both turned on me. "Do-gooder, huh," Royal growled. "Or she thinks she is."

"Ha. She doesn't know anything about us or this city." Conway shook his head. "A neophyte."

Outside, the rain had temporarily stopped, or at least resolved itself into a steady drizzle. I could see moonlight streaking oyster shell color across the clouds and onto the dark sea.

Conway and Royal had called it. I was a neophyte and a do-gooder. Ostensibly to help Lisa and earn some extra bucks and put a little purpose into my purposeless life, I'd entered politics.

And by doing so, I also entered into close contact with insane and/or insufferable people whose great hope and ambition was to sit around in those stuffy city council chambers twice a week every week into the wee hours saying insane, insufferable things, turning on one another, and then embracing one another, and every once in a while getting yelled at by outraged citizens.

By proximity and proclivity, this whole political trip very likely meant I was insane myself. I couldn't quite believe I was insufferable, but insane sort of fit. It would certainly explain why I had sex with a stranger I ran into in the street to whom I felt a ridiculous, almost overwhelming attraction and affinity, but who couldn't be bothered to call me afterward.

I could've gone home and brooded, or made up campaign slogans or something, but instead I took a brisk walk along the Strand and over to Lisa's place. By the time I reached The Shack, I was determined to put some positive political spin on the evening at least for Lisa's sake, if not my own.

The lunatics I'd just spent my evening with aside, politics was at least sort of lively. I mean it was more lively than if I had been sitting at home already and brooding.

So I put on a smile and threw the club door open. Or I tried to. The door wouldn't open. It was stuck or something.

I hammered on it. It was inconceivable that Lisa had locked the front door on purpose. And it was only then that I realized the parking lot was virtually empty, except for Lisa's car and a van with a big four-leaf clover painted on it; and there was no bass line thumping behind the walls, and the marquee wasn't lit, just the light over the door and the floods in that parking lot.

A wave of something like panic washed over me. All at once I was in an episode of *The Twilight Zone*. Where was the good Irish rock and roll vibrating the walls? Where was the crowd of happy, normal music-loving people, unconcerned with any politically sanctioned potential distribution of condoms?

I kept knocking, and it seemed like it took forever for Lisa to open up, and when she did she was holding a carton of ice cream against the side of her head.

"They say you should use frozen peas, but we don't have any. So I'm using chocolate-chip mocha," she said.

Chapter Six

I was so glad to see her I just hugged her. She hugged me back, one-handed, still holding the ice cream against her temple with her left hand.

She stepped aside to let me in. The club was dead empty, and a feeling of dread crawled in my stomach. "What happened?" I asked.

She dropped down in a booth and closed her eyes. "Sorry. Head just hurts, that's all."

"How did you hurt your head?"

"*I* didn't hurt it," Lisa said. "It was the guy who attacked me and robbed me."

"You were attacked and robbed? What happened? How—"

"The police just left," Lisa said wearily. "Give me a minute."

"I'm sorry," I said. I squeezed her hand. She managed something close to a smile and squeezed back.

"Right after I dropped you off. I was just opening up," Lisa began. "The band showed up, bass player asked if I could open the back door so he could pull his van right up to it, not get the equipment wet. I'm like fine, I go in the back, unlock the door in my office. The guys come in, back and forth, I thought they were still bringing in stuff. The phone was ringing—you know how it is. I got busy."

I glanced over at the stage. Three skinny guys in their mid-twenties were packing up their instruments, looking nervous and guilty as if whatever had happened was their fault.

"I had my back turned to the door, doing paperwork. There was a knock. I called out, 'It's still open,' and next thing I know something hits me on the head, like a club or something, and I'm on the floor, and somebody I can't see has a knee in my back and what felt like a gun against my neck."

"Jesus."

"Yes"—Lisa nodded—"I started praying. I asked him what he wanted, and at first he didn't say anything. Then he said, 'You can't take me out,' in this real husky voice."

"That's a weird thing to say," I remarked. "Why not 'Give me all your money'?"

"I didn't think about questioning his dialoguing skills," Lisa said. "I just screamed. And meanwhile, the band was running their sound test. So nobody heard me."

Lisa set the ice cream down on the table. "I felt him cock the trigger on his gun. I said, 'The safe's open, just take the money.' He reached up and snagged my cash box with one hand, still kneeling on me, and he said, 'You've been warned,' and then he jumped up and he left."

"Did you see what he looked like?" I asked.

"I only got a look at him from behind, wearing a hooded sweatshirt, gloves, not much to go on. By the time I stood up and looked outside, there was nobody there. I thought I heard a car pull away."

"I'm just so glad you're okay. I'm so glad, Lisa."

Fresh tears started up in Lisa's eyes.

"Did he get a lot of money?"

"No, I don't keep that much around. Robbing me after the show, not before the show, would've made a lot more sense. For only a couple hundred bucks, what was the point?"

I shook my head. "I guess the real point is that you keep the back door locked at all times from now on. The band gets wet, too bad. And you should get yourself like a bouncer, too. A big guy, scares off any potential trouble."

"Yeah," said Lisa, giving a shuddery sigh, "the cops suggested a better alarm system, security, all that."

Maybe one of the cops was Chuck. Maybe he was working tonight. *Maybe I ought to stop thinking about him and move on.* Life, big, messy troublesome, Lisa-got-robbed life was happening all around me and I kept ruminating about a man I hardly knew.

"Just need to see him, that's all." I was speaking out loud again, like I was having an argument with myself, and not winning.

Lisa looked puzzled. "Maybe it's being hit on my head but—need to see who?"

"A bouncer," I said, recovering as quickly as a self-described insane professional communicator and political hopeful could. "People need to see one out front. Lets everybody know someone's around keeping an eye out."

"I guess," Lisa said. "I'll have to run an ad in the paper."

"Let me call the company that handled security at KCAS's Rockin' Holidays concert last year. If they don't want a little gig like this, I'm sure they can recommend somebody."

I was all business now, partly rising to the occasion of Lisa's need and partly to cover up my Chuck obsession. Some people had OCD, obsessive compulsive disorder; I had apparently developed my own version of OCD, obsessive Chuck disorder.

"Sure, call them for me." Lisa rubbed at her forehead. "But tomorrow, okay? I'm not up to talking to anybody else tonight."

"Maybe we should get you an X-ray or something."

Lisa gave me an actual genuine smile. "No, I think a warm bath will do. Used to be a nurse, remember? And a paramedic looked me over and pronounced me quite fit for everything but skydiving."

"And to think I already rented the plane," I joked.

"A plane—that's not a bad idea." Lisa seemed to forget all about her headache. "Hire a plane to go over the beach, if it ever stops raining. Do some skywriting."

"Skywriting?"

"Sure, everybody always reads skywriting, even if usually all it says is 'Will you marry me?' or 'I love you.' You've gotta price how much it would cost to write 'Vote for Jessie Adams.'"

"Certainly no point in pricing 'Will you marry me?' or 'I love you,'" I said. I swallowed a sigh. "Come on. No security experts or skywriting tonight. Let's get you home."

I spent the night at Lisa's house, moral support not just for her, but for me. I fussed around with pillows and ice cubes and aspirin and described in hilarious detail the other contenders for city council. I did not think about Chuck, not once. Well, maybe once, but just before I fell asleep.

The overnight drizzle turned into yet more full-fledged rain by morning, and woke me early with the unfamiliar sound of it pouring down Lisa's gutters.

Lisa was still asleep, so I took a shower and watched CNN for a while with the volume turned way down, waiting for the local weather report and the now somewhat standard dire predictions of mud slides and closed streets.

I sat at her kitchen table with a bowl full of cottage cheese and granola and a large glass of calcium-enhanced orange juice and called the security service I knew.

They referred me to a local South Bay guy named Big Dave who handled the kind of gig Lisa needed.

Dave returned my phone call within minutes, sounding nicely authoritative. Within an hour, Lisa was up and dressed and he met us at her place. He looked like he'd just walked off Mt. Rushmore or something, there in her cozy cottage living room among the hand-quilted pillows and wicker furniture and black-and-white photos of the old fishing pier and the club in its heyday.

Dave had arms that looked like they were cast in bronze, short sandy hair, and hard blue eyes. He also had lots of freckles, which were the only thing that made him look like he might not squash you like a bug just for fun.

But once he finished questioning Lisa about the attack, he relaxed a little and smiled, and his eyes grew less hard.

"You hire me, I promise you, I'll be there for you. Won't let you down."

Lisa conferred with me for just slightly more than two seconds before she hired him. "You think he's as good as he seems?" she asked. "I don't usually jump into a relationship so quickly but—"

"Me either," I said, a little defensively.

"But sometimes circumstances just dictate that fools rush in."

"I hear you."

"I like the guy."

"Me, too," I said.

Once hired, Dave jumped into action.

"I'll go into the club with you and get you set up with a security camera. Something not too expensive. Hook it up myself. See if there's any other needs I can advise you on," he told Lisa.

She hesitated and he threw in, "Off the clock. Won't start workin' officially until this evening's little shindig for her."

He pointed a thumb in my direction and not much of a smile. The smile he reserved for Lisa. "I have your back now," he said.

I couldn't help hoping there'd be a brown car waiting when Dave dropped me off at my place, but of course there wasn't. There were also no messages on my answering machine.

It was time I accepted that I'd merely had a one-afternoon stand and there were more important things in life than brooding over such an occurrence. Still, as I was changing for work, the doorbell rang and I ran for it. I really, really ran. Squeak chased me and Sally chased Squeak.

And midrun I stopped and checked my hair in the mirror and then there was a second knock and

I tripped over Sally in my overeagerness to answer it. She growled and cast me one of her most exasperated looks, as if I was the one who peed on rugs. I answered the door, breathless.

It wasn't Chuck. Nope, it was none other than Ned Rutkin, poised and pink-faced in another designer suit nice enough to have belonged on another body. He was standing under an umbrella with a stack of glossy brochures in his hand.

"Well, hello, I'm running for city council and—"

"I know you are, Ned," I said, not bothering to keep the irritation and disappointment out of my voice.

"You've seen my signs then—" He'd already put one of the brochures in my hand when he recognized me. I saw the brochure had a very nice picture, sort of a superimposed picture, of Ned standing right next to JFK on his PT boat. I had a picture taken of me kind of like that once, only I was standing next to Elvis in the Madame Tussauds Wax Museum, Las Vegas.

"Well, it's Ms. Adams," he said, adjusting his voice and his smile to dimmer wattage. "You certainly did appear out of the woodwork to challenge those of us who've been hoping for a slot on the city council for years now."

"So I'm keeping you on your toes, Ned?" I asked.

"Always on them." He chuckled. "I've served on the Chamber of Commerce, you know. Along with working on the City Planning Commission. I served on the school board for six years, even though I have no children or interest in education. My wife and I both are extremely active investors in progressive—"

I interrupted, still smarting from the fact that Ned was not Chuck.

"Listen, Ned, if you think I find your expertise intimidating, you're wrong," I lied. "In fact, I find it all kind of boring. Like maybe a lot of the voters around here do."

Ned snatched back the brochure like he was afraid I might just superimpose myself on the PT boat, substitute my name for his, and Xerox it a thousand times.

"Sorry to upset you," Ned said unctuously. "I'm sure you'll realize that the best person for the job will win."

Ned had not particularly upset me, and I sure didn't want his stupid brochure. What I did want was Ned's umbrella, which was a nice expensive black one with a wooden handle carved like a duck.

But before I could act swiftly—snatch the umbrella and slam the door—he was already scurrying away down the stairs wishing me "Good luck in your endeavors."

"You, too," I called after him. "Especially with that PT boat thing."

I fed Squeak who was most insistent, and ignored the puddle Sally had just made by the door—which I was certain in her mind I deserved for tripping over her. Why couldn't she at least make herself useful and pee inappropriately on command, like right on Ned's shiny shoes?

I threw on a baseball cap and pulled my jacket up around my neck and went out into the rain. I unlocked the door of my sway-backed, aged Corolla, climbed inside, inserted the key, and said a quick prayer, but naturally, it did not turn over. I let it sit and tried it again and then I gave up.

I couldn't see the bus coming so I stopped in at the corner grocery again for one of my favorite doughnuts. I wasn't exactly dying to see Tad, but sometimes one has to make sacrifices in order to achieve the important things in life, like grape-filled chocolate-glazed doughnuts.

Outside the store there was a big banner over the doorway that said ELECT TAD! A NAME YOU CAN TRUST! The letters were kind of faded and the message so generic I had a feeling he'd used it in his previous election attempts.

Inside, Tad was wearing an even more faded-looking ELECT TAD, THAT'S ME!" T-shirt, and stocking a bunch of miniature pies with BENNI iced on them in red, white, and blue lettering.

"Hi there, girl," he said. "You gonna get elected?"

"Not sure. How about you?"

"Oh, mos' def I'm winning." He raised his fist in a kind of salute. "You see Ned's brochure?" He pulled it out of a trash can behind the counter. I got a good look now at the words coming out of JFK's mouth in a bubble. "Rutkin is best."

"What an idiot. Thinks people can actually read his Pacific Rim languages stuff. 'Niktur si tseb.' Like Kennedy would've said that."

It took me a beat, but then I remembered Tad's comments about dyslexia when we first met.

"Never know," I offered.

Tad leered across the counter at me. "What I do know is we are both a lot cooler cats than most of the other dogs in this dog-and-pony show."

I gave him a tepid smile. My head was spinning from the mixed metaphors, which couldn't possibly be blamed on dyslexia.

"Anyways, you and I should *both* win IMO, but since we can't, maybe we can sleep together and that'll accomplish the same thing."

"How's that?" I asked, reaching around the pies for a doughnut. I've found that the best way to react when hit upon by someone so completely inappropriate that it's not even offensive is to simply act as if what they've said is perfectly reasonable and you'll consider it. Sometime in the future, like a hundred light-years from now.

"Politics makes strange bedfellows." Tad winked. "You've heard that expression."

I made no response at all, just handed him a five.

"Well, *I've* heard it, anyway," he amended, like maybe I wasn't as bright a bulb as he thought I was.

I changed the ludicrous subject while he rang me up. "Speaking of politics. Why are you stocking pies that promote Benni Cardell?"

He looked mystified. I couldn't resist throwing in, "Do you want to sleep with Benni, too?"

"Oh, Benni. *That* chick! That's what it means on the pies, wow. Really bad icing letters, took me a while to read 'em at all. I thought it was one of those acronyms. For some kinda pie filling, like blueberry banana or something."

He looked positively contemplative as he gave me change. His fingers grazed mine just a little too long and I kind of snatched my hand away. Now he seemed amused.

"Don't be jealous. She's too old for me, girl. Somebody just dropped the pies off in a basket, asked if I'd display 'em and I said, 'I dunno. How much are they?,' and the dude said they're free, so I said sure. There was a bunch of flyers stuck to the bottom of the tins, but I just tore them off, didn't bother to read 'em. Truth to tell I am not a big reader, I prefer TV. I priced the pies to move—you know, a buck each. I'm an entrepreneur even before I'm a politician. Two birds in one stone though. Dumping her flyers and making a couple bills on her baking, pretty slick without even realizing it, huh. Wasn't there a poem once about birds and one stone in a pie and a king or something?"

"Blackbirds in a pie," I said. "Six and twenty of them."

"With a stone though, right?"

"Could be."

"By Robert Snow?"

"No."

"Frost, that's the guy, stopping by the woods on a frosty evening, you've heard that."

I just pocketed my change.

"Well, *I* have anyway." He shook his head at me, really sure now that I was not as bright as he'd thought I was. "Wish Salome would bake me some pies. Or better yet, come jumping out of a cake. You and me and her! Now that would be a menagerie."

"Mos' def," I said, copying his style and heading for the door.

"You ever used to be a Las Vegas showgirl?" he called after me.

"Um. No. A little short." And probably a little bit flat-chested and a little bit not interested.

"Well, Salome, she's plenty tall enough. Six-two that lady, and built. I like 'em all sizes though. Don't be jealous just 'cause she used to walk a runway."

I figured it had to be the dyslexia again. "She's a 'purveyor of holistic health care products,'" I said, my hand on the door. "She's not a showgirl."

"She was. The Folies Eregreb. I think that's the name of it."

I turned around, surprised enough to actually

look at Tad who was kind of sizing me up, half-leering, half-squinting. He got a hold of himself.

"Bergère," I said.

"Yeah, sure she had a brassiere, or at least those little tassel things. Ned showed me an old newspaper ad. Ned kinda likes me but fears me, you know? Shares confidences, knows me well enough to know I'll only tell like the select few. He said it was when she was younger, you know. But kinda led me to believe she is still not disinterested in entertaining gentlemen. I think it's true. She's still pretty hot. I'd like to see her in a diamond g. And maybe some feathers. You have a diamond g? Feathers?"

"Nope." I left Tad without another word and walked on down to the bus stop.

Doughnuts were bad for my health anyway. It was time to give them up.

In front of me, I saw Ned crossing the street, shiny shoes splashing around the edges of a cavernous puddle, heading self-importantly toward the police station. Doubtlessly, the mayor's choice was going to glad-hand there, too. Impress with his stellar, boring credentials. And maybe tell everybody in uniform that Salome was a showgirl. I wondered if it was true. I also wondered what he was saying about me. I wondered if by simply going into The Place Chuck Worked, Ned could possibly find out about me and Chuck, and tell Tad, who would then doubtlessly tell the world what I really was, a slut who slept with stray cops.

The bus came fast and I sunk down in my seat with my doughnut. It must've been candidate sighting day though, because at the Playa Vista stop right before hitting Pacific Coast Highway, I saw Ida

Pinckney and Royal Garritty in some sort of conversation inside the coffee shop.

Actually it looked more like an argument than a conversation. He was wagging a hammy finger in her face, and she was drawing back from him, looking very quavery and upset. Royal's lips were drawn in something like a sneer, although maybe he was just about to devour the platter of biscotti on the table between them.

Tad was right about one thing. Politics made very strange bedfellows indeed. And then I thought, sighing, there were bedfellows who were merely strangers.

Chapter Seven

I played a lot of straight-ahead rock and roll, some Steve Earle, some semi-current Stones, some Magic Numbers, a little Nine Inch Nails. No Nick Drake, no Badly Drawn Boy, no 1970s Jesse Winchester. No more love songs, absolutely not.

I changed from jeans to another outdated, conservative skirt in the ladies' room, and went straight from the station to Lisa's place, renewing my makeup on the bus. I entered The Sea Shack with a perfect politician's smile and low turn out expectations.

But to my surprise, The Shack was packed with my supporters, at least assuming any of them actually lived in Playa Vista and were registered to vote there.

The crowd might've just come for the music of a very popular local band, and the free food thrown in on top of that, and not cared at all that half of tonight's admission fee and half the cost of every coffee drink was going directly to my campaign and was tax-deductible. Still, seeing all the cars jammed in the lot and filling up the curbside spaces, and inside, finding the tables full and standing room three deep along the bar, I realized I was going to be able to cover my campaign filing fees and pay Lisa's sign guy, too.

Who knew, maybe I could afford a flyer, something glossy and faked like Ned's. Me with say, Bruce Springsteen, our arms spread triumphantly to welcome a sellout crowd. Oh, and maybe I'd have Kurt Cobain with little angels' wings glued to his back hovering over me waving a magic wand.

In lieu of such wizardry, Lisa had a hand-painted sheet strung up behind the stage, reading VOTE FOR JESSIE ADAMS! SAVE THE SEA SHACK. Low-tech or not, it made me feel like, well, like a celebrity or something.

I didn't see Lisa or Big Dave immediately, but I did spot my program director, Sandy. Since he was coming down, he could've offered me a ride, saving me from the vicissitudes of public transportation. But apparently I'd been sacrificed in favor of a date, a girl with long purple fingernails and silver hair, with whom he appeared utterly besotted, stroking her shoulders, touching her cheek. She didn't look like she minded the attention, but she did look rather bored.

When he wasn't handling the girl, Sandy was handing out KCAS buttons and stickers and passing around a jar marked DONATIONS. Somehow I didn't think the donations were going to end up in my hands. Still, I appreciated the fact that he'd shown up at least, and dropped the cash for two admissions.

"Funky outfit," Sandy shouted at me, giving me a thumbs up. I glanced down at my calf-length skirt and the blouse with a little knit vest thing I'd pulled from the bowels of my closet. If Sandy liked it, I evidently looked as lame as I felt.

"Have something for you," he called out. I ignored

him. If he expected to give me a big KCAS button to wear at my campaign rally, he was out of luck. He forgot about me fast anyway, becoming occupied with fondling purple nails again, who was now moving from that bored look to one of semirepulsion.

Theodore was also there with a surly-looking teenage boy, doubtlessly the D-minus.

I found Lisa busy behind the bar. She waved a bottle of vanilla bean flavoring at me and I crossed the room to her.

"Where's Dave?" I asked.

"Checking out my new security camera. A friend of his came over and installed it this afternoon." She slid a couple of lattes across the bar to a well-heeled couple in designer denim.

"By the way, I saw you on tape earlier."

"On the security camera?"

"Paranoid! Cable access reran the debate this afternoon. Right after they reran last year's high school graduation." She was gesturing at the TV over the bar, a remnant from the days when the bar served something harder than espresso and there were Sunday afternoon football fans showing up to drink it.

"How was I?"

"Well, kinda purple. I don't think the footage was white balanced. So your skin was purple. Everybody's was though, so don't feel bad. And Tad's tattoos, they were strobing out. The security camera's a lot better, honestly."

"How did I sound, then?"

"Well, until the band started and I couldn't hear you, you sounded good. Like you do on the radio. Smooth and persuasive. But not phony. I mean at least not as phony as anybody else."

She mixed up a mean-looking iced cappuccino and gave it to a guy with a ponytail and a turquoise ring, who sniffed it and sipped it like he was at a wine tasting. "A hint of nutmeg," he said to me, like I cared.

But in case he was a voter, I smiled like I did. Not as phony as everybody else quite *yet* was the real story.

I shook his hand, I introduced myself, and he nodded. "I'll try to remember to vote," he said. "But ever since my alien abduction I get these memory lapses."

I laughed like I thought he was very amusing, but he didn't laugh so I kind of had the feeling he might be serious, and I edged away from him and back toward Lisa.

"Anyway," Lisa went on, "Dave's decided to hang in the parking lot tonight, watch everybody coming and going, and leave his friend on the inside. He wants to make sure everything runs smoothly tonight. No extra charge for the extra set of eyes, he said. He's really wonderful."

I smiled. I could tell Lisa might possibly think Dave was wonderful in a way that had nothing to do with club security. Well, good for her. One of us ought to meet a guy who was worth meeting.

"They're *both* being just wonderful," Lisa went on. "Incredibly on top of things. Here's Mr. Jackson now. Let me introduce you—"

I turned toward this Mr. Jackson and saw not Mr. Jackson but . . . Chuck. Yes, he was always on top of things. Including, recently, me.

So his last name was Jackson. He wasn't wearing a suit and tie anymore, and he looked less like a cop and more like a body builder or something, a more slender, swarthy version of Dave. His shoulders and chest were all pumped up and strong and broad beneath a just slightly tight black T-shirt that he was wearing over just slightly tight black jeans and battered sneakers.

I suppose I was turning purple again, just like on cable access.

"This is the friend I was telling you about, who's running for city council." Lisa smiled. "Jessie Adams."

"So it is," Chuck said.

I could feel him taking me in, and I felt foolish in my knee-length out-of-date-skirt, I realized every other female in the entire room was wearing tight hip-riding jeans and camisoles and tank tops and miniskirts. I felt like I'd wandered into the wrong party. I wanted to say, You know, I am hipper than this, I do own spaghetti-strap tops and dangling earrings with lots of beads.

"Chuck Jackson," said Chuck, his eyes drifting away before they quite reached mine.

"You already *know* me—my name that is, I guess," I said. I sounded not exactly pleased by that fact, and a little puzzled frown line appeared between Lisa's brows.

Despite how much I had longed, absolutely longed, in the past thirty-six hours to see him, to hear from him, now I longed for nothing more, than to never ever see or hear from him again. But here he was.

The phone behind the coffee bar rang and Lisa picked up.

"The Sea Shack," she said cheerfully.

Chuck stepped uncomfortably close to me and muttered, "City Council? Thought you were a DJ."

"Club bouncer?" I returned smartly, my face still hot. "I thought you were a cop."

"I am. I moonlight for Dave on occasion."

So indirectly it was my fault he was even there. Of course absolutely directly it was my fault that I even cared, one way or the other.

Lisa slammed the phone down on the bar. The frown line between her brows was deep now and she looked kind of pale.

"Oh, shit," she said.

"What?" both Chuck and I asked. We inched away from each other.

"Prank call," Lisa said, "I guess."

"What do you mean you guess?" I asked.

"After last night—I'm still jumpy," Lisa replied.

"After what Dave told me happened last night, you should be," Chuck said. "Now what just went down?"

"This man—I guess he just—threatened me."

"Threatened you how?" Chuck and I said simultaneously, and took a larger step apart, as if we were contaminating each other's minds or something.

Lisa was too upset to notice. She rubbed at her eyes. "He said, 'I just have to tell you something. You're not smart enough to take me on.'"

"To take me on—" Chuck repeated. "That's all he said?"

"Yeah." Lisa tried to shrug it off. "And the guy who broke in here, he said, 'You can't take me out.' Probably a coincidence. But he had a hoarse low voice. Like the guy who robbed me."

"I had a funny phone call myself. Yesterday," I said, biting my lip. "Almost forgot about it, with so much going down."

"Yeah, I bet," Chuck said, and his eyes flashed with

wicked amusement. "So much." Then he turned serious. "What kind of voice did your caller have?"

"Also low and raspy. Tom Waits like," I told him.

He nodded intently like he knew what Tom Waits sounded like when he growled "Looking for the Heart of Saturday Night," but I bet he didn't even own a single one of his CDs.

I didn't even think Chuck was really listening to what I said; he was just looking at me and nodding. Looking at me really intently, like he was absorbing me or something. I had to look away. I looked at the stage.

The lead singer of The Dublin Five was tuning his guitar. He had long blond hair and blue eyes and it occurred to me that there were an awful lot of musicians out there with long blond hair and blue eyes, and that all of a sudden I wasn't all that excited by the prospect.

"So. Two funny phone calls," Chuck resumed. "One to each of you. Both with the same kind of voice as Lisa's intruder. What did your caller say?" Chuck asked me. "Try to be exact."

I rubbed my forehead with the back of my hand. What I remembered all too clearly was thinking it was Chuck calling. And then how he never did call.

I made an effort. "He said he was warning me, that politics were tough—it doesn't sound that bad, but when he was saying it, I felt like it was a threat."

"Of course it did. This is all connected," Chuck said.

"My robbery has something to do with the election?" Lisa asked, surprised.

"Definitely," Chuck and I both answered, and took another step apart. If we kept saying the same thing at the same time, pretty soon we were going

to be at opposite ends of the bar and shouting over
The Dublin Five's drumbeats.

"That's bizarre though, isn't it? An election mugging? Threatening phone calls? Over Playa Vista
City Council?" Lisa asked me more than Chuck.

"Exactly," we both said.

We both gripped the bar railing as if we were pre-
venting ourselves from each taking another step
back. Agreeing was almost as bad as saying the same
thing at the same time.

"This is just a little seaside town—" Lisa began.

"With million-dollar homes. With contractors
waiting for the right zoning to allow them to swoop
in and build some more and knock you out of the
ballpark," I reminded her.

"Maybe literally," Chuck added.

"So it stands to reason that someone could be
very concerned about me winning," I said.

"You're going to *win?*" Chuck asked.

I spun on him. He seemed almost amused by the
idea.

"Well, that is the plan," I said.

"You think you have a better chance than Ned
Rutkin? He has signage, a whole PR machine, tons
of access, connections you wouldn't believe,"
Chuck said.

I was really sick of Ned and his signs.

"It's not that I have a better chance. I'm a better
candidate! People are gonna see that!" I was getting
quite worked up for someone who hadn't even considered *being* a candidate until seventy-two hours
ago. "I could do a lot more for this town than the
pie lady or the showgirl or the foreclosure thug or
the environmentalist who wants to turn the harbor
into a swamp, or even Mr. Connected Rutkin."

"And then there's Tad," Lisa said.

"You know what they say, third time's a charm. Local boy. Maybe thirteenth run for office is a charm for him," Chuck said. He had that amused look on his face again, and I knew he was pulling my chain before he asked, "Who's a showgirl?"

I stuck out my tongue.

He laughed. I did not laugh.

"Getting serious again, I think these crank calls and the attack here at the club are tied in to the perception at least that Ms. Adams is a political threat."

Ms. Adams, was it? And just a *perception* that I was a threat? I wanted to smack Chuck, but before I had a chance, the front door opened and a couple of wiry tough guys in denim jackets walked in.

They were both scowling, and one of them had an ominous-looking scar running down his cheek and the other one was wearing a skull ring in his nose. They looked like they'd forgotten this wasn't punk night. They were aggressively pushing past the roped off PLEASE WAIT HERE sign Lisa had strung by the entrance. Lisa started toward them, but Chuck took her arm.

"I'll welcome these dudes," he said, and he strode across the room.

"What do you think?" Lisa asked me.

"I don't think we have to worry about anybody pulling something tonight, not with this crowd, not with your—your security around."

I was trying unsuccessfully not to watch Chuck, weaving his way through the tables to the front door. He had this way of walking—cocky, arrogant, graceful somehow. A wave of something like longing passed through me.

"I meant," Lisa said, "what do you think of Dave's friend Chuck Jackson? I think he likes you."

"How could he like me?" I tore my eyes off Chuck now. My cheeks were burning. He liked me? Lisa thought he liked me! But wait, why did I care if he liked me? We'd just crossed paths again, that was all. Just because we'd crossed paths did not mean anything would ever again come of this particular alignment of the space time continuum.

"I don't know *how*, but he does. I mean it's really obvious," Lisa said. "He can't take his eyes off you."

She didn't say so, but the way she was looking at me now, she seemed to be implying I couldn't take my eyes off him, either.

"He couldn't possibly like me," I said stiffly. "He just—uh—met me. He is not my type. Is he my type?"

"No. But there's some kind of chemistry. Really."

We were both watching Chuck now, conversing with the two tough guys. He had his arms crossed and his body was all coiled up, like he was a cougar about to pounce or something. Then one of the guys took out his wallet and there was an exchange of greenbacks. Chuck's shoulders relaxed, he shrugged, pointed them in the direction of the bar.

"I guess he cleared them," Lisa said. "Boy, I wish I could afford to have somebody like him or Dave— Dave's a really great guy—around all the time. Maybe if you win this election and I stop sinking so much into 'improvements' around this place at the beck and call of the politicians, and put more into advertising, and business picked up, I *could* have a guy like Dave around. Just knowing he's outside, watching over the place. Well, it makes a difference."

She sounded wistful. It struck me that she hadn't even looked at a man, much less had one give her safety tips, since Bob passed away. I squeezed her shoulder.

"You've been doing everything on your own a long time," I said.

She flashed me a quick, bright smile. "It would be nice not to be the only one responsible for breaking up fistfights between couples who've had too much espresso, that's all."

The two guys in denim stepped up to us at the bar. "Your door fella said you were out of seats but you were allowing standing room at the bar if we bought a coupla drinks and contributed to the cause."

"Sure thing," Lisa said, and she started behind the counter.

But there was Chuck again, putting the cash he'd collected into the register behind the bar.

"I want to stay near the phone, in case you get any more funny phone calls," Chuck said. "Why don't you go relax a little? You've been working all afternoon. Jessie and I can take over for you here," Chuck said.

My eyes met his again. He was smiling. I almost couldn't help myself. I smiled back.

Lisa was surprised. "*You* want to make mochas?"

"Seriously, cop trick. Blend in with the scene," Chuck explained.

Lisa looked from him to me, like there was something she couldn't quite figure out. There was a lot I couldn't quite figure out, but I gave her a steady smile.

"He's right. I know where everything is," I said. "You need to rest, and if I don't keep busy I'll get nervous before I make my little speech tonight."

"Okay. Sure, you guys cover things," Lisa said. She

walked over toward the stage, but shot a meaningful glance at me over her shoulder.

"What'll you have?" I asked the chirpy, skinny
denim guys as I joined Chuck behind the bar.

"Two strawberry sugar-free frappés," the one with
the scar said.

Chuck looked deeply uncomfortable. "Coffee I
know. Strawberry frappés—"

"I've got it," I said.

I opened a small refrigerator, took out some un-
thawed frozen strawberries, and dumped them in a
blender. I took out milk, sweet and low, and ice,
measured and poured it all into the blender.

Then I waited.

"Why don't you turn on the blender?" Chuck
suggested.

Right. He had no clue how to make a strawberry
frappé, but now he was going to give me tips.

"Because the band is playing. It would be rude to
run the blender now. I'll turn it on when the song
ends."

In the meantime I got out a couple of glasses,
straws, napkins, plastic spoons. Anything but look
at Chuck. Anything but talk to Chuck.

"You're being weird," he said. "Are you always this
weird?"

"Yes," I said.

"I can't believe it's you. Here. I thought, can't be
the same Jessie—"

"Considering how you didn't call and all."

"I would've."

"Right." I busied myself putting the lid on the
blender.

"Listen, when we—ran into each other, I'd just
gotten off a twelve-hour surveillance, and called my

boss an asshole, which by the way he is. He didn't like my attitude. And I don't like his. While I was still at your place, I got a call. He pulled major rank on me. Called it disciplinary action and he sent me right back out on the same surveillance again. After I left you, I barely had time to feed my dog before I had to turn back around and do that second twelve hours. And after that, I crashed. Worked again. And tonight, before I could call you, Dave called me and"—he spread out his hands, placating— "here we are."

"What were you surveying anyway?"

"Hookers," he said.

I locked eyes with him.

"I work major crimes. Around here, a call girl ring, that's major crime."

"Ah," I said. "Call girls. Were you out trolling for some the other day?"

"It doesn't happen all the time, like you said, does it, what we—"

"You were an aberration," I said, and I didn't say it like being an aberration was a nice thing, or like I was being funny, or anything. I was mad. I wasn't even sure why I was mad.

"That kinda hurts. An aberration. *You* weren't. I mean, you personally. I don't mean that every woman I run into I—"

"It won't happen again," I said.

"Never?" There was that little twitch of a smile that I'd seen in my apartment, like he was sharing a kind of secret joke with himself. It was very endearing, that smile. Sort of vulnerable and rueful. I didn't let it get to me.

"Not with me it won't," I said.

"Okay." He nodded. "Okay. We have other things

to think about anyway, right? I'm here because Dave wants to make for damn sure there isn't any more trouble at this club. And he thinks there could be. So we're both keeping an eye on your friend. And if you're getting funny phone calls, I'd like to keep an eye on you, too."

"I'm not paying you."

"I didn't say you had to. But it could be fun. Sounds a little kinky, actually. Kind of a call *boy* operation."

He had that smile again. And that smile had the effect of making me want to touch it. Touch his lips with my fingertips and then his lips with my own. I steeled myself. Resistance was not futile.

At last the song ended in an upbeat, long-drawn-out D major chord and enthusiastic applause. I turned on the blender, and timing it perfectly, I flicked it off again before the opening chord on the next song was struck.

"Very respectful," Chuck said.

I couldn't tell if he was making fun of me or not. Irritability rose up like hackles on my back. I poured the strawberry frappés into the two glass mugs.

"I remember when this place used to serve beer in glasses like that," Chuck added. "I used to come down here sometimes, after work. I think I saw you do a set once. With some blond guy with long hair, playing guitar. He was looking all moony at you."

"Huh," I said, because it was altogether too weird that he was here right now, but he hadn't called and we'd had sex and I was really totally attracted to him and he wasn't the type of guy I would usually be attracted to, and on top of all that he'd seen me sing with Jack once it must've been like two years ago in this very place, when we'd first met, and now it was like Chuck knew me intimately, well, I suppose he did.

Oh, God, what if Lisa hired Dave permanently and Chuck was like part of the package and I'd have to run into him over and over again? No, I couldn't handle that. I'd just never show my face in this place again.

As I would have to show it, I realized, to everyone in this room after this set ended, because this was my own fund-raiser and he would be here tonight, even if he wasn't any other night, watching me, and it wouldn't just be some stage fright dream that I was up there at the mike without any clothes on, because he could at least imagine me up there at that mike without any clothes, without even really having to imagine.

I set the mugs and the spoons and napkins on the bar in front of the two guys. My hands were trembling just a little.

"There you go," I said, even more chirpy than before. "Seven dollars. And that goes half to the house and half to my campaign, but you can write the whole thing off, I won't tell."

"No whipped cream?" the one without the scar but with the nose ring asked.

I opened the little fridge behind the bar and took out the big metal can, shook it, and sprayed and got—nothing. I tried it again, in case I had somehow done something wrong, although how you could screw up spraying Reddi-wip was beyond me.

"Let me try," Chuck suggested, and I just glowered at him, while he looked at me like I was an idiot who couldn't figure out how to spray whipped cream.

His fingers brushed mine as he took the can, and

I could feel the heat of his skin, and the heat stayed with me even as his fingers were busy shaking the can and ending up with nada.

"Empty," he agreed.

I wanted to smack him again. There was, I realized, no logical reason for me to be so angry at him. Except that I was really angry at myself. For wanting to see him so badly and for feeling so strange about actually seeing him, and for feeling that there was something between us other than what there was— a moment of mutual base interest.

"I'm empty," I said to the frappé guys, referring to the whipped cream and not my emotional state, although it was an appropriate way to describe both.

"I'll have to get some more from the kitchen, I guess?" I said, kind of leaving a question in my voice, like, if you really want me to, because I don't really want to.

The guy with the skull nose ring smiled apologetically. "I appreciate it. I don't like 'em without whipped cream."

I crinkled my nose. I was a political candidate and a professional communicator and starting to get depressed besides. I was not a waitress. At least I had not been for at least three years, since I was also an underemployed musician.

He slapped a fifty on the counter. "No change necessary," he said. "Political contribution."

I thought about making Chuck go, since it was his bright idea to help out behind the coffee bar, but then he was supposed to be keeping an eye on the room and keeping things safe and everything, so I went.

Hitting the kitchen got me away from Chuck

anyway, which was a good thing. It gave me a chance to breathe and not watch him rub a towel back and forth over the bar like he would see the answer to all his life's questions if he just rubbed hard enough.

Naturally, I wondered what he was thinking about, and at the same time I was thinking of him rubbing his hands like that against my hips. Oh yeah, it was time for a break from Chuck.

I stalked into the kitchen, opened the big fridge, and pulled out an industrial-sized can of whipped cream. I stood there for a long minute with the cool air from the fridge hitting my face. I felt calmer now. I felt the heat that had risen up in my cheeks, and never really left from the minute I saw Chuck, finally dissipate.

At last I turned away and nudged the refrigerator door closed with my shoulder. And at that moment, the kitchen door swung open behind me, and maybe because of the phone calls and the Lisa-mugging and everything, or maybe because of this mood I was in over Chuck-the-aberration, I jumped and dropped the whipped cream.

Well, almost dropped it. Chuck made a quick grab and set the can on the counter, very lithe, very competent. And then he grabbed me. Just as quick, just as competent. He had me in his arms and he was kissing me like he had been wanting to kiss me for years or a day or at least hours, and couldn't believe he finally had the chance to kiss me now. And I was kissing him back, the same way.

"Oh yeah," we both said, between kisses, on my lips, eyes, cheeks, neck, and back again.

He deftly slipped a hand up the back of my

blouse and unsnapped my bra. "I'm a fast learner,"
he whispered.

"Oh," I gasped.

"Oh—" he gasped in return as his lips found
mine again and our tongues moved in and out between our teeth.

He pressed me tight against him. I could feel the
heat and hardness of his body, I could feel myself
sinking into his arms, sinking deeper and deeper
like I was in quicksand and I liked being swallowed
up. And I did like it, very much.

How could I have possibly wanted him to go
away? How could I have possibly not remembered
this feeling he made rise up inside me, from the
tips of my fingers straight through my rib cage and
deep inside some hidden place in my heart? A
thrill, a chill, a rightness, a heat. Oh, God. If only
he felt just a little bit the same way. Just a little bit.

I was letting him move me back against the refrigerator, letting him pull my carefully chosen, lace-
trimmed, conservative candidate's blouse out of
the waistband of my skirt and slip his hands beneath the fabric, rub up against my skin, slip his fingers inside my loosened bra, his fingers so warm,
my skin still refrigerator cool. I felt him warm me,
I felt his fingers flick against my nipples, and I felt
them quicken and harden and a flood of warm feeling and cold feeling both rippled all through my
body and I arched up against him. God, I wanted
him. I wanted him right there.

Apparently, he did feel that way, at least a little
bit, too, because he was rocking up against me, he
was lifting up my skirt, he was slipping his hand between my legs and inching down the waistband of

my stockings. We were both breathing so hard and fast we didn't hear the door open again behind us.

"Oh!" said Lisa, the kitchen door swinging back with a jolt against her hip.

Chuck and I pulled apart, I was sure that my face was once again that cable-access purple.

Chuck on the other hand was more or less sanguine. He smiled at Lisa and straightened his shirt. "We just needed a—condiment."

He hoisted the mega-whipped-cream can.

"Ah. Yes. A condiment," Lisa said.

Chuck was already pushing open the swinging door, holding it for Lisa to precede him, giving me the moment I needed to rearrange myself, tuck in my blouse, smooth my hair, pull up my stockings, catch my breath, avoid Lisa.

How embarrassing was it to be caught messing around with your best friend's assistant bouncer, whom you'd appeared to have met only moments before and not entirely approved of? More or less embarrassing than admitting you'd met him, oh, two days ago, and on that very first day having just met him, you'd already seen him naked? That was a tough call.

Chapter Eight

When I emerged from the kitchen, Lisa was leaning against the wall near the stage with a strange look on her face, as if she was Alice in Wonderland and she'd just passed through the rabbit hole. I figured I had to explain somehow, even though I had no exact idea myself what was going on with me and Chuck.

It was all Chuck's fault for putting me in this situation of having to explain something that had no explanation. He was the one that kissed me. I only kissed him back. Over and over.

I frowned across the room at him, but he gave me the hugest smile I had ever seen on any person anywhere and I found I was smiling back like a complete and utter idiot.

Still smiling, I drew a deep breath and leaned in close to Lisa.

"I know him," I said.

"Biblically speaking, I gather," she replied. "Why didn't you tell me?"

"I didn't have a chance?" I said it more like a question than an answer because that wasn't really true, but it could pass as an answer if she let it. She gave me a quick once-over and let it pass.

"I thought he was so not your type," Lisa said. "Where did you meet him?"

"In front of the police station," I said, my face hot.

"When?"

"Um. Day before yesterday. Um. When I filed for the city council race. We uh—we talked. And stuff."

"Well, I think he's an improvement. Over Jack. So for what that's worth—"

"Thanks?" Again, the question mark crept into my voice.

Lisa shrugged. I could tell she was a little bit mad at me for keeping this thing with Chuck a secret.

I felt like I should stay and try to make her understand what was going on, but honestly, what was I going to say when I didn't understand myself?

Besides, there was Chuck smiling at me, and I was more or less compelled to go over there and stand beside him and say something intelligent, something endearing, something that would clarify my feelings and his feelings and whatever it was that was going on between us. And then once I did that, then I could explain things to Lisa.

So I went over to the bar, and we were both giving each other these goofy smiles.

"Wow," I said. That was certainly intelligent and clarifying.

"Yeah," he said. He took my hand in his and smoothed his fingers over it. He seemed to think that was all that was necessary by way of communication.

"We should talk about this," I said. "Don't you think?"

"Why? Because you're always talking?"

"What does that mean?" He was annoying me again.

"I mean you intellectualize, you express yourself uh, verbally—for a living," he said hastily, picking up on my recoil. "And I don't know what to say. How much do we really have to talk to know that—something just feels right? Really right. There's something going on with us. Something really, really going on with us."

"Yeah, but what? I mean we barely even know each other. Logically, what's happening here?" I demanded.

Green eyes dancing mischievously, he brushed his fingers against my lips, silencing me. His hair was kind of messed up—it was probably perpetually messed up—and I just wanted to run my fingers through his curls and smooth it.

"Logically? I don't know. Illogically? That whipped cream? I'd like to rub it all over your body and lick it off before it melts. I'd like to take some of those strawberries, a little chocolate syrup, make a sundae out of you and eat you up. Then I'd like you to turn me into whatever kind of desert you've ever really wanted to take a great big mouthful of and—"

"Pie!" The screechy voice made us both jump and spin toward its owner, none other than Benni Cardell, grinning her big tight-lipped grin across the bar.

"You don't have any pie in this place. Hello there, Miss Jessie. Don't you look pretty. I just got here and your friend told me she'd look for you, but I guess she forgot why she was looking for you because you didn't make it over to my table in the back there, now did you?"

"Uh. No." I could see why Lisa would forget. Even if she hadn't caught Chuck and I more or less in flagrante, Benni wasn't someone you wanted to remember.

"You're blushing. My goodness, don't be embarrassed that one of your more experienced fellow candidates came out to get a gander of you and have a good time. I like a band as much as anyone, and I certainly wanted to see this place, which I gather is a place destined to become kind of another place, due to the changing infrastructure of our city."

"I think that's still open to conjecture," I managed.

She turned her attention from me to Chuck and stretched her lips into a tighter, upward curve. To say that she was smiling was kind of a stretch. It was more like a grimace.

Chuck squared his shoulders, flexed those taut pecs a little.

"This your boyfriend?" Benni asked bluntly.

"Friends," I said. "Good friends."

"And you are?" Chuck said.

"Oh, shucks," said Benni. "I like to bake pies. And run PTA's, I was known as PTA Benni for about seventeen years. While my kids were in school, you know. After that I was in charge of youth group sing-alongs and bake sales for a variety of local charitable ministries. I've stuck with all the Boy and Girl Scout troops, offering my help whenever I can with environmental projects and arts and crafts. And I've had my foot in the back door of politics, or rather the kitchen of politics, ha there, baking up my own special creations for a long time. A behind-the-scenes kind of person. South Bay Women's League. South Bay Ladies Club. South Bay Mothers United. Lots of support in this community. Everybody knows me. I'm the pie lady!"

She gave a long laugh. Her laugh fit with the overall sort of horsey look of her long face, kind of like that of a horse neighing, except several decibels lower, in direct contrast to her screechy voice.

"Uh-huh," I said. "Yet I didn't know you before the other night."

"Me neither, I'm sorry to say," Chuck said gallantly. Meanwhile, his hand slipped behind my back and kind of caressed my butt.

Even though we hadn't talked things through, even though I didn't know what was going on between us, I gave in and laughed. He laughed. Benni looked puzzled.

"What humor am I missing?"

"None," we both said, and this time, though we were speaking in unison, we did not draw apart. That would've meant his hand wouldn't be stroking my butt anymore and I liked it there.

"You all don't know me because you haven't been involved in this community."

"Oh, I'm pretty involved," Chuck said, "although usually with miscreants."

Benni looked blank.

"I don't know Miss whoever," Benni said. "Which does surprise me because I really do know almost everybody—who is anybody—in this town. Anyway, what I meant was that you haven't been really involved, deeply involved." Benni was focusing on me. "What coffee with the elementary school principal did you attend? What Little League game did you referee? Did you ever staff the Coalition of Kids Who Love the Beach? Chaperone a Youth League dance?"

"No," I said. "But I guess I'm missing how this is relevant to my candidacy."

"Oh, honey, honey, honey. Sugar, sugar."

Inevitably "You are my candy girl, and I can't stop loving you . . ." ran through my head. I bet I knew an old pop song, or a new one, to complete practically any phrase ever uttered.

"What *I'm* missing is whether or not you support Jessie's candidacy," Chuck said cooly.

"Oh, for goodness' sake! I'm her competition!" She socked him on the arm heartily.

"Care to make a donation?" Sandy had made his way up to us with his giant change jar. Purple nails was nowhere to be seen, she'd apparently given in to her semirepulsion and fled.

"For what?" Benni asked, almost flirtatiously.

Sandy scratched his hairy belly. I could tell he was eyeing her—Benni? God, Benni!—as a consolation prize. Not that he was a great prize himself, but still.

"For Jessie's campaign. You get a KCAS bumper sticker and glow-in-the-dark pin. I'm the KCAS program director"—he puffed out his chest proudly— "not to mention the purveyor of Sandy's Sunday Afternoon Brunch Beat all-requests oldies."

"Really?" said Benni, having ignored Sandy's references to my campaign. "Oldies, how fun. I like to sing them myself. Beatles, Beach Boys, Doobies, Rod Stewart, you know 'Tonight's the night . . .'" she warbled.

Sandy seemed charmed.

"Music just isn't as good now as it was in, say 1973," Benni said, breaking off from her song.

"That's for damn sure," Sandy agreed.

I rolled my eyes but no one noticed.

"I love to sing oldies," Benni said. "My son bought me a karaoke machine for my birthday. I bring it everywhere I volunteer, and I volunteer a lot. I use it for a little extra pizzazz, you know.

People say I'm pretty good, that sometimes, with a little vocal enhancement I sound just like the original artist," Benni enthused. "I should bring my machine down to this club and perform sometime."

"I bet Lisa would love that," I said, oozing sarcasm.

Benni ignored me, googling her eyes at Sandy. "So you work with Jessie, here."

"Definitely. I came down tonight to bring her the best in vibes. And this big jar here—it's my way of supporting the midafternoon delight of our airwaves," he said clapping his big hand on my shoulder.

"Noontime delight," Chuck whispered in my ear.

I went all hot and cold and goose bumpy just like that.

Benni eyed Sandy with a sort of glazed-eyed devotion. "You remind me of my ex," she said. "Do you like pies?"

"I love pies!" Sandy exclaimed enthusiastically.

"Well, come on over to my table," she said. "I have a few little pastry pleasures with me tonight. And I want to hear everything about the radio business. It sounds really exciting. And disc jockeys . . . I've always admired them. Having to sit in those little booths all by themselves, right? Are you all by yourself when you do your show? Do you get lonely, Sandy?"

Support for my political efforts forgotten, he trailed her across the room, where I saw her pull a little packaged baked good out of a large canvas satchel and hand it to him. He was practically drooling.

Too late, I remembered Sandy saying he had something to give me. It was probably just tickets to some concert I didn't want to attend. Whatever it was, I'd ask him about it when I saw him at the station again. I had no desire to spend any more time in Benni's company.

"Now that the pie lady is spoken for, as I recall we were discussing ice cream sundaes . . ." Chuck began.

But we were once again interrupted, this time from the stage.

The lead singer hushed the crowd's applause. "As you all know, this is a special night. This is not just another Friday. This is a special Friday! We're proud to be a part of a rock the vote effort here in Playa Vista. Get out there and vote! When's the election?"

No one answered, so I was forced to shout out "March 12!"

Benni, I noticed out of the corner of my eye, was whispering to Sandy. Kind of creepy. Even if purple nails had decamped early, there were a lot of other girls that Sandy, regardless of looks, but with the force of his . . . well, not personality, but persona anyway, as a radio station program director, could've hit on before descending to the depths of Benni. Although pie was a very persuasive tool of attraction to Sandy. He'd been known to devour ten at a time of the little apple ones from McDonald's.

"March 12, you heard her. That's our candidate Jessie talking. She's going to come up here and say a few words now. Remember, she is *the* candidate whose name you want to remember when you hit the voting booth. Jessie—what's your last name?"

Oh, that was real slick. I sighed. I felt Chuck sigh beside me.

"Adams," I called out, and I slipped around the bar and inched my way toward the stage. "Common wisdom is that most people have to hear something three times before they remember it, so maybe you'll introduce me three more times here."

To his credit, the singer led the other members of The Dublin Five in a little chant repeating my full name and accompanied by a little drum roll and then I was up on the stage, to a smattering of not-very-enthusiastic applause.

"We're certainly voting for this lovely lady," the lead singer said, with an Irish brogue that up close and personal, I believed was unnatural in origin. He bussed my cheek.

I smiled, a little too enthusiastically, because he leaned close and whispered in my ear that he would like, very much, to be alone in a voting booth with me.

"That would be illegal," I whispered back, and took a long step away from him with the mike in my hand.

"This is a great turnout tonight," I said. "Give yourselves a hand." Dutifully, because that sort of thing always works, the crowd applauded.

"I want to thank my good friend Lisa Murray, the owner of The Shack, for putting on this event tonight. I want you to know that I'm running for city council not only to support the preservation of this wonderful musical institution, but for a lot of other reasons, too."

For a moment I blanked on what my other reasons were. I saw Theo and his son, both sitting there yawning like they wished they were anyplace else; I saw Sandy staring at Benni, his arm draped casually across her shoulders as if he'd forgotten she was my rival or didn't care; I saw Benni sitting there grinning at me like I was as stupid as she thought I was.

Then I looked behind the bar, at Chuck, and saw him nod at me confidently, like atta girl, I could do it, the same way he probably looked at his four-legged friend Jessie when she caught a stick or something. Still, that encouraging smile worked. What he was encouraging me to do, exactly, I wasn't sure, but it very likely involved taking off all our clothes again.

I cleared my throat and putatively my head, and went on.

"I honestly believe I can help you keep this community healthy and vibrant. I don't think that anything good can come out of new zoning that exiles businesses like this one in favor of more and more unaffordable housing. I think we need to consider the needs of all the people in this town, not just special-interest groups."

I waited for the thunderous applause but none came. "That's all," I said, because maybe people were still waiting for me to finish.

Lisa started clapping and then others joined in, got a real rhythm going.

"Wonderful," the lead singer said. "Is she not?" And then the band was kicking it to "In the Name of Love."

Usually I would welcome any excuse to stay in the spotlight a little longer, but tonight I just kind of wanted to slip away. So naturally, the lead singer linked his arm with mine and as his brogue grew thicker still, he shouted, "Join us in a chorus." So much for slinking away.

Thanks to the arm linkage I stayed for *every* chorus until the song ended and the singer called, "Good night, fair lads and lassies."

With relief, at last I was able to unlock my arm

from the singer's. "Most bonnie lassie," he said to me. "Quite a voice ye have."

"Are you from Ireland originally?" I asked him.

"Not in point of fact. But spiritually," he said. "Spiritually I will always reside there in the land of the shamrock. In the here and now I am one of your most loyal constituents."

"Well, it's good to have your vote," I said.

"Well not my vote exactly. I don't live actually in Playa Vista—more like Van Nuys, that fair city, to be most accurate."

He was so full of crap that I was almost surprised I wasn't engaged to him.

Lisa was already at the door, reminding people to vote for me, so I jumped on in and joined her, shaking hands. There seemed to be a lot of people whose spirit resided in Playa Vista, but who technically lived in Torrance or Hermosa Beach or El Segundo or L.A. proper, not to mention quite a few Dublin Five fans from the wee fair isle of the San Fernando Valley. But there were some locals.

I really got into all the handshaking and smiling. I was pretty good at it, really, it felt natural. All I had to do was say, "Vote for me, Jessie Adams. Don't forget now," which honestly came just as easily as "Tune in to me weekdays, two to six, KCAS FM." I could probably do just as well with "Buy my new CD, available at music stores near you," except that I didn't have one.

Unfortunately, Benni seemed to have found the locals faster than I did, because almost every one was already holding one of her minipies with campaign flyer attached, even while nodding affirmatively that they'd vote for me.

Benni appeared to have scattered her pies and

fled, possibly with Sandy, which would be both interesting and grotesque to consider and gossip about with Theodore at the station on Monday.

Chuck went out into the parking lot and had some kind of a confab with Dave, then Dave watched the front and Chuck took the back while Lisa and I cleaned up.

"You brought in a big crowd tonight," Lisa remarked.

"The band was the draw," I said, "and you know it."

"Oh a lot of people came to support the club—and you," Lisa added hastily. And then in a softer voice she added, "Like apparently Chuck Jackson. When are you going to fill me in?"

"Tomorrow? When I'm maybe a little bit more sure of what's going on myself. Okay? It's been a long night."

"I'm betting it'll get longer," Lisa teased me. She didn't seem like she was mad at me anymore, so I busied myself putting chairs on tabletops, hoping the clatter would keep me from having to make any further response to Lisa without getting her mad at me again.

Apparently recognizing that I wasn't going to spill any beans more interesting than those in the chili right then, Lisa told me she'd do a fund-raising count at home tonight, and she'd bring the proceeds over to my place in the morning.

"You don't have to tell me what the deal is with you and Chuck Jackson. Don't worry about it. I won't force you or anything."

"Good," I said.

"Until tomorrow. If you don't tell all then I'm gonna keep the money we raised and—and give it to Ned Rutkin."

"You're so funny," I said.

"You're so into this guy," she countered.

As we doused the lights and locked the door, I felt my heart start pounding in my chest because for all I knew, during the time we were inside throwing away paper cups, Chuck had been sucked up into the sky by aliens and no one but me would even acknowledge that he ever existed.

But actually that didn't happen. Dave stood by the front door looking serious and stoic; when we emerged, he barked something into a walkie-talkie and Chuck strolled around from the back. They both flanked us over to Lisa's car with the vigilance of the Secret Service.

The moon was swathed in clouds and sending out just the faintest rim of phosphorescent glow, but it wasn't raining at the moment, and the streets were sort of pretty, all shiny and wet, at least if you discounted the enormous puddles that looked as if you needed hip waders to cross them.

"You riding shotgun?" Lisa asked me.

I hesitated. Dave was sort of glowering at me, like I'd kept him up past his bedtime. Chuck was giving me that half smile of his that made my fingers start to tingle.

"I think I'll maybe walk home," I said, "I'm still hyped up from the fund-raiser."

"That *must* be what you're hyped up from," said Lisa sagely. She looked at Chuck. She winked. "Thanks for helping us out."

"No problem." He winked back.

Dave leaned in Lisa's car window. "I'll swing by your house in a couple minutes. Just to make sure everything's copacetic."

"I really appreciate that," Lisa said, and a warm

glance passed between them. Dave squeezed her arm and she smiled and drove away.

Dave crossed the lot and unlocked his car. "The candidate gonna ride with us, then?"

"Yeah," said Chuck, taking my arm proprietarily.

"Okeydoke. I'll drop her first"—he waved a thumb at me—"then I'll leave you back at your car, then check on Ms. Murray. Come on, guys. Get a move on."

"Just take us both to my car," Chuck said firmly. "I'll make sure Jessie gets home."

"Oh," Dave said, drawing out the syllable, like boy, he was thick.

Now Dave and Chuck exchanged a chuckle. And then a wink. Okay, that was really enough with the winking stuff.

"Always workin' it, huh? You're too much," Dave said to Chuck.

"I hope not," Chuck returned.

They both laughed like boys in a locker room, as if I, the object of desire, wasn't even there. Maybe I was overly sensitive after the winking and all.

Chuck threw me an amused glance, like I was supposed to find this all very funny too, but I didn't.

In fact, suddenly I realized it would've been better, all told, if he had been sucked up into the sky by aliens.

Because suddenly, it was clear to me. It wasn't that Chuck was afraid he was a commonplace occurrence for me, it was that *I* was probably a commonplace occurrence for Chuck. I wasn't one in a million, I was one *of* a million. That's what all this laughing and winking was about. That's why it didn't bother him that he had no idea what was really going on between us. There was nothing really going on. Beyond the obvious thing that was going on.

Sure he liked me. Sure there was chemistry. Sure he knew how to turn me on. It was business as usual. Something so wild and crazy and wonderful as what passed between us was far too good to be special and true. I was beyond dim for not realizing that.

I was still out there, excuse the word, *campaigning* for Prince Charming and Happy Ever After and The One, in a world of hooking up and hanging out; in a world where Chuck was "workin' it."

So I shook his hand off my arm. "I don't think I really need a ride," I said. "Truly, I'd like to get a little fresh air."

There was a beat of dumbfounded silence from the guys that made me feel just the slightest bit back in control again.

"With everything that's been happening around here?" Dave asked, like I sure was stupid.

"Wait—" Chuck said, but I didn't. If I waited I might see him and Dave grin at each other again, grin over what Dave could so easily imagine was going on between me and Chuck, because of course it happened all the time! The reason Chuck didn't call me for thirty-six hours was because it was probably happening with someone else at that particular time, maybe one of those call girls he was busy observing.

"Good night," I called out, and even that felt like I'd said too much.

Chuck sprinted across the parking lot after me. "I don't get it. I thought you liked that whipped cream idea."

"I did," I admitted. "But the whole idea of just jumping in to dessert—I kind of think first you should sit down and share a meal. Conversation. A glass of wine. Vegetables. Maybe you're used to girls who go straight to the sugar rush, but I'm—" I wasn't sure what I was, so I stopped and kind of lifted my hands and dropped them again, at a loss for everything—words, gestures. Some professional communicator I was. I was now talking about a dinner menu when what I wanted to talk about was a relationship. Which obviously I wasn't going to have with Chuck.

"Baby, I'll give you plenty of sustenance," he said, his voice light and joking, which was the wrong tack to take with me at that moment.

Dave was sitting in his car with the engine running. He tapped lightly on the horn.

"You better go," I said. "Dave really should keep an eye on Lisa. She was the one, after all, that was attacked. Me, I'm fine. So someone called me on the phone and said some goofy stuff. It's no big thing."

What I wanted to say was "You'd better go unless you can show me you care for something other than taking off my clothes and putting your lips on my lips, your tongue against my tongue, your hands against my—"

I felt my resolve to ditch him and spend an evening that could've been absolutely incredible instead alone and miserable, weakening. Still. I had my pride. Even if I made myself sick with it.

"Good night," I said firmly.

Chuck glanced from Dave's idling car to me and back to Dave again. "Just let me walk you home. I won't make a move on you. You don't want me to."

"I'm fine," I repeated, keeping my eyes firmly on the oil rainbows floating in the parking lot puddles.

"I know you are," he said softly.

I looked up at that, but he was already loping across the parking lot, already climbing into the passenger seat in Dave's car, already giving me a two-fingered salute, that half smile on his lips.

The car turned left out of the lot, and I was alone now in the dark wet night, just as I said I wanted to be. Was I saving myself from heartbreak or causing it? Was I doing the right thing or just what I thought was the right thing to do?

I walked as fast as my heels could clatter across the parking lot and down the sidewalk, feeling regret and loneliness and self-reliance all crashing into each other in my head. But who needed Chuck anyway? The only thing I needed right now was votes.

Ordinarily I took a shortcut up a little alley behind the Dive and Surf Shop, but tonight, after the threatening phone calls and Lisa's robbery and Chuck telling me I should accept a ride, and my own inner demons, I stayed on the sidewalk, past the dry cleaners and the car upholstery shop and the scuba school, businesses all doomed by the proposed rezoning. I made a mental note to stop in and chat with the business owners, see if I could get their support for my campaign, put my signs in their windows or something. That would be a much more productive use of my time than lolling around with Chuck until he inevitably rejected me.

I crossed the street at the crosswalk and passed the gym I sometimes, when I paid my membership dues, worked out in. The windows were lit up and there was a lone fat guy on a treadmill, staring out past me at nothing. There but for the grace of God and a few extra pounds went I. Running in place and staring out at the empty night like an exercise zombie.

Then I was on residential streets, eyeing the mix of 1950s cottages and 1970s tall and skinnies, otherwise known as two-on-a-lots, and the million-dollar stucco monstrosities that had already eaten up most of Playa Vista, our district being the lone, scruffy hold-out. I realized that since some of my voter base was likely to come from the monstrosities, I shouldn't come down altogether too hard on them, though. I might alienate them. I should stick with the idea of how keeping a mixed-use neighborhood nearby would make everyone's quality of life better, even those people living inside their minicastles.

I mean how good would life be if they had to take a limousine or something all the way into Hollywood to hear a local band? Well, actually, that didn't sound too bad. But wouldn't it be a drag to have to send your maid all the way up to the Marina to get your dry cleaning? At least for the maid.

I began to realize just what an uphill battle I was facing, how maybe the people that were rapidly becoming the new Playa Vista didn't care about the past or landmark music clubs or a real community; all they wanted was a nice view and a big house, and more of the same all around them. Wasn't that what everyone wanted? Their own small slice of paradise, and damn anyone else whose alternate version might clash?

In the same way, Chuck wanted his version of me, a kind of fairy-tale easy date, ready to play; he didn't want a contradictory, contrary woman who was used to serial musicians sweet-singing her, slowly, at the pace of a languid ballad with many, many verses, into bed.

I supposed Dave had dropped Chuck off by now and was driving past Lisa's. Maybe Dave and Chuck had gone over to her house together, and they were even now all sitting around having a wonderful conversation or watching an old movie or discussing me, my love life, my lack there of. I could almost picture it happening. Chuck getting the inside scoop on the crazy lady who turned her nose up at the very idea of *dessert*. And coming to the conclusion that he and Dave should go leer at somebody else. And since I had already more or less decided that he must have a plethora of somebody elses just waiting in the wings, it wouldn't be very difficult to discard me. I was trouble.

It occurred to me that love, or what passed for it nowadays, was a lot like being involved in politics. In both instances, you had to be careful what you said and be careful how you looked and certainly not get caught making out in the kitchen of your friend's music club. And there was always the nagging worry that you'd picked a lame duck as a running mate.

But all of a sudden, I had a nagging worry of a different kind. I thought I heard footsteps behind me. Even in a fairly sleepy little bedroom community like Playa Vista, even if someone wasn't already making threatening phone calls and attacking your best friend, a woman alone on a dark street at night reaches in her purse for her pepper spray, which due to the presence of lipsticks, sunscreen, and spare change, can be difficult to find.

I turned, weapon in hand at last, but there was no one behind me. Just a low clap of thunder, and far on the distant horizon a pretty, pearly white torch of lightning off to sea. And then, naturally, it started to rain again. Like a car going from zero to eighty without hesitation, it was not just raining, it was deluging.

I was only two blocks from the big hill that was 190th Street and two more from my place. It wasn't the end of the world or anything to be getting rained on yet again; but it did seem even more incredibly stupid of me to turn down Chuck's offer of a ride.

I heard the footsteps again. I swore I heard them. I spun around, but I couldn't see anything now but the rain, which was coming down like a silvery curtain behind me. I jogged up to a streetlight and stopped under it, catching my breath. Now I was really getting soaked, but I liked just standing in the light for a minute clutching my pepper spray.

L.A. is a city of drivers, not walkers, and it was no different in the suburb of Playa Vista.

They drove to the grocery store, they drove around in circles looking for parking spaces by the pier that they could've walked to in less time than it took to find a space. They drove to Tad's corner grocery and double parked there. They drove to Lisa's club. Everyone drove, I drove. Except that my car wasn't working now, and I had just literally and figuratively refused to get in another car in which I was not in the driver's seat.

Maybe that was why the men I had loved took my advice and air play and food and even my bed to sleep in when they weren't on the road, and never really gave that much in return. Maybe I never gave them a chance to give. Maybe I didn't want anyone to give me anything. Maybe that was why I picked the men I had picked. I had to be the one in charge of this whole love thing. Maybe the real reason I wanted to get away from Chuck-whom-I-hardly-knew was because he wasn't asking for anything from me. Well, other than the sex, which he didn't even think he had to ask for. He thought that was just guaranteed, didn't he, with that smile of his.

Thinking of the sex with Chuck that I obviously wasn't going to be experiencing that night drove me out of the light and back into the dark street. But I wasn't walking now, I was running, which like walking, nobody did on a street in Playa Vista.

Playa Vista runners used an indoor track at the gym, the high school track, or after having driven to the beach, found a parking spot and the quarters required to retain it, the hard pack of sand along the harbor. In dry daylight. In good quality sneakers or barefoot. They did not run home at night in the rain in uncomfortable high-heeled shoes. Only I did that. I was exactly what I told Chuck he was— an aberration.

I jogged past the high school, dark, its stucco splotted with rain. The big hedges in front of fenced and locked gates rustled in the wind. At least I was pretty sure it was only the wind doing the rustling, even if I inadvertently let out a little cry.

If it wasn't just the wind, it was surely a stray cat or dog or one of the possums that ambled around sometimes, or some high school kid ripe to scale the fence, up to no good with a spray paint can.

Still I ran in earnest now. I could see the traffic up ahead on 190th Street, I could see Tad's store across from it, lights on but closed for the night; and there was my street, my duplex, my home, a door I could lock, blinds I could draw, a car I couldn't get to start.

Now that I was really running, man, I was absolutely sure there was someone running behind me. I could hear the footsteps for real and they were gaining on me, gaining on me as I hit the curb at 190th. I could've turned again, sure, and made my stand with my pepper spray and a good knee to the cajones, but without even thinking about it, I picked flight instead of fight, and I just rushed on into the rain-slick street.

But of course, there was an SUV, one of the big chunky ones that are almost the size of a small house, movie theater marquee lights etched along its spoiler. It was coming right at me with halogen headlights blazing near-lavender.

I knew I had to jump back and I was going to jump back. I was about to, when someone pulled me back, yanked me off my feet in fact, so that one of my shoes flew off, flew right into the path of that oncoming SUV. Horn blaring, that vehicle flattened, I mean absolutely flattened, it road-killed my shoe.

The pepper spray dropped out of my hand and rolled down the hill after the SUV.

I turned to my attacker, my nails out, ready to go for the eyes; teeth bared, ready to go for the nose or the ear.

"Don't," Chuck said, and he grabbed my hands in his and just held me and I felt his heart beating and I felt mine beating, and I wanted to cry.

But I didn't cry. "What the hell are you doing?" I asked.

"Saving your life, I think."

"Ruining a shoe, I think."

"You were running right out into traffic," Chuck said. "Why were you doing that?" His hair was so wet the curl was just about drenched out of it, and it looked much longer and softer as it fell about his face.

The rain was pounding down on us, so hard it almost felt like a hailstorm. I just wanted to go home.

"I just wanted to go home," I said out loud, my explanation sounding more petulant and lame than it had in my head.

"I'll walk you," he said simply.

It was almost necessary for him to put his arm around me because I was out one shoe and I was limping. We both looked down at my flattened pump lying in the road and neither one of us apparently considered picking it up.

"So other than . . . say a passion for jaywalking, why did you start running across the busiest street in the South Bay in a blinding rainstorm?" he asked me.

"I thought I heard something, in the bushes. And then behind me—"

"Well, that was me," he admitted. "Behind you. Not in the bushes."

We made our way to the median in the middle of the four-lane street. A couple of cars sailed past us, throwing up big fountains of dirty water.

I took off my other shoe while we waited for a break in the traffic. What was the point really, in keeping one shoe? Now at least I could ruin both stockings equally and walk without Chuck supporting me.

And yet he still kept his arm around me and I didn't object, as the last car splattered us and we stepped off the median again.

"Where's your car?" I asked him.

"Still at Dave's. I didn't think I could follow you covertly in wheels," Chuck said.

A car whizzed down the hill in the lane next to us. We froze, waiting for it to thoroughly splash us with mud and oil slick before finally making it to the other side.

"Look," I said, "I really appreciate you coming after me and keeping an eye on me and all but—"

"No buts. You're almost home now. We'll get you home and you'll let me come in and dry off and maybe wait out this deluge before I have to walk back to my car."

"It could go on like this all night."

"It could," he admitted.

We were silent for a moment, wrapped up in all those two words entailed.

"You lied to me," I said. It just came out; I didn't really mean to say it.

"That's funny, coming from a politician."

"I'm not a politician. I mean not really. I'm just—"

"Helping your friend," he said. "I know. Lisa told me all about you. And what she didn't tell me, she told Dave, who told me."

Maybe it was the hard stinging rain that was making my cheeks burn.

We'd made it down the block past Tad's grocery store and we were standing right in front of my duplex now, where we seemed to get stuck.

"I didn't know you were you when Lisa was talking about you—she just said her friend, her good friend was helping her out—wait, what is it you think I lied about anyway?"

"You tried to make me believe I was something special. I admit you had me going, too, until I saw you and Dave winking and laughing. You might as well be honest now. What am I, flavor of the week or just the weekend?"

"You put your life in potential jeopardy tonight, whether from an assailant or bad drivers, because

I winked at Dave? Because you think in some way I am disrespecting you? Because I didn't say, 'Dave, drop us at my car first because I need to be alone with this lady, the love of my life'?"

"I certainly don't consider myself the love of your life," I said huffily. Although wouldn't that have been amazing and kind of neat, and wasn't I yesterday afternoon acting as if I thought he might in fact be the love of mine? What a sap!

"I mean even if you were, why would I let Dave in on something I hadn't let you in on yet? Why are you so bent out of shape? It's not like I said something embarrassing about you, like I couldn't wait to do it on your bathroom rug again," he said.

"That's true," I admitted.

We both kind of stopped whatever else we were thinking about and stared at each other. Because of course, at least on my part, I actually couldn't wait to do it on the rug again. Not that I'd admit it, or let it happen.

"Look, we can talk about this another time. You can call me or—"

"Call you? Not come up now and finish this conversation, however inane it may be?"

"What's inane about it?"

He flung his hand over his face, dashing water from his eyes. Water was beaded on his lashes. He had very long lashes over those very green eyes.

"You getting all worked up because I shared a-a jocular moment with my buddy. And saying I lied, when I have done nothing but tell you the truth, that I was on a stakeout, that I was pretty distracted with work issues, and that's why I didn't call you yesterday or last night or this morning or appear on your doorstep with some ubiquitous bouquet of roses and tell you that I didn't really believe you did what we did all the time, even though you said that and more or less led me to believe you were telling the truth, and okay, I admit, that kind of made me nervous. A little. Not a lot. So you were the one who lied, not me."

He was out of breath now. I started to protest but he waved his hand at me, asking for silence. "But we can discuss this when I'm not in danger of drowning and I don't expect to see Noah's Ark gliding up from the fucking harbor. Yes, yes, yes you're special, okay? At least I think you are because of the way I felt from the first second I grabbed you in my arms to keep you from rolling backward downhill. I felt like you were just it, just the one, just someone I had to be with because I was meant to be with you and you were meant to be with me. Okay?"

"Ah," I said. "Well."

"And I'm not ashamed of or embarrassed by what we did Wednesday afternoon and I cannot believe you are, and I cannot believe that you don't feel we should be upstairs right now doing exactly what we did before, except this time you should show me which door does not lead to your bathroom."

In a feeble attempt to hang on to my steadily washing away self-control, I said, "You just keep telling me what I should and shouldn't do, and I'm not sure I like that."

"Oh, God," he muttered. "I sort of thought you understood. That you saw things the way I saw them. And now all evidence is pointing to the fact that you are one of *those*."

"One of those what?" I didn't like his tone.

"Those kind of women. Who insist on everything going her way. Nobody can have everything go their way. Life isn't like that. It's not an—an election or something! We're not going to take a poll from passersby on what chance we have as a couple, or what comments I make that might or might not be politically correct or offend you! Are we? Or is that why you're keeping me standing out here in the rain?"

"No such thing as a sure thing, huh?"

"Well, I felt pretty sure the other afternoon, to be honest. And like fate had intervened most fortuitously when Dave asked a favor, and even though all I wanted to do was crash—and scare up your phone number—I agreed to help set up a security system and wham, I find you again. But you sure have a way of putting the brakes on. Right now I'd really appreciate it if you'd take them off. I'm not *telling* you, mind you, I'm *asking* you. Come on. You're barefoot, the rain is coming down harder, and if there *was* someone back there in the bushes, there might be a reason just as good as wanting to spend the night with me."

He was right on all counts, but being right doesn't always mean you get your way, either.

I pulled out my keys. I went up the steps in front of him. The stairs were all slippery and had little puddles in the middle, and in my tattered stockinged feet I slipped midway up. He caught me again, his arms around my waist.

Okay, so it felt really good to feel his arms around me. Okay, for almost two days I just wanted to feel Chuck's arms around me like that again. Nothing else, momentarily at least, mattered except that he was back here on my porch with his arms around me and I liked it.

"You keep doing that," I said, and it was more like, I hope you keep on doing that.

He smiled. Oh, that smile. He smiled and he touched my cheek and he kind of shook the rain out of his curly hair because it was dripping down his nose, and he kissed me. And I kissed him back.

"I'm coming in," he said.

And I wanted him to, I really did. Still something perverse in me made me put my palms on his chest and push him away. "It can't be this easy."

He looked astonished. "You want it to be hard?"

"I mean it can't be this easy for you. You think you can just have me because we—"

He put his hand right over my mouth. He pointed at my front window. There was a shadow standing behind the curtain. Unless Sally or Squeak had grown like six feet, it wasn't the shadow of one of my cats.

I nodded, I understood. He took his hand off my mouth and grabbed my key from my hand. Pushing me behind him, he shoved the key in the lock, pulled the knob, and opened my door, wide.

Chapter Nine

"After you," Chuck said loudly, as if he were letting me step in front of him, but instead I stayed out on the porch, behind him and to the side.

He slipped in my hall while I huddled out there on my porch, and I saw the shadow inside my apartment connect itself to a thick dark form and shove Chuck hard against my wall.

Chuck made a grunting sound, which didn't sound good. I screamed. The guy lunged for the door and I screamed again, and the shadow man was about to hurl himself at me but I slammed him with the side of the door. Wham, it was a good hit, the edge of the door glanced off my would-be assailant's head with a really nice solid thunk before he turned and swatted it back at me.

I pressed against the porch railing and he just grazed my arm with it, but I could tell that he was strong by just how much that hurt. That was about all I could tell, because the guy was huddled under a hooded sweat jacket that drooped over his forehead like a monk's cowl. He was all shadow.

Now he was throwing himself past me and down

the stairs, and sans pepper spray, I was powerless to stop him.

I dashed into my kitchen.

"Chuck!" I shouted. "Are you—"

"I'm okay." He was lifting himself up off the floor where he'd fallen. "Got me in the gut, used something looked like a wooden cudgel, a club, I dunno. Hit me on the head with this first—"

He gestured to an enormous copper-bottom spaghetti pot usually hanging from a hook at the entry to my little box-car kitchen, now lying on the floor at Chuck's feet. I had never used the pot, but I'd purchased it as a tremendous bargain at the Rose Bowl swap meet back when I thought Jack and I were a couple, and someday whenever he stopped doing the road house thing with his band, I'd make us a nice, romantic Italian dinner centered around the spaghetti I was going to cook in that pot.

From my bedroom I heard my cat Sally yowl, so I knew she was okay, and then Squeak the kitten made a kind of chirruping sound, like he did when he hoped I was going to feed him, so at least whatever this guy was after, he wasn't some sort of Cruella de Ville of cats.

I was about to express my relief to Chuck, but he wasn't there. He was already out the door and leaping over the railing, his black T-shirt and black jacket shining wet like seal fur. He landed hard but he didn't fall and he made it down to the street only about a block behind our assailant.

I kind of expected Chuck to say "Halt in the name of the law," or something like that, but he didn't. Neither one of them made a sound other than the clatter and splatter of their footsteps on the wet street. I was the only one shouting, like I was watching a video game instead of reality, "Get him! Get him!"

They were disappearing around the corner, in the opposite direction from Tad's grocery. Briefly, it occurred to me to grab my cell phone, pray for service, and call 911, but instead I scooped up the spaghetti pot—if it worked as a weapon once, it would work again—slipped my feet into a pair of flip-flops I kept by my porch, and slammed the door shut behind me. I went chasing after them both, bringing my pot with me like I was going to find some lobster as we all went racing downhill toward the harbor, toward the police and fire station and city hall and the site of my debate.

I could see Chuck was gaining on my intruder, but then the guy zigzagged behind the chain coffee place in the mini-mall. It was as closed as Tad's place now, the only light coming from its familiar green illuminated sign. The guy banged into the Dumpster, which slowed him; Chuck was steady behind him and gaining as they moved behind the coffee place and out of sight.

I was definitely not fleet of foot, in my wrecked stockings and rubber sandals and knee-length skirt, so I lost sight of them, lost the sound of their footsteps, heard only my own feet slapping on the pavement, my own ragged breathing, the ping of the rain against my big old pot.

I wanted to cry out but I didn't. I just swung around the side of the building, panting. Above the sound of my own rough breathing rose the sound of tires on wet pavement. And then there was a car barreling straight at me, brights on, blinding.

I pressed up against the side of the building, as tires squealing, rear end fishtailing, some large dark square car, a hybrid maybe, came right for me. It was hard to believe the driver of such an environmentally sound vehicle was trying to run me down in a rainy parking lot. It flew past me, windshield wipers flipping back and forth wildly.

With the headlights blinding me and the rain, I wasn't that certain of my aim, but I threw my pot, hard as I could, and sent it crashing against the driver's side window.

The vehicle slowed for a moment, and during that moment I thought how stupid I was, how I always wanted to have the last word, how the driver was going to back up now and flatten me against the wall like a bug.

But the reverse lights didn't come on and the driver surged out of the parking lot and up the hill again away from the harbor, and along with a dented pot rolling back toward me I got a glimpse of an empty rear license plate frame and the name on the frame, Pahalu Motors, Oahu.

"Chuck," I screamed. "Chuck!"

"Right here," he said, and I jumped about two feet straight up in the air. He was practically right up against my shoulder. He'd stepped out of an exit door alcove a few feet away. He had a gun in his hand, but he hadn't fired it.

"You scared me," I said, because somehow I'd missed him in the rain and the dark.

"Oh, it was *me* who scared you," he said, wiping the rain out of his eyes with the back of his hand. He set the safety and slipped the gun inside his jacket.

"You okay?" we both asked each other at once.

"Yeah," we both answered.

"Kind of an echo back here in the alley," Chuck

said. "I could've hit the tires, but I didn't know quite where you were. I didn't want to risk losing you." He took my hand in his. "And I don't. Want to lose you."

"I don't want to lose you either," I said. "I mean I just found you."

And we laughed. And then things were okay with us, I could feel it. All was forgiven—him not calling, our mutual carping, me keeping him out in the rain.

We left the spaghetti pot back in the alley and walked on up the hill.

"Should we—report this, call the police, something?"

"Baby, I am the police."

"Okay, then," I said. "What next?"

"Well, I didn't see the guy except to notice he walked kinda softly and carried some kinda big wooden stick—and he was wearing gloves along with that baggy sweat jacket, so I'm making a well-educated guess there's no prints at your place. And as to the car, I didn't even see the plates."

"There wasn't one in front, just an empty frame for a dealership in Oahu."

"You remember the name?"

I spelled it in case my pronunciation was bad.

He stopped right there in the street and took a small, damp steno pad out of his inside jacket pocket and scratched the name on the wet paper with a stubby pencil.

"Okay," he said. "Something to go on."

"That's good, I guess," I said.

"That's very good. But not as good as the fact that we're both in one piece."

I nodded. We were both pretty winded in our uphill climb, and the rain was still sluicing down.

"You could've been hurt," we both said.

"Vulcan mind meld," he said, placing his fingers lightly on my forehead. "I noticed it back in the club. You know, like Spock—"

"In the original, best, cheesiest *Star Trek*."

He shot that adorable smile at me, and he cleared his throat, and since we were about dead even with the police station, just about where we'd met, I thought he was going to say something poignant about our first meeting.

But all he said was "This would be a good time for one of us to say 'Beam me up, Scotty.'"

He slung an arm around my shoulder. My flip-flops were slipping off my feet and slowing us down, but it didn't really matter anymore; we were as soaked as two people could get, and yet in a weird way, as comfortable all of a sudden. Maybe it was almost being run over. All my prickly defensive feelings had just kind of washed away in the down-pour. Life was too short and all that.

"You watch the reruns on Sci Fi Network, one A.M.?" he asked me.

"Yes," I admitted. "Sometimes."

"That musician you were dating, he watched with you?"

I wanted to ask him just how the hell he knew about the musician, but I assumed the information came from Lisa or indirectly from Lisa through Dave or maybe he put it together from seeing me singing with Jack in the club that time, so I let it go.

"No. When he was in town, I was usually watching him do a gig somewhere that time of night."

"You broke up when exactly?"

"Well, just about a week ago, officially." I swallowed; this sounded bad. "But he was on the road with his band since before Christmas, so I was long over him when you seduced me." That sounded a little better.

"*I* seduced you? I think you were the one who started things rolling."

"Me?" My cheeks burned so hot that there in the rain I thought steam was rising off my face. "I followed *you* up the stairs? I begged you to let *me* in?"

"I never beg," he said. "Okay. We both just wanted each other. At the same time. The Vulcan mind meld thing, right?" He squeezed my shoulder, affectionate.

I drew a deep breath. "Right. So how about you? Who do you watch late-night sci fi with?"

"Nobody. Last girl I dated worked in the morgue downtown. She wanted to get into forensics. She had all the *CSI* shows on TiVo. We broke up before Christmas. Sort of like you and the musician did. She wanted me to go with her to the state medical examiners convention over New Year's. I dunno, it was a turnoff. All those people getting drunk and smelling just faintly of formaldehyde."

I laughed. "Sounds like a bar I once sang at."

"Dave likes to act like I'm some kinda ladies' man, always on the prowl. And I'm not going to tell you I wasn't that way ten, fifteen years ago. Then I got married. That changed things."

"Married?" I kind of slipped out from under his arm.

"Divorced. Three years now. She left me. For another guy. You work late nights, sometimes you come home and well, you're alone even if she is sleeping on her side of the bed. She left me the dog though, and you want to know the truth, the dog always loved me more. Toward the end, being incredibly totally truthful, I loved the dog more, too.

Anyway, it might be different for girls, but for guys, your marriage busts up like that, you have to act like you're doing okay, you're fighting off the babes, no big thing you got dumped, you have 'em lined up and waiting. Especially when you're working in a putatively macho job environment."

I didn't know quite what to say to all that, so I just said "I like that you use words like *putative*."

"You think all cops are dumb doughnut eaters or something?"

"I don't think about cops at all. Except in relation to 'No, Officer, I did not make a rolling stop' or 'I'll turn down the music now, of course.'"

He laughed, amused.

"Were you ever not a cop?"

He glanced sideways at the police station, now slipping away behind us in our trudge uphill.

"Yeah. I was in high school. Then police academy, then LAPD, then the quieter, simpler life, here by the bucolic beach. Like the word *bucolic*?"

"Yeah," I said.

"Dave thinks it's time I retired early, like he did, before I rub yet another set of supervisors the wrong way. Be his partner. I never thought the personal security industry was very exciting, but tonight's proved me wrong. In lots of ways."

He squeezed my hand. I squeezed his.

"So," he said. "Now you, unlike me, you have some real job diversity going on."

"Yeah. Very part-time musician. Disc jockey, newly minted city council hopeful."

"What happened to professional communicator?"

"I think I checked the bullshit at the door." And speaking of doors, we were just about abreast of my own again.

"Then let me check mine. Here I am, a certified hunk, at least according to Dave, winner of the LAPD major cases special service award two years running, smart enough to use big words that impress you, and yet, night after night I go home to nothing more than a six-pack and a take-out pizza and the *Starship Enterprise.*"

"That spaceship can get a little lonely, rattling around in there all by yourself."

"It'll be a lot more fun, sharing that pizza and the final frontier with *you* tonight," he said. He gave that smile of his, which back in the days when he was a ladies' man, must've sealed many such bargains. "There is no way you're turning me out again," Chuck added firmly.

Damn, now there he went telling me what to do again. I felt myself bristling. He had to learn that just didn't work with me. Nobody I ever dated ever told me what to do. They didn't care what I did. Of course really, how good was that in the long run?

"No way I'm not staying, right?" Chuck prodded me. A little bit of doubt had crept into his voice.

"No way," I agreed at last.

Chuck took my keys and unlocked my door for the second time that evening, and this time, he turned on the lights, too. I picked up the picture of me bent over the keyboard of a piano at a college recital that had fallen from my wall in the scuffle between Chuck and my would-be assailant. The glass was cracked but not shattered, so I just set it on the kitchen counter. I left my flip-flops by the front door, peeled off my ragged stockings, and threw them out. Chuck took off his own sneakers and socks.

I hung our jackets in the shower to drip there and left the rest of my wet clothes in a heap in the tub and threw on a sweatshirt and jeans. I was shivery now, and considering Chuck and I had almost been run over, and confessed to watching late-night TV alone, the cute little robe didn't seem necessary.

Wiping his face with a dish towel, Chuck searched around my place for anything resembling evidence, but all he found was something that looked like a piece of crumbled-up cookie on the kitchen floor, which Squeak had no doubt dragged out from under my refrigerator.

There were muddy footprints in my hallway that weren't mine or Chuck's, but they didn't go back any farther than my kitchen, so either the guy had just arrived when we did, or he wanted to hang out right there in the entrance so he could grab me fast. The prints were fairly large and indistinct.

Chuck examined my door, which bore no visible sign of forced entry. "Cheap lock like this. Maybe even just a credit card. You need to get a locksmith out here, get something more serious."

"That my landlord will not reimburse me for."

"Write it off as a campaign expense."

After he'd reassured himself there was nobody lurking in my living room closet—if there was, he'd have to be really skinny and a midget besides what with all the free CDs and cat toys and stuffed animals I'd hauled around since I was a kid, and the big sombrero and the piñata stuffed with candy that had hardened into something I didn't want to think about that I got in Tijuana a few years back.

Finally Chuck gave it up and took off his T-shirt,

wrung it out, and left it over the shower rail. I had a lot of extralarges around that I used as sleep shirts, so it was nothing to find him one that fit his very ripped pecs and his six-pack abs.

So with Coldplay on tap, he stripped off his jeans and wrapped a towel around his midsection and we settled down on the sofa. I figured we had virtually no secrets left now. It wasn't the intimacies of sex so much as the incredible intimacy of letting anyone I was kind of at least dating, see that closet.

He reached for my phone and ordered us a pizza and beer, and I knew he wasn't kidding about those nights alone; the guy on the other end of the phone knew Chuck by the sound of his voice, and evinced surprise at a different delivery address.

The towel slipped down a little as he hung up the phone, and I saw a dark bruise rising on his abdomen—the hit he'd taken from the guy who'd come to hit me. I felt grateful and tender.

Had any of my serious relationships ever been serious enough to take on a fight for me? My boyfriends had uniformly thought of exercise itself as nothing more strenuous than bringing the amps in from the car or shaking their hips against a tambourine. Although the situation of defending me had never actually arisen, I was pretty sure there was no one I had a relationship with before who would've chased some bad guy down a rainy street and into a dark alley. For me. But Chuck had.

"So," Chuck mused, "what did this guy want? What was he doing here? And since the engine was already running, who picked him up in that car?"

"And was the driver trying to kill us, or was he just a bad driver?" I added.

"He was trying to scare us, anyway," Chuck said.

"If he'd wanted to kill us all he had to do was back up when you threw the pot at him."

That thought had occurred to me, too, but I'd chosen not to dwell on it. With Chuck presenting the idea I suddenly got a lot more scared than I'd been when the car was actually rocketing down the alley right at me.

I shuddered and Chuck wrapped an arm around me.

"You look good in fuzzy gray," he said. I stopped shuddering. I laughed. "I don't think I even combed my hair," I realized.

"You didn't," he said, and he ran his hands through it with his fingers. His own was standing straight up on end again, and I smoothed it, and for a few moments there we were like monkeys grooming each other. And it was nice. It was so nice, our lips were edging together for a kiss.

Then the doorbell rang and we jumped apart.

It was the pizza, and to my surprise my downstairs neighbor, Art, was doing the delivery.

"Hey," he said to me.

"Hey there," I said back.

"To think I live right downstairs and you've never ordered any pizza from me before. Must be a special occasion tonight." He smirked, eyeing Chuck.

".Not really," I said.

"No? My mom said you must be having a party or something. She said people were runnin' up and down your stairs and you were waving a drum around, chasing after some guy."

"A pot. I had a pot."

"You were chasing this guy here without the pants?"

"No. There was a break-in," Chuck said.

"Wow, wait'll I tell Mom." Art looked all excited. "News like this makes me need my meds." He looked happy about that. He gave a high-pitched giggle crossed with a snort. "Anything stolen?"

"No," I said.

"Guess you don't have much worth stealing," he noted, deflating, staring around my place. "Mom said you must be pretty broke or you'd order from my place of business instead of Domino's like you usually do, and only when they have their fifty percent off coupons in the mail."

"Your mom is pretty observant," I said, taking the pizza and setting it on the kitchen counter. He was losing any tip I would've given him, that was for sure.

"She is, yeah. Burglar better watch his behind around her. She's got a sweet little twenty-two she keeps under her pillow. She's always on the look-out."

Chuck lit up. "Think she saw anything more than Jessie and the spaghetti pot tonight?"

"Dunno," Art said. "Mom keeps things close to the vest." He pummeled his flabby chest with his doughy fists.

"Would your mom be willing to talk to me?"

Art looked at Chuck in the towel. "Maybe if you put some pants on."

Chapter Ten

Mrs. Palazo was already peering out her front window, staring at our feet coming down the stairs. Art introduced us and explained our reason for appearing before her semi-bedraggled at nearly midnight. She shrugged, with her eyes narrowed, like this sort of thing was entirely to be expected from the likes of me.

"So, attempted robbery, nothing taken," she said, spreading a dish towel on a kitchen chair before letting Chuck sit down in his rain-soaked jeans.

"Right—" Chuck began.

She shot me a sharp-eyed look. "Wish somebody'd take your car. Kind of an eyesore, those radio station bumper stickers and some kinda rock band logos and all. Just sitting there."

"It'd be hard to steal since it doesn't run at the moment," I noted.

Chuck kind of motioned me to be quiet, so I took the third of three chairs in the kitchen. For the record, the apartment was clean and neat and bigger than mine with two bedrooms, decorated with Hummel figurines, Hummel prints, and a plethora of ceramic lighthouses. I didn't mind the light-houses, but the Hummel stuff with the big staring sad eyes made me understand why Art craved his meds.

Art kissed his mother's cheek. "You'll be okay? I have to go."

She smiled benignly. "Don't work too hard."

As Art left she told Chuck, "His job is so demanding. All the deadlines, you know. And then there's the ladies. Can't keep the ladies off my boy."

She gave me a suspicious glance. "Even those most inappropriate."

Thirty-some-year-old pizza delivery boy already balding, hooked on "meds," and living with his mother in an apartment full of Hummel figurines, and right, ladies, including myself, must really go for that. Of course if he was a cute blond musician, I might've, in the past, overlooked the other flaws.

"Moving on," Chuck said. "Your son told us you might've seen something earlier, something that would help me in my investigation—"

"Are you a real policeman?" she interrupted. "Doesn't seem like you're real. I mean why are you bringing the alleged victim along with you to question me?"

Chuck smiled. "Safety concerns," he said smoothly. He left out the fact that I just wanted a look inside my neighbor's apartment.

"Oh," she said sagely. "Oh-kay. That must be it. But yeah, I saw something. And if you say it was a burglary, well oh-kay, but that guy had a key."

"A key?" Chuck and I both said, doing that Vulcan mind meld thing again.

"I saw him take it out of his jacket pocket before he went upstairs and unlocked the door. It was on one of those silver key rings the mayor handed out last election. You running for office and all, you oughta consider getting yourself some key rings," she suggested to me, reeking superiority.

"Thanks for the suggestion," I said politely. I was too busy thinking about the guy having a key to my door to take any serious offense to her tone.

"You really are observant," Chuck flattered Mrs. Palazo.

"Oh, yes. I see everything."

"That's great. Can you describe the man with the key?" Chuck asked.

"Well, he was medium build. And wearing a hooded jacket, so I couldn't see his face. And baggy jeans."

"No hair color, anything like that?"

"Hidden."

"And did you hear anything?"

"Just the door opening and closing. No walking around or anything. Then you two coming home, arguing about something. Then thumps and bangs and groans and running. And when the first fellow ran—followed by you—I guess I did see something."

"What?" we asked.

"Teeth. Man had his mouth open, panting or something, and you could see teeth. You don't always see teeth. I used to work as a dental hygienist back in the day. The guy had an overbite or something."

"Okay," Chuck said. "That could be helpful." He didn't look like he thought it was very helpful, but still. "One more thing," Chuck said. "Earlier maybe, when this person with the key first showed up, any idea how he got here? Walk? Drive?"

"Walked. Heard a car pull away down the block.

Couldn't park right here of course, not with her car just sitting right in front of the driveway—"

"Well, you've been great," Chuck interrupted. "We don't want to keep you up, it's getting quite late, so we should be going." He slipped a sodden business card out of a card case in the pocket of his jeans and handed it to her. "If you think of anything else," he said.

I stood, too. Mrs. Palazo whispered to me as she walked us to the door, "Not that I'm voting for you, mind you, but a word of advice anyway. You'd think, under public scrutiny, you wouldn't be having so many men, some of them with keys, over to your apartment."

"So, who could have a key to your place?" Chuck asked me.

I was one beer and two slices down, and I'd been waiting for the question, to which there was only one answer. Jack, to whom I'd given a key on just such a ring as that described by Mrs. Palazo.

"My ex-boyfriend. The guitar player you saw me with that time at Lisa's. He didn't give me my key back."

Sure someone could've stolen my landlord's master key and put it on a mayoral election promotional key ring and then snuck into my apartment. But I had to admit that was unlikely.

Chuck was frowning steadily. "So your ex-boyfriend sneaks in to surprise you in the dark and then attacks me and tries to run us both down?"

"I don't think so. He'd never throw a punch or risk getting one thrown at him. He jammed his finger once opening a can of tuna, and he had to ice it immediately so it wouldn't affect his ability to play guitar." I left out the other obvious reason it couldn't have been Jack. I knew he didn't care enough about me to sneak into my apartment and try to run us down.

"So who would he give the key to that would want to hurt you or us, and why?"

"No idea."

"Call him," Chuck said.

"Now? I don't even know if he's still in town."

"Now. If he's around, I want to have at him."

I hesitated, not because I would feel bad if letting Chuck have at him meant that Jack, with his crisply pressed jeans and his waitress, would feel a little, um, threatened, but because I really didn't want to talk to Jack. Even more, I really didn't want to see Jack. I also didn't really want Chuck wondering what I saw in Jack versus what I saw in him, which was the part I wasn't all that sure about myself yet.

I scrunched up my face, preparing to object.

"Don't tell me I'm trying to make you do something you don't want to do, and ordering you around and acting like a cop and all the stuff I know you're thinking of saying," Chuck warned me. "I know you don't want to do it, and I know I'm telling you what to do, and I know I'm acting at least half like a cop and half like a could-be-jealous-at-any-moment asshole. But it's still important. Someone more or less tried to kill us tonight. And if your ex is the only one with an actual physical key, and the person who tried to kill us came in here using a key, then we have to start with him."

"Okay," I said, and I picked up the phone and then I realized I couldn't remember Jack's phone number. I hung up the phone and got out my address book. For some reason this made Chuck laugh. It made me laugh, too.

"Don't clue him in," Chuck said, "that anything happened. Just say you met somebody new—true enough, right—and he needs a spare key. See what he says. I'll listen in, and we'll take it from there."

Chuck opened another beer for me and I took a long pull of it, and then I dialed Jack's cell phone. Chuck hit speaker phone, and there he was listening in as Jack answered, sounding a little fuzzy. There was loud music in the background.

"Jack," I said evenly, "it's Jessie."

"Jessie!" he said halfway between shock and warmth. "We're havin' a party. Wanna drive on up? We're in Santa Barbara tonight! Got a new manager! He sees the future of rock and roll and it's not me, but he sees a lot of potential. A lot!"

Jack was definitely high. He'd just taken a hit of his personal favorite drug of choice, narcissism.

"I bet the new manager's great. But, no, don't want to drive up now. It's late."

"Oh. You miss me, sorry you left things so negative?"

"Uh, no, not exactly."

"'Cause we can still hang out, see each other time to time, just, you know, stop thinking this is more than it is or was, no more of the unofficially engaged, exclusivity stuff, and it could be fun. Could be better even."

I saw Chuck's hand twitch.

"This is kind of the opposite of missing you," I went on. "Actually, Jack, this is kind of awkward, but uh—"

"You want to have a baby and you want me to be the sperm donor?"

"No. Not that." The words came out in a rush now. "I met somebody new that I really like and he needs a key and you have my spare."

"You know, Jessie, I don't know exactly why you're calling me this time of night, but I get the feeling there's something sort of ulterior going on, like maybe you do need a sperm donor or something."

"I do not—I just need that key," I interrupted hotly, but Jack, sounding even fuzzier, just laughed.

"Listen. I already left it for you in an envelope this afternoon. Shoulda given it directly to you, I know, but to be honest you were so pissy with me the other day, I didn't need any more of your bad karma comin' down on me."

"Where did you leave it?" I asked. "By my front door or in my mailbox or—"

There was a burst of laughter and the music played louder in the background.

"Look, I can't even hear you right now. It's in an envelope, okay? You know, we're kinda trying to have a good time here. I gotta go—"

He hung up on me. I replaced the receiver carefully. I took another long swallow of beer to wash down that pesky pride thing.

"So. He left the key in an envelope. Anyone could've taken it," I said. I twisted the beer can, avoiding eye contact with Chuck.

"I have to agree that from the sound of him, old Jack there isn't a very likely suspect," Chuck said.

"Old Jack," I repeated. "He's actually not that old."

"Just an expression," Chuck offered. "But I think I've got him pretty well pegged."

I looked at Chuck now, I had to see if he had me

pretty well pegged too, and if that was a bad thing or a good thing or no thing, really.

Chuck smiled. "I'm just glad you dumped him, that's all."

I smiled back. I was glad Chuck said I dumped Jack instead of that Jack dumped me. He was probably just being nice about it, but I was glad he was being nice, too. Or maybe I was just glad I was with him.

Chuck stood up and wedged a kitchen chair against my door, and then effortlessly, using only one hand, he moved my kitchen table in front of that. I think he might've been showing off.

"No matter how somebody other than ol'—than Jack—got your key, this should do the trick for tonight."

The cats liked this arrangement and were each perched on opposite ends of the table, claiming it. I hoped Sally would not go so far with the claiming process as to pee on it.

"Don't worry," Chuck said. "I got you covered."

I nodded. I felt like he did. And it was a little presumptive maybe, but it was really kind of nice.

"So this guy who got my key, because Jack just left it by my mailbox with my name on it, this guy who's trying to scare me or kill me, why is he trying to do that?"

Chuck dropped down on the sofa again and reached for his third slice of pizza. "I'm not sure. The people you're messing with, politically speaking, don't need to do stupid things like make threatening phone calls or rob Lisa or break into your apartment. They just buy the election. Or try to discredit you in some way. I'm sure you've done something embarrassing. I mean everybody has."

Zebra
Contemporary
Romance

Zebra Contemporary

To start your membership, simply complete and return the Free Book Certificate. You'll receive your Introductory Shipment of FREE Zebra Contemporary Romances, you only pay $1.99 for shipping and handling. Then, each month you will receive the 4 newest Zebra Contemporary Romances. Each shipment will be yours to examine FREE for 10 days. If you decide to keep the books, you'll pay the preferred subscriber price (a savings of up to 30% off the cover price), plus shipping and handling. If you want us to stop sending books, just say the word... it's that simple.

If the FREE Book Certificate is missing, call 1-800-770-1963 to place your order.

FREE BOOK CERTIFICATE

Yes! Please send me FREE Zebra Contemporary romance novels. I only pay $1.99 for shipping and handling. I understand that each month thereafter I will be able to preview 4 brand-new Contemporary Romances FREE for 10 days. Then, if I should decide to keep them, I will pay the money-saving preferred subscriber's price (that's a savings of up to 30% off the retail price), plus shipping and handling. I understand I am under no obligation to purchase any books, as explained on this card.

NAME _____

ADDRESS _____ APT. _____

CITY _____ STATE _____ ZIP _____

TELEPHONE (_____) _____

E-MAIL _____

SIGNATURE _____

(If under 18, parent or guardian must sign)

Offer limited to one per household and not to current subscribers. Terms, offer and prices subject to change. Orders subject to acceptance by Zebra Contemporary Book Club. Offer Valid in the U.S. only.

Thank You!

CN027A

THE BENEFITS OF BOOK CLUB MEMBERSHIP

• You'll get your books hot off the press, usually before they appear in bookstores.

• You'll ALWAYS save up to 30% off the cover price.

• You'll get our FREE monthly newsletter filled with author interviews, book previews, special offers and MORE!

• There's no obligation – you can cancel at any time and you have no minimum number of books to buy.

• And – if you decide you don't like the books you receive, you can return them. (You always have ten days to decide.)

Be sure to visit our website at www.kensingtonbooks.com.

Zebra Book Club
P.O. Box 6314
Dover, DE 19905-6314

"Uh-huh." The most embarrassing things I'd ever done I'd done with Chuck. "Like Ned telling Tad that Salome was a Vegas showgirl," I said to cover.

"Disappointing to find that out, really," Chuck said. "I mean it would've been really cool if it was you. Showgirls do those things with the tassels that—"

He saw me looking at him like I was ready to smack him, and he switched topics.

"Anyway, this guy, whoever he is, keeps telling you and Lisa that you can't take him on." Chuck rubbed at his chin. "It's like a challenge as much as a threat. It doesn't make a lot of sense unless the guy's just some crazy out there."

"In which case it could be anybody at all. Which is kind of scary."

Chuck pushed the pizza away and kissed my lips, gently. "Don't be scared," he said.

"I'm not," I replied, because when he kissed me like that I forgot I was scared. I forgot just about everything else except the kissing.

"Feel less like clawing my eyes out for the remark about the tassels?" Chuck grinned when we came up for air.

"Yeah."

"I could get you some tassels. And a how-to-move-them DVD or something."

"Ha."

"You laugh now. I think there's an art to it. There's an art, after all, to lots of things."

His fingers moved up under my sweatshirt and gently caressed my skin.

"I didn't think you were wearing a bra," he said happily, rubbing my nipples between his thumb and forefinger. "This makes things much more . . . convenient."

I teased his lips with my tongue.

He slipped my sweatshirt off my arms and broke from me long enough to pull it over my head, and then he tossed it aside.

The kitten pounced on it where it dropped and started wrestling with it.

And then Chuck closed the pizza box and drew me up from the sofa, and he led me into my bedroom, and we sat down on the bed.

He nibbled on my ears and stroked my nipples stone hard, and then took them in his mouth, first one and then the other. Then he went back to touching them again, keeping them full and firm and wet.

He pushed down the band of my jeans and peeled them to my ankles, and I stepped out of them. He nibbled his way around the edge of my underwear and then slid it carefully down my thighs and over my ankles and lifted up first one foot and then the other, kissing my ankles as he tossed my underwear away.

He pulled off his T-shirt and I unbuckled his belt and unzipped his water-stained jeans.

I slipped onto my knees and kissed the place on his abdomen where the guy in my apartment clubbed him, kissed around the bruise and down and then I took him in my mouth.

He drew in his breath sharply. "You're a fun date," he said. "Even if you don't do tassels."

After a while, I climbed onto his lap and we necked and nuzzled some more, me rubbing up against his chest, his hands skating over me like he knew all the right places to just graze and I guess he did know, judging by the little sighs and moans that were issuing from my lips whenever he wasn't kissing me, and whenever I wasn't moving my mouth down between his firm thighs again. We were kind of prolonging things as long as we could.

Then he lifted me gently off his lap and onto the bed beside him, and pulled off his jeans altogether. He lay down, plumping pillows up behind him, and drew me against his chest. We just lay there, naked and both of us still a little rain damp, listening to our heartbeats. Then he reached for the remote on my nightstand and clicked on the TV.

"After," he said, and though I admit I was a little bit surprised, it was really kind of fun, lying there like that, in a state of suspended excitement, watching the *Starship Enterprise* in faded color.

This was more or less a galaxy I'd never been to before, probably because I'd never been with a man like Chuck. So annoyingly in control. So sure of what I wanted. Why was he so sure, anyway? I wasn't sure. I wanted to talk to him about that, about us, but instead here I was watching TV with my head on his chest, waiting to complete our lovemaking.

The episode was the one about the Tribles and we'd both seen it enough that we could quote the dialog. So we did that instead of talking, really talking, and during the commercials we made out. At the first break, he rubbed his hand between my legs, and all along my thighs. I ran my hand through the damp curly hair thick on his chest and down, and down until I was holding his sex and rocking him between my palms.

At the second break, he slipped his fingers inside me until I cried out, and I forgot all about the wanting to talk to him part; talking was not at all what I wanted to do with my lips anymore. At the third commercial, I climbed on top of him again and he pressed himself up inside me and okay, we did not really watch the rest of the episode very closely, but we knew how it turned out, just as we'd *both* known, all along, how the evening itself would.

Chapter Eleven

Chuck was up before me and I could hear him in the kitchen, rummaging around my fairly barren refrigerator and mixing something in a bowl.

I heard him talk affectionately to the cats and then groan. Sally must've performed her special morning greeting, but hopefully she hadn't done anything extra special on Chuck's leg.

I really wanted to take a shower and comb my hair and maybe slip on an attractive camisole, but before I could do anything at all about overhauling my appearance, Chuck was right back sitting on the bed beside me. He was wearing just his underwear, his hair looking like a cross between Don King's and Albert Einstein's, standing straight up on end. A slight dark beard stubble shadowed his cheeks again. I found his morning look kind of endearing—well, not just kind of, but very endearing.

My other relationships all involved guys who were concerned about their stage presence, even when they were off stage. Witness Jack's always pressed, creased jeans. My flautist spent sixteen minutes every morning doing his hair, which was exactly fifteen minutes longer than I spent towel drying and combing mine. My lead singer went to tanning salons, and on top of that, used bronzing gel.

Chuck didn't have a stage presence. He was just Chuck.

He was completely unselfconscious and he made me feel that way, too, offering me one of two plates of scrambled eggs drenched in salsa, a couple of leftover slices of pizza, and a couple of forks.

"You don't have any bread," he said.

"I know." I smiled, and took up a big forkful of eggs. I was hungry and they were good.

"Coffee's on," he said. "Cats are fed. I'm gonna have to go feed Jessie pretty soon," he said, shoveling down the eggs in about two bites. "The other Jessie," he amended. "Take her for a walk. I can be back in forty-five minutes. You'll keep the table against the door and won't let anybody in but me, even though it's daylight and I'm relatively sure nothing's gonna happen this morning. But we have to change your lock right away obviously. I guess I'll just bring Jessie over here. Wonder how she'll get along with the cats. . . ." he mused.

"The question is how Sally'll get along with her," I said. I was imagining the yowling, growling, snarling and biting from her side of things, and I could only hope that Jessie was the sort of motherly female dog who wasn't a true bitch.

"Sally's the cute one who chews your toes or the matted one who pees by the door?"

"Pees," I admitted. "She's seventeen and she was thrown out in the rain by a really obnoxious family when they moved from down the street, and I'm certainly not going to throw her out, so I kind of have to live with her imperfections." I was feeling just a little defensive.

"I like that about you. Able to live with imperfections. Loyal. Kind-hearted. But you should know she peed twice this morning, unfortunately the first time on your copy of the *Daily Sail*." The coffeemaker timer beeped, so he walked out of the room, carrying both our scraped-clean plates.

While he poured the coffee, I tucked my hair behind my ears and rubbed the sleep out of my eyes, then folded the sheet around me so that for a moment I could imagine I looked like I was wearing a nice toga or something, instead of just all tangled up in the covers.

He came back into the room carrying two mugs of coffee, a section of newspaper tucked under his arm. "But I managed to save the South Bay section so you could read all about your campaign."

It was only then, when I wasn't so occupied with trying to make myself look halfway attractive, that it occurred to me. "I don't get a paper," I said. "I mean, I buy the *Sail* at the corner store sometimes, like when I'm running for office or I'm looking for a movie showtime, but that's about it."

"Well, you got a paper today," he said, dropping it down on the bed. He slurped his coffee and stepped into his jeans. "If it was your neighbor's, I don't think they'd want it anyway, with the cat pee and all."

I watched him tugging his jeans over his hips. He grimaced a little when he came to the bruised and swollen spot where my intruder had clubbed him. I felt a strong urge to get out of my carefully draped sheet, sympathize, and then tug those jeans right back off again.

He saw me looking at him and he smiled. He leaned forward to kiss me on my forehead.

I leaned up and kissed him on the lips. We stayed locked like that for a long time. It felt natural, as if we'd been greeting each other like this every morning for a year. Or in another lifetime maybe. Yeah, maybe it was that, maybe in another lifetime we'd been married for like eighty years or something. It felt like in about another thirty seconds he was going to tell me he loved me, and like I might say the same thing back to him, casually and completely naturally, as if we *had* been married for eighty years in another lifetime.

He looked at me tenderly. I looked back at him, my breath catching in my throat.

"If we have time later, maybe I'll take a look at your car, since it's not running. I mean theoretically, if it doesn't run and it's parked on the street, it should be towed," he said.

I guess he wasn't on the verge of professing true love. Well, naturally, neither was I, right? Like the song goes, I was just letting my imagination run away with me.

Besides it was nice of him to offer to work on my car, except for that part about how it should be towed. Chuck headed back into the living room to retrieve his shoes and socks.

"Really should canvass the neighborhood, see if anybody saw anything besides Mrs. Palazo. I'm not on duty again until six A.M. tomorrow, so I should be able to fit everything in."

I tried not to feel crabby, but yeah, I felt crabby all of a sudden. How could he look so tender and talk about my car and canvassing the neighborhood? I was used to guys who professed their passion for me after having slept with me, told me over and over how wonderful and beautiful I was; they flattered me. Okay, maybe ultimately their flattery wasn't very sincere, but it would still be nice to be paid just the slightest bit of attention. Especially by someone who for a minute there was looking at you like you were indeed all that.

Chuck came back in my room again and sat on the edge of the bed next to me with his sneakers in his hand. He wasn't paying any attention to me at all. He wasn't even looking at me now. Still, as he slipped his feet in his shoes, he said, "By the way. I'm not big on early-morning endearments and stuff like that. My mind starts going and you know, it's like I'm already off someplace else. Working on a case or something. Today, working on what happened here last night. But it doesn't mean I don't think you look hot this morning."

I stopped feeling so crabby. "You, too," I said, and we made eye contact. We took another minute for a little more kissing.

"Yeah, have to carve out some more time for that, too," he said.

He turned his attention back to his shoes, and sufficiently appeased, I looked at the cover of the newspaper's South Bay section, and below the fold to the article on the city council race.

"'Record number of candidates file; some have no political background,'" I read aloud. "'Will they gain needed experience in time to seduce voters?'"

"You've certainly seduced me into voting for you." Chuck laughed.

The debate wasn't mentioned at all, but the reporter had either attended or watched some of it on TV, because there was a quote from Benni about pies, and one from Salome about unity, and from Tad about the harbor fill-in. I turned the page for the jump, hoping the reporter pulled a quote from me. And a typewritten sheet of paper fell out on my lap.

I thought it was a flyer that wasn't very professionally done, an ad for carpet cleaning or a weight-loss center. I almost just tossed it away on the bed. But something about it, maybe the fact that it was damp, and I didn't want Sally's incontinence issues to affect my sheets, made me look at it before I threw it aside.

In bold type, unevenly spaced across the top, it read "You're not as smart as you think you are." That got my attention. So I read the smaller type below. "You should get out of the race. Before the shadows fall at five and you are *no longer alive.*"

"What the hell is this?" I said.

"Is what?" Chuck asked.

I waved the paper at him. He wrinkled up his nose, and took it like it was toxic waste or something.

"Whatever it is, your cat really peed on it."

"Read it," I said, a little bit hysterical. "I mean I guess I should be proud that somebody considers me a serious enough political contender that they're interested in killing me, but I'm starting to get seriously creeped out here."

Chuck scanned the paper for a moment. "To be honest," he said, "so am I."

He jumped up, and pulled me with him. So much for the artful sheet.

"Get dressed and come with me to my place. I don't want you alone here," Chuck said, "not even for forty-five minutes."

Despite the fact that he was ordering me around again, given the circumstances I let it ride.

I was in and out of the shower in about thirty seconds, and then I called Lisa to see if she'd received any bizarre letters in her morning paper.

"No, nothing like that. But talking about bizarre, what's going on with you and—"

"Now's not the time. I mean he's um, right here—"

Lisa gave a little squeal. I barreled on. "Talking to Dave on his cell. I think he wants Dave to go over and watch your back while he, uh, watches mine."

"I bet it's not just your back he's watching," Lisa teased.

Actually, once again, he wasn't watching me at all. When he was finished talking to Dave, Chuck called information and got the number of the Hawaiian car dealership. Since it was still six A.M. in Hawaii, he didn't get any further than leaving a voice mail message for the sales manager about important police business.

He was still in the process of leaving that message as he took my arm and led me out of my apartment. It wasn't a sunny day but it wasn't raining as yet and the clouds rolling around were a thick whitish gray like distended pillows, the kind that my fellow candidate Benni would go on about pulling the feathers from.

We'd jogged halfway down my street when Chuck hung up and finally looked at me again in my simple jeans-sneakers-camisole-matching-sweater ensemble. I thought I looked pretty swell for just throwing this outfit together.

I didn't get a compliment though, I just got a "Good, you're wearing sneakers," and suddenly the low-level jog went to a full run east toward Torrance, where we arrived out of breath at a white-stucco, red-roofed office building in the parking garage of which Chuck had left his car. The run took fifteen unconversational minutes, punctuated only by Chuck encouraging me to "Hurry up." I decided he wasn't big on endearments while exercising, either.

I was panting and sweaty now and really annoyed that I'd worn the fuzzy sweater, which was dry clean only. I felt like I had signed up for one of those exercise boot camps without remembering that I had.

"Sorry to rush you. But the most important thing is keeping you safe," Chuck said. "I wanna get that note to the lab for analysis. I'm hoping our perp might be a little bit surprised to find out you're dating a cop."

I confess the word I fixated on was *dating*. We *were* dating, weren't we, even if we hadn't been out on an actual date. I wiped the sweat off my forehead and settled back for a short ride west again.

First stop, the police lab, where because it was Saturday, and the tech was taking his grandson fishing, Chuck was told he'd have the results Monday.

"Makes you miss LAPD, despite all the extra chances of getting shot at. One tech and he's fishing," Chuck groused as we drove down to the ocean ourselves.

People were so glad it wasn't raining that they were out walking along the Strand and biking along the Strand and just standing around the Strand, all staring down at the dead fish on the beach that the red tide and the storm had brought up. Staring, like the dead fish were something really cool.

Chuck had a studio apartment in one of the anonymous-looking high-rise apartment buildings that dotted the harbor: SEA VIEW APARTMENTS— STUDIOS—GAS FIREPLACES—OCEAN VU. Beneath that

sign swung a smaller one that read NO PETS AL-
LOWED, so I kind of pictured Jessie the dog as being
small and quiet.

Chuck unlocked his door, and Jessie gave an
enormous bark and circled Chuck like she hadn't
seen him in forever, and then she leapt up against
him, nuzzling his neck in a way that was not unlike
me nuzzling his neck.

He laughed and pushed her back, which resulted
in more furious barking, and then she turned her
attention on me. When she was raised up on her
hind legs and had her front paws on my chest, she
was taller than me. Small and quiet, Jessie was not.

She was part mastiff and part lab or something.
She sniffed me like maybe she was wondering if I
was what Chuck had brought her for breakfast.

"Nice doggie, nice Jessie," I said, trying to keep
the tremor out of my voice. If unknown assailants
didn't kill me, my new lover's dog might eat me.

But at the sound of my voice, she dropped down
and lay right at my feet. If she was a cat she would've
purred, but she wasn't a cat, so she just turned huge
sleepy black eyes up at me and whined. She rolled
over on her back and put all her paws up in the air
and wiggled them.

"She wants her tummy scratched," Chuck told
me.

I knelt down and started scratching. Who knew
what she'd do if she didn't get what she wanted?

"I never can train her not to jump up on people,
but other than that she's perfect."

"She seems . . . very nice," I managed. And truthfully,
who could resist being won over by those big dark eyes
looking up adoringly?

Chuck walked into his tiny avocado-green kitchenette, and Jessie got up off my feet and followed the sound of the can opener.

"You want to meet some cats?" he asked her.

Despite how sweet she seemed, her gargantuan size and the way she plowed into her dog food made me hope she didn't want to *eat* any cats. Although there was one occasion when Sally peed on the score of a song I'd been up all night writing, which I'd foolishly imagined might be a great calling card piece for me, and which I'd even more foolishly set down on the floor, that I might've looked the other way.

Jessie gobbled her food and Chuck disappeared into the bathroom, where I heard running water and the scratch of a razor.

I looked around. He was a minimalist in terms of furnishing. His living area featured a small TV and two large pillows, both on the floor. Along with the 1970s-era green appliances, his kitchen also boasted a built-in breakfast nook for two. Through a window at the far end of the nook, you could indeed see the ocean below, lapping against the boats in the marina.

Beneath the table was a mat with Jessie's water and food bowls, and next to the table there was a hook on the wall holding Jessie's leash.

On the other side of the kitchenette was the bedroom area, taken up with a full-size mattress on a box spring on the floor, covered with a fake fur bedspread in a terrible zebra stripe. There was a CD player and an alarm clock on an apple crate and a small stack of CDs. Naturally, I went to take a look at those. Jazz, not to my taste exactly, but stuff I actually had heard and respected, local boy Chet Baker, Miles Davis, Michael Chucks. And some blues, Leadbelly, The Nighthawks, which explained Chuck's faint recognition of KCAS's eclectic format. Again, not to my taste, but it wasn't like he listened to Justin Timberlake or old AC/DC, or Cher. I breathed a little sigh of relief.

On the other side of Chuck's bed there was a dog bed of sorts made from a box and a blanket, and another apple crate turned upside down and filled with dog toys, and that was that.

"Too much furniture is bad luck," Chuck said gruffly, emerging from the bathroom, cheeks clean-shaven. "At least for me. My ex-wife came with a full living room suite from Levitz, and I told you where that relationship ended up."

He threw open his closet. He had a couple of duffel bags, a sleeping bag, and a Coleman lantern on the top shelf, neatly folded jeans on the second. He had a clear plastic box holding rolled-up socks and underwear, a couple of cheap suits and dress shirts on hangers, four or five identical black T-shirts, and a tie rack with three identical striped ties.

His sparse, orderly closet put my own cluttered disaster to even greater shame. He took out a fresh pair of jeans and a blue T-shirt and stripped and put them on. He took another pair of jeans and another T-shirt and a dress shirt, tie, and khaki slacks and folded everything very economically into a duffel bag. He threw his shaving kit on top of those clothes and zipped it up again.

"I'm ready to move in with you," he said.

"For the weekend?"

"Longer than that. Like permanently."

"What?" I thought he was joking.

"I think it would be a lot safer if you weren't alone right now, and your place is bigger than mine and management here said I had to get rid of my dog or find a new place anyway."

It wasn't really very romantic, and he was doing that telling me rather than asking me thing again. Apparently, along with not offering endearments first thing in the morning or while jogging, he wasn't big on offering endearments prior to announcing we were going to live together, either.

"Hold on," I snapped, feeling just a little bit taken for granted. "You're moving in? I mean *really* moving in? Because it's safer and you need a new place for your dog—"

He stepped close to me and kissed me. "Not just because of my dog."

I just sort of shut up then, because the truth was, as long as it wasn't *totally* because of his dog, and the pronouncement was accompanied by another long, sweet kiss, I didn't really mind.

Jessie sat on her haunches in the back seat, leaning her head over my shoulder. She was panting and drooling at the same time, not unlike the boy I took to my high school prom.

"She really likes you," Chuck said.

"I'm glad she approves."

"You have no idea how loud she can bark if she doesn't like someone."

I had some idea but I didn't say so. He seemed to take this as a point of pride.

"Anybody tries to mess with your place again, she'll pin 'em down and hold 'em until I call her off."

Part of me liked the idea and part of me still worried that she might perceive *me* as messing with my place and hold me down, but he didn't say that during the holding process she was going to bite off a nose or anything, so I figured I was okay.

When we pulled up in front of my place, or rather next to in front of my place behind my broken-down car, Dave was already waiting at my apartment with a big toolbox. He stared at Chuck and I, puzzled, as if he was seeing something completely unexpected, like the sun coming out. Maybe it was because Chuck was carrying his duffel bag in one hand, and Jessie's dog bed/crate filled with toys in the other, or the fact that I was holding Jessie or she was holding me by her leash.

Lisa was there, too, helping a slightly bent older man in a beret unload stacks of yellow-and-black signs from the camper shell on the back of his truck. My campaign signs. I'd forgotten all about them.

"You didn't buy stakes," Lisa chided me.

"Yes, I did. But I have to keep them in a secret place so I can kill vampires."

"I guess we'll just have to staple the signs on telephone poles," Lisa said.

"It's illegal to put them on poles," Chuck warned me.

"Slight problem with police protection," I noted. "Police overprotection."

Dave and Chuck and Lisa all chatted, and reassuring myself they couldn't possibly be talking, or laughing, now they were laughing, about me, I conferred with the sign maker. He had extra stakes in his van, and they'd only cost me twice what they would have if I'd remembered to order them in the first place.

"In spite of the stakes, ha, going up," Lisa told me, "you have thirty-one dollars left over from your fund-raiser. After you pay yourself back for the campaign filing. If you don't pay yourself back and you let it sit on your credit card for the next five years until you've paid MasterCard at least nine thousand dollars in usury interest, then you have twelve hundred and sixty-one dollars left over."

"Cool," I said. What else was there to say? We were talking about signs and campaign expenses when clearly what Lisa wanted to talk about was me arriving back at my own apartment with Chuck and his dog and Chuck's duffel bag and dog crate.

We carried the signs and stakes into my apartment and I shut the cats in my bedroom so Dave and Chuck could get busy with the front door. Or at least get busy examining Dave's tools and several different lock sets and a dead bolt, and argue earnestly over which was the best. I noticed Dave kept throwing puzzled glances my way and back at Chuck, and Chuck kept ignoring them.

Jessie the dog was temporarily tethered to a little palm tree in front of the duplex, which she was circling warily. She looked kind of puzzled, too. She kept rearing up on her hind legs; so many people to jump on and too little leash. The leash didn't keep her from barking though. I saw Mrs. Palazo peering out the front window from behind her curtains. I waved. The curtain fell.

We finished bringing in the signs. Boy, there sure were a lot of them. It was really rather daunting to think about having to do something with them other than stack them up on my sofa so there would be someplace to walk. Chuck saying my apartment was bigger than his was only true so long as there were not two hundred and fifty signs, a new large wooden crate, and four extra people in it. The cats were whining and scratching at my bedroom door, and Jessie was barking and barking outside. My jaw clenched.

Was I really going to just let Chuck move in with me? Just up and move in, with no discussion about it, no planning, no engagement or even a going-steady ring? Even Jack, who never lived with me, gave me a ring. It was just a junky ring that he bought from a street vendor at the annual Playa Vista Memorial Day arts and crafts fair, and I'd lost it by the time he left town around Thanksgiving, but still.

And things were going to get awfully crowded with Chuck and his dog. Would I ever have enough space to write a decent song again? To mope about whether or not the song I had written was indeed decent? To listen to homemade garage band CDs dropped off at the station in the hope of discovering some great new talent? To wonder if I had any talent and if anyone would ever discover me? To wonder, if I was struck by lightning during L.A.'s greenhouse effect-expanded rainy season, if anyone would even notice I was gone?

My jaw unclenched. Someone would certainly notice now. For one thing, they'd have to move my charred body just to reach the door.

After a little while, Chuck and Dave finished with my door, and Chuck unleashed Jessie and brought her upstairs. Jessie pulled all of her toys out of her crate and wrestled with them. Then we all stood around my living room looking at the big pile of signs.

For a moment everyone was silent. The cats weren't whining behind the bedroom door; Jessie wasn't barking, she was just gnawing quietly on a rubber bone. I think everyone, even the dog, was

waiting for Chuck and I to make some kind of declaration or something.

"Well," said Chuck, breaking the awkward silence, "now no one has the key to your apartment
anymore."

"Including me," I pointed out. Chuck handed me
a key. We all watched him tuck the spare in his own
pocket.

"Someone had the key to the old lock?" Lisa
asked.

"Jack," I said. "But it wasn't Jack breaking in here
last night."

"How do you know? Maybe he missed you."

I rolled my eyes at Lisa. "He was having a party in
Santa Barbara when I called him."

"You called him?" Lisa asked.

"I made her," Chuck said.

"So we could question him," I threw in.

"Makes sense," said Dave.

Lisa looked doubtful.

The scratching and whining behind the bedroom door resumed and grew more violent.

"We can't leave the cats in there all day," Chuck
said, even though I thought maybe that would elim-
inate the potential for Jessie the dog to devour
them. He opened the door. "Come on. Meet your
new friend," he said, and he set them free.

Although the canine and feline discussion that
ensued was not understandable to human ears, I
would not have been at all surprised to discover
that it involved something along the lines of "So, he
spent the night with her, and now he's moving in?"
and "You know, my name is Jessie, too, and I was
here first."

Certainly Chuck and I coming together was the

major if now unspoken preoccupation among the two-legged creatures filling my living room. Dave and Lisa were glancing from me to Chuck and Chuck to me and then back at each other. Chuck and I were kind of smiling at our respective pets and then at each other, but we stopped when we saw them looking at us.

"Intense," Dave managed.

Lisa gave another giggle. I was not used to so much giggling from Lisa, and it kind of unnerved me.

"Yes, I'm moving in," Chuck said. "Let's move on."

"Wow," Lisa and Dave said, both of them chuckling wisely.

I didn't say anything. I just didn't know what to say. I mean every time he said the words *moving in*, it sounded so permanent. Everything was happening so quickly, right now my head was spinning faster than an old-fashioned LP turntable set at 78 rpm. Bam, ran into Chuck, had great sex with Chuck, bam, almost got killed, spent the night with Chuck, felt bizarrely comfortable waking up with him, bam, was threatened in a weird creepy difficult to fathom note, bam, Chuck was living with me. Along with his dog. Who had the same name as me.

I kind of shook my head as if to clear it, and as if picking up on the whirling confusion in me, Dave said, "Aren't you moving pretty fast here, Chuck?"

"No," said Chuck, looking at me steadily, as if willing me to agree.

The thing was, I mostly did agree, which also made my head whirl. I managed to make my spinning head nod in agreement with Chuck, which seemed to be enough to get everyone to shut up about it.

"Now," said Chuck to Dave, with exaggerated patience, "why don't we focus on the problem at hand? I read you that note over the phone. You said you'd give me your thoughts on it."

"Could've been directed at you," Dave suggested to Chuck. "That was my first thought. You tend to rub people the wrong way sometimes, and it had that aggrieved kinda tone."

"No. It was inside *her* paper."

Dave cracked his knuckles and I jumped like the earth was quaking at the sound. "I'm just trying for some levity. Look, both these ladies have had break-ins and been threatened. Both these ladies have had phone calls with words indicating a similar threat. The note read like the work of a crackpot, but in my opinion we're supposed to write it off as a crazy person, when really it's the work of someone with an actual plan."

"Could be," Chuck said. "Or it could just be a nut."

"We'll watch out for you both," said Dave. "You made the right call when you called Big Dave." Dave gave Lisa's shoulder a comforting squeeze.

Actually, I'd made the call, but what did that matter now? I waited for Chuck to say I'd collided with the right guy when I collided with him, but he didn't say that.

Instead he said, "Jessie's a good girl. Yes, she is."

Lisa looked surprised but then realized he was talking to his dog. Sally and Squeak were both sniffing her, Squeak offering joyous little meows, Sally sort of growling, but softly. Jessie rolled over on her back and put her legs up in the air again, which seemed to be one of her favorite positions. Chuck patted her on the belly. "My Jessie just loves getting her tummy rubbed."

"I bet," Lisa whispered to me.

Chuck and Dave decided to install a sensor-triggered light over the front door that went on like a spotlight whenever anyone stood on my porch.

"Isn't that overkill?" I asked.

"Dave put one up at my house too," Lisa said.

"Deterrent," Dave muttered, really absorbed in his task. "Hey, Lisa, maybe—another cup of coffee? You make great coffee."

"Sure thing," she said, smiling like she'd just won the Publishers Clearing House sweepstakes.

Lisa and I went into my kitchen. It was lucky Dave only wanted coffee, since it was all I had left in my cupboard except cat food, since Chuck had appropriated the eggs and salsa this morning.

"What's up with you and Dave?" I asked.

"He came over last night and we sat up late talking."

"Just talking?"

"*Talking*. He lost someone, too. An accident, not illness. But both of us, we've been on our own for a while. So, we're moving slow. He did spend the night, but he crashed on my sofa. He's not like your Chuck."

"*My* Chuck?"

"Well, if he's moving in here with you, I guess he's yours, all right. Are you sure—?"

"Sure I am."

"Okay, then." She looked like she wanted to say something more, but she just bit her lip and got some cups out of my cabinet.

"I don't get it myself, you know," I said. "That's why I'm not saying more, it's because I don't know what to say, I haven't known since I met him. I feel really connected to him. And I think he feels that way about me, too. But sometimes he's so . . . presumptive. He doesn't ask, he just tells. Like he just kind of told me he was moving in. This morning. No discussion or anything. But I didn't say no. I mean I couldn't say no."

"By all means then, live together because you couldn't say no! It'll be perfect," Lisa said, amused. "You know, you were *engaged* to Jack and never once in a year did it come up that you'd live together."

"He was always on the road and—and he never asked. And I never really wanted and—"

"But you want Chuck Jackson. Even if he didn't ask your permission first, it's like, boom. After knowing him four days."

"Well I met him four days ago, yeah. I can't say I've really *known* him more than say a day and a half."

"I repeat," Lisa said, laughing now, "by all means, live together."

"There's something that outweighs, well, how short a time I've known him, or how much I want to stop him from saying or doing things that are just absolutely maddening, I mean there's something more important than that—"

"Good sex," Lisa suggested. "Don't sign a long-term-lease agreement."

"No, it's not good sex!" I protested.

Lisa raised her eyebrows.

"I mean it is good, but that's not the reason he said let's live together. Why I agreed."

I tried to think what that reason was, but it was all

tangled up in his dog needing a new place to live and someone breaking in my apartment and threatening me and he said he'd keep me safe, or at least his dog would.

I sighed. "I don't know why I agreed. I just wanted to. Okay? Really lame, I know, I just wanted to. Be with him. Skip the whole dating and listening to him sing to me part."

"He sings?"

"I don't know. I don't think so. I just meant I want to skip the part I usually get all wrapped up in. Going to clubs and mooning over someone, and them courting me and me courting them, and dressing up and holding hands and reading record reviews and talking about sixties rock influences and the Nashville sound and did rap kill pop and are Amy Rigby's rhymes cute or silly, and all that stuff! I don't want to build a relationship, or fake a relationship or invent a relationship. I want to just have one. I want it to feel *real* for once."

"So does this seem real? With Chuck?"

"Yeah," I said. "Yeah, it does." Maybe a little too real, when you considered how small my apartment was and how short a time we'd known each other, but still.

"Well, then, maybe it's a great idea living together. Who knows? I mean it's not like you're sixteen and you're doing this. Ostensibly, you're old enough to know what you're doing even if I don't think you've ever known what you were doing in a relationship before."

"That's kind of funny, because this is the first time I don't have any idea at all what I'm doing."

"Maybe you're in love," she suggested. "You want to be, anyway."

"Well, sure."

"I don't think you've ever really been in love. With the idea of love maybe, with a pretty ballad the guy sang, but not with the guy."

"You could be right," I admitted.

"I'm going to encourage you to, well, go for it," Lisa said. "As long, of course, as it doesn't affect your political campaign."

Chuck and Dave finished making my apartment into a security fortress in under an hour, and then Pahalu Motors returned Chuck's call.

"No, I don't know the model or the year of the car in question. It was an SUV, most likely dark gray in color, under two years old, boxy shape. I'm thinking hybrid, but I'm not positive. Yeah, start with a fax of the full list of SUV purchasers over the past two years. I'll get you an official request for records, but it's gonna be Monday. Thing is, I need those records sooner rather than later, if you could do me a favor."

Dave answered his pager and called a client.

Lisa was talking on her cell phone to someone about booking a private party at the club, someone who wanted her to take a meeting on it that afternoon.

Sally and Squeak chased Jessie around the apartment and they appeared to be having fun, although at rather great and repeated risk to the lamp on the coffee table.

I knew I should be on the phone calling someone about something, or chasing the cats and dog around, but I wanted to sink down on my sofa in exhaustion. Except there was no place to sink because of those signs.

The signs I was going to go around town and distribute with merry goodwill. Except I didn't feel like doing it. I wanted a little time to feel stunned and/or excited about this Chuck-moving-in thing. I wanted some more sleep. I wanted whatever creepy guy was mugging or trying to mug Lisa and I to go away, far, far away so that I wouldn't have to worry about that anymore.

This person wanted to hurt us if not kill us, and there was Lisa talking about a private booking, and I had to put up signs so I could make myself more of a target, oops, candidate.

With everyone on the phone and Chuck's dog and my cats racing around, I literally thought about sneaking off somewhere by myself, but then what if my stalker was around just waiting to nab me the first minute I did something stupid like go off alone to study the chaos of my life. Besides, if I studied it, what good would that do? I had signs to put up.

"Okay, it isn't like we made plans to lie in bed and drink Bloody Marys or something, although that would be nice." Chuck was helping me pound about the hundredth campaign sign into the ground. "But I already had a lot of other stuff on my plate today."

"I know," I said. "But it seemed like a shame with Dave shepherding some wealthy couple's kids to Disneyland not to let him take Lisa along to visit Mickey. And you wouldn't want me putting up these signs all by myself."

"I wouldn't?" Chuck sighed.

I'd also kind of thought that with time alone together maybe we could talk just a little bit more about the moving-in thing. It wasn't that I was having second thoughts about agreeing so easily, at

least not exactly, it was that I really thought we
ought to discuss *why* we were living together. Just a
little. The way last night I'd wanted to talk about
why we were so attracted to each other. It was one
thing, though to just go with being attracted and
not question it; it was another to just move in together blithely ignorant. Wasn't it?

It was kind of a big step, living together, and I already knew he liked things to be easy, but maybe
this was just too easy. I wanted to be reassured. I
wanted to know what he was thinking, really thinking, about us.

But three hours into the sign staking, the opportunity for discussion and reassurance, for finding
out exactly what Chuck was thinking, hadn't presented itself. Or maybe I didn't really want the opportunity to know what he was thinking exactly,
because I didn't know what I was thinking exactly
myself.

Meanwhile, my signs sprouted like mushrooms in
the damp ground on every street corner, in front of
the gas station, the minimart, the surf shop. My
signs were cheek and jowl against Ned Rutkin's,
Benni's, Salome's and Royal's because there were
only so many public spots available to stick them, so
it looked like the candidates were all friends or
something.

The other candidates' minions had hit the streets
earlier than Chuck and I, taking full advantage of
this break in the weather. They were working faster
than we were, too, because their signs didn't have
to be personally attached to stakes the way mine
did, because of a candidate's stupidity in not ordering them that way.

Ned's sleek, plastic, virtually weatherproof signage was being expanded every moment by what appeared to be professional sign installers, or possibly handlers of toxic waste. The guys bearing his signs wore white jumpsuits and popped out of minivans and were in our way and out of it again before we'd stapled a single sign to a stake.

Royal had five teenage boys, thick of build and chunky of neck who appeared to be relatives, or maybe young clones, distributing his signs. Salome had a group of really pretty women and men, some of whom were waving at passing cars. I wondered if they were all former members of a Las Vegas chorus line. Chuck seemed to be wondering something about them too, because he kept glancing at them suspiciously from time to time, or at least at the miniskirts some of the women were wearing.

Benni's crew was made up of a massive but glum-looking group of boys and girls in Boy and Girl Scout uniforms.

"What kind of a badge is a sign badge?" I heard one boy ask another.

Tad was, I guess, relying solely on the huge faded banners draped front and back around the grocery, or was still sleeping in after a night of something I didn't want to think about. Ida and Conway didn't have signs, at least not yet.

Jessie was a great help with our drudgery. She dug some convenient holes so we didn't have to, and even more holes when we didn't want her to. She barked at all passing cars, and there were a lot of passing cars. When most muddy she jumped up on me and licked my chin. All was forgiven though when she peed on one of Ned's signs.

My simple yellow-and-black motif stood out pretty well in a field that was otherwise all red, white and blue, or red and white or blue and white. Salome's said VOTE 4 SALOME AND PEACE, MARCH 12, with a peace sign and a heart and a dove at the bottom. Royal's read LET ME MAKE YOUR DREAMS COME TRUE—ROYAL GARRITY. Ned Rutkin was THE PEOPLE'S CHOICE. Benni's sign included a pie painted like a flag, and the catch phrase DON'T SETTLE FOR JUST A SLICE.

My signs just had my name on them. I really believed in the adage "Keep it simple, stupid." Also, my signs cost a lot less with just the name. Also it had never occurred to me to have a slogan. If it had, I could've thought of something really spiffy. Like "I'm the Best" or "Strawberry Fields Forever," or—boy this would've been really, really good—"Born to Run."

Because of all the rain, at least the ground was nice and soft to stick the signs in, although on the downside, as it started lightly sprinkling again, I could see the edges of mine begin to curl. Soon they'd warp. Ned's would be pristine, of course, as plastic perfect as he was.

We'd put up well over a hundred signs, which meant we still had another hundred signs and the two hundred posters that Chuck was obdurately against me stapling illegally to telephone poles, though many of the other candidates had done it, and Chuck couldn't tear them all down. He did try, though.

"Can we knock this off now? Get something to eat?" Chuck asked.

"Sure. Just want to stop by Lisa's."

I papered the front door of the club with posters, and left some more in her mail slot with a note that she should put them up behind the stage.

Back at my place, I stuck a bunch of them all over on my stalled car.

Chuck looked like he was going to object to that, but instead he groaned, "Food. Have mercy."

"Okay, food," I agreed. "We'll have to go out somewhere to get some, because one thing you should know about me before you move in is that I'm not really big on grocery shopping."

I thought maybe this would lead naturally into a moving-in discussion, but it didn't.

"I'm not either," he said. "But I suppose if we want to 'live long and prosper' we should start ordering healthy stuff from the organic grocery on Pier Avenue over the 'Net or something. You can make great salads with that stuff."

Now he was going to tell me how to eat! And even if baby carrots and pesticide-free arugula was good for me, I started to take umbrage.

"We're going to order organic vegetables? I'm going to make salads?"

"I'll make them, I don't care. Right now though, let's just grab some burgers," he said.

He should've really asked me if I wanted Thai or El Pollo Loco or if I wanted to just grab some burgers, but I was too hungry to get annoyed about that, and it had no bearing whatsoever on the whole living together thing.

"Okay," I said, like he'd asked me instead of just announcing that we were going the fast-food route. "I'll burn off the calories doing door to doors anyway."

"You and me both."

I was momentarily charmed. "You're going to campaign with me?"

"I'm going to investigate for you. The election is one thing. Surviving it is another."

"Maybe I can shake people's hands while you ask them if they saw anyone try to run us over last night."

"I think we should canvass different doors. And you should take Jessie with you, in case you pick a door with a nut behind it."

There he went again, telling me what to do. Of course he was right, so how could I object, without sounding like a nut myself.

It started to rain again. Just a soft drizzle but we both knew where that led. He unlocked his car, which was parked behind mine, and Jessie bounded inside, and I was about to follow her, when a car pulled up right next to us.

"Jessie Adams," the cheerful guy behind the wheel called out. He had spiked short brown hair and lots of freckles. I'd never seen him before in my life. He looked way too perky to be the break-in guy, but he still made me kind of shrink back up against the car. Chuck stopped short and glared at him.

In the face of that glare the guy's perkiness wilted. I wiped my hair out of my eyes. Why was I always standing around in the rain with something unexpected—Chuck, a crazy person behind the wheel of an SUV, a perky person—coming at me?

"Hello," the guy said. "You *are* Ms. Adams?"

"Yes," I said cautiously in case he was from some former credit card company dunning me, or a record company exec wanting to sign me, or someone new about to threaten my life.

"I'm Brian Harrigan, with the *Daily Sail.*"

"I'm not interested in subscribing," I said curtly.

He laughed like I'd made a joke. Chuck took a step closer to the car like he definitely hadn't. Jessie picked up on something either in the guy or Chuck's manner and she started barking. Loudly.

Brian spoke hastily. "Remember? I spoke to you a few days ago."

I was really trying to remember.

"About your candidacy," he prompted me. "Boy, that dog sure can bark."

Chuck tapped on his car windshield twice, lightly, and Jessie shut up.

"I won't keep you long. I know it's raining," he said, perfectly dry himself inside his perfectly dry car. "I just thought I'd swing by and see if I could get your reaction," he said. "I've been calling all the candidates but you didn't answer your phone."

"We were out," Chuck said shortly. He was still glowering.

"My reaction?" Oh, probably to the newspaper article that gave each of us council runners our one paragraph of fame.

I'd scanned mine long enough to see that I was identified as running on a "preservationist ticket," and despite my effort to come up with a more sophisticated description of myself, I was described as a "disc jockey." Sometimes it just didn't matter what you did, you ended up as you, after all.

"Of course, my reaction," I said, trying for a friendly, accessible, candidate-like tone.

The rain had picked up to a steady pace and I was really getting wet now. I could slip into Brian's car, but then that would leave Chuck out in the rain. Or I could get into Chuck's car but that might make Brian think I wasn't very friendly, which of course would be reinforced by Chuck and Jessie the dog staring him down, which they were both doing.

So I just sucked it up and brushed the rain off my

face and tried to smile at Brian. He had a little notebook out of his pocket, not unlike Chuck's little
notebook. He started scribbling away as I spoke.

"Well, I'd just like to say that while I firmly believe
in preserving our vital commercial district and in
particular an historical musical landmark that
brings in great tax revenue for this city, I also believe that we must preserve a general quality of life
here in Playa Vista. To make certain that our de-
scendants have a real community to live in."

"That's what you want to say?" Brian sounded
quite surprised. He'd stopped writing in his little
notebook a while back.

"Well, yes," I said. What exactly was wrong with
that? I thought I sounded pretty pleasant and political and all that. Considering I was standing out in
the rain, it wasn't that bad. Jessie started barking
again, like she was annoyed. Honestly, I was getting
a little annoyed, too.

Brian mumbled something that sounded like "In
regard to the dearth."

"In regard to the dearth of what?" I asked over
the barking.

He said, "Of whom?"

And I said, "What does that mean?"

Now his voice sounded less chipper and more
somber and he said, "You have not been informed."

Clearly not.

Chuck gave a firmer rap on his windshield and
Jessie the dog was quiet.

"I hate to be the one to break the news to you,"
Brian said, and there was this gleeful undertone
that made me think he was actually kinda looking
forward to it, what with him being nice and dry in
his car and me waiting expectantly and patiently,

the candidate in need of good press, out there in the rain.

"What news is that?" I asked calmly.

"About the passing of your fellow."

"The passing of my fellow?" Now I was really confused.

"Fellow candidate," he continued, savoring every word. "Conway Marcus has left us."

"He's left us." I knew what he meant but I couldn't quite grasp it. "I'm so sorry," I managed adroitly. Everything I said was very likely going to be used for attribution. "What a terrible loss." Conway was the old guy with the combover and the weird tie who was fighting with flat-skulled Royal.

"Any other comment?"

"I didn't know him well but he seemed like a wonderful person," I said. "Some of his ideas appeared to be very heartfelt and I'm sure he did the community a lot of good."

After all, he didn't seem to like Royal, and that had to be good for the community right there.

"All right then." Brian sounded deeply disappointed.

Chuck stepped up next to Brain, and leaned in the window, dripping on him. "What was the cause of Mr. Marcus's demise, do you know?"

He had his badge out now and was shoving it in Brian's face.

There was just something about having a badge shoved in your face that made people nervous, I guess. Because Brian was now nervous.

"Mr. Marcus suffered a . . . a collapse in his home, was taken to the hospital, and passed away. They're saying overconsumption, you know, of alcohol, led to heart failure."

"Hmmm," said Chuck, like he believed Brian was holding out on him.

"Can I ask just one quick question," Brian asked. "Of you, sir?"

Chuck grimaced, clearly part of the problem here was that he was used to being the one who asked questions, and he didn't like being on the answering end of things.

Brian was undeterred by the grimace. "Is there a reason that a police detective is accompanying this candidate around?"

"We're friends," Chuck said gruffly.

"He's helping me put up my signs," I said.

"You're putting up your own signs?" Brian looked as shocked as if I'd said I'd just run into Chuck on the street one day and had sex with him and now, a few days later, he was moving in, and we hadn't even talked about it.

As soon as Brian pulled away, Chuck and I finally drove off ourselves.

Chuck made a quick cell phone call asking for Conway Marcus's address, and I felt a sinking feeling in my growling stomach. I knew we weren't going out for burgers, or even going to order good quality organic vegetables over the Internet.

Conway lived only a few blocks from me, in one of the tall and skinny houses that were the rage of the residential streets back in the late seventies and early eighties. His entire block was made up of these homes, twenty-five-feet wide and one-hundred-feet deep, unattached town homes with garages and short driveways in front and no sidewalks.

Conway's was easy to spot because there was a police car in the drive with one officer inside, and one standing outside, holding a black umbrella over Ida Pinckney.

"Wonder what she's doing here," I said.

"Go find out," Chuck suggested, striding over to the cop who was still in the car.

"What's up?" I heard Chuck ask as he turned up the collar on his jacket.

"They're running a blood alcohol analysis now on Mr. Marcus. Won't have the results 'til Monday but it appears he had one too many. Many too many."

Meanwhile, Ida looked up at me, like she was looking for an excuse to stop talking to the second officer. She smiled at me hopefully.

"Ida," I said, "I guess you've heard, too." Kind of lame, but that was really all I had to go on.

"I was with Conway last night. I dropped him off at home," she told me.

"Oh." Now I felt really lame. Ida and Conway were friends? Or something even friendlier?

She spoke to both me and the policeman. "I didn't want him to drive home when he seemed so out of it. We were both attending a Sierra Club meeting. But he . . . seemed unwell."

"I can imagine," the policeman said, almost but not quite hiding a smirk.

"You're getting soaked to the bone," Ida said to me. "Let's get you back to your car—if you're through with me, Officer?"

"Yes, ma'am." He headed for the patrol car and Ida and I made for Chuck's sedan.

She whispered in my ear. "I hope you don't mind, my dear. But I've had it with the questions. That Conway was a drunk is already well documented in police records. He had to do an awful lot of glad handing to keep a lid on that news, and he's not around to keep things quiet now."

Behind us there was the sound of a car door being closed, and some more conversation passed between Chuck and the second officer, and then the police car pulled away.

"Is there anything I can do?" I asked her.

"Is the man who drove you here a police officer too?"

"Yes," I admitted.

She sighed. "Here he comes then."

Chuck's footsteps rounded the house and he joined us beneath the awning. "Mrs. Pinckney. It's nice to meet you. Detective Chuck Jackson, Playa Vista po—"

"Yes, yes. Conway was inebriated at the time of death. I would love to keep it out of the paper, but I am sure it won't be kept and his family will all be humiliated. I did my part to get him safely home, but"—there was a little catch in her voice—"but I should've known something was wrong. He could barely stand."

"I'm sure you did the best you could," Chuck said. "You say you should've known something was wrong. What do you mean by that?"

"Conway was quite . . . incapacitated. He kept muttering that he'd 'underestimated.' Then he laughed and said, 'I think I've had too much to eat.' Those were apparently his last words."

"To eat?" Chuck repeated.

"I assume he meant he'd had too much to drink," she said impatiently. "He wasn't exactly making a lot of sense. I told my daughter this morning that I should come by and check on him, and I have, and I've discovered this—sad event. You may not have thought very much of him," she said to me, "but he was a friend of my late husband's, and a gentleman, and he had some very good ideas at one time. I'll miss him."

"I'm sorry," I began, but she waved her hand to stop me, her eyes teary.

"Not as sorry as I am," she said. Then she turned on her heel and walked down the street, her umbrella tilted against the wind.

"What do you think?" I asked Chuck as we climbed into his car.

He wiped the rain out of his eyes. "I think there's no point in bothering the Marcus family right now. I think Ida's telling the truth, but I feel, in my gut, that Conway's demise involved foul play, and it's a little on the odd side that Ida, as Conway's political opponent, would be so nice as to bring him home and save him from public humiliation. Still, I think I've gotta wait for the medical examiner to see if there were any exigent circumstances. And most importantly, I think we really need to buy an umbrella."

Chuck seemed to be thinking a lot. About everything, I thought, except us.

Chapter Twelve

The city clerk had left a message on my answering machine.

"We at the city clerk's office feel that due to the sudden and unexpected death of your fellow candidate, it is appropriate to discuss all ramifications and are calling a meeting today in the city council chambers at five P.M. We hope to see you there."

"Five o'clock," I said.

"Yeah, like in the note. Like maybe somebody knew there was going to be a meeting, and why. Like maybe they were trying to scare you away."

The rain was really coming down again. Looking out my window down to the corner I saw one of my signs curling up under the onslaught. And the black ink was running on the posters I'd plastered on my dead car, rendering my name very Goth.

"Maybe they have scared me away," I said to Chuck. "I mean, what's the point in going to the meeting anyway?"

"No, you'll go. And I'll go with you," he said. "If the perp shows up, man, I'm ready to call him out."

Chuck opened the bag of fast-food burgers we'd just picked up, like everything was all settled.

He really did seem to think that if he made a pronouncement, that was how it was going to be. I wanted to argue with him about it, except I knew he was right, once again. It was really hard to call him on stuff that he said that I agreed with. There wasn't really anything to be afraid of at that meeting, not with Chuck by my side. Unless whoever was after me was on the other side and they both started shooting.

But that was pretty unlikely, so nope, there was no point in discussing attending the candidate meeting. But there was still some point in discussing our relationship.

Chuck seemed blithely unaware that anything at all needed to be discussed. He handed a burger to me with his right hand and one to Jessie the dog, drooling in anticipation, with his left.

"I have to talk to you," I began.

Chuck was staring into the middle distance, chewing obdurately, like he was trying to figure something out, and not exactly liking what he was figuring.

"Talk about what?" he asked, a delayed response that told me his attention wasn't entirely on me.

I decided the timing wasn't right for a "Let's discuss our relationship" conversation.

Instead I asked him, "Why don't you like that reporter from the *Sail*?"

His eyes barely grazed my face. "Because Clark Kent, Jr. is a dork," he said. "That's why."

He went back to staring at my wall again.

I started humming the old Missing Persons song, "Life Is So Strange."

Life was very strange indeed and I couldn't even bring myself to comment on it.

Chuck put his feet up on my coffee table and gave his dog another burger. He took another one for himself and broke off a few more pieces and tossed them to Squeak, who was wagging his tail like he thought he was a dog now.

Sally wasn't interested in the burger. She was huddled by the front door and I knew exactly what she was going to do, and that right after she did it, I'd be hitting the kitchen for pet stain deodorizer and a handful of paper towels. So I guess my destination wasn't entirely unknown, like it said in the song.

Chuck was still staring off into space. I broke off my song, but he didn't seem to notice if I was humming away or not.

It occurred to me that he wasn't so much deeply absorbed in staring into space as he was concentrating on anything but me. He was avoiding me. It was either because he, too, was having second thoughts, or at least one and a half thoughts about moving in, or because "You know something you're not telling me," as I accused him.

Chuck swallowed, and focused on me. "Don't let's have some stupid argument."

"No, let's not. Is it about Conway Marcus? Or the scary note in my newspaper? Or this meeting at five o'clock, not four-thirty, not six o'clock, but five?"

"I wouldn't keep anything from you that you needed to know," he said.

"Maybe *you* should go into politics. You'll inform me, then, on a need-to-know basis?"

He ignored my jibe, and got very busy wiping his hands on a napkin. I tried a different tactic.

"Why's Brian a dork?" I asked.

Chuck laughed and relaxed a little. "Well, I sent

him an e-mail about a year ago regarding some . . .
questionable activities on the part of friends of the
very councilmen whose ranks you're hoping to
join. Since Brian had come to me for information
about a couple of cases and I helped him out, I figured he might be interested in looking into those
activities. As a public service."

"And to help you out a little, maybe?"

"Sure."

"But he wasn't interested?"

"Oh, he was interested. So interested that along
with his own request for a meeting, he accidently
forwarded my e-mail to the council, the mayor, and
several other community players! Of course my
lieutenant wasn't wild about hearing from the
people who help keep him in office that his subor-
dinate was shooting off his mouth.

"That marked the first—but not the last—time I
called my boss an asshole. And that's part of the
reason I spend so much time these days eye-balling
the local call girl operation."

"Questionable activities, huh? What kind exactly?"

Chuck rubbed at the back of his neck. "About a year
ago, a c.i. I had—that's a confidential informant—
told me there was a big real estate deal about to go
down here in Playa Vista. That the council had some
friends who wanted to buy up all the businesses, replace 'em with condos, megahouses, and maybe a
sweet little boutique hotel. They wanted to increase
property values and sell bonds for development and
give a big kickback to certain contractors. None of this
is illegal. None of this is even out of line with the way
things are going everywhere in this state. It isn't a community anymore, it's a business venture."

He drew in his breath. "Okay, off the soapbox.

The people who were behind all this development stuff, and who had contributed, I might add, to the councilmen's campaign coffers, they were using money from the sale of illegal substances."

"Drug money," I said.

"It was a trail I was following when I worked vice in L.A. A frustrating, dirty, bought-out trail no one wanted me to follow, and that's a big part of the reason my marriage fell apart, and a big part of why I left LAPD and moved down here for a quieter, simpler life. Then boom, I'm hit in the face with it again. Certain names came up, names I'd seen before. It's like the whole scene followed me into my new, so-called laid-back lifestyle. So, I go to my boss to tell him what I know, and he won't even listen."

"Was this before or after you started calling him an asshole?"

"Before." Chuck looked pained. "When he wasn't interested, I decided I'd take it to the press. And I e-mail Brian, and like I said, he screws it up, my boss and I get it on, and then everything gets very quiet. Until Drew Bartlett calls me. You know, the councilman who 'resigned.'"

"I know who he is," I said shortly. How dumb did Chuck think I was anyway? Although less than a week ago when Lisa first mentioned Drew, I had no clue who he was.

"Drew was the only one who got that e-mail who wasn't ready to skin me alive. Drew mentioned Lisa's club to me, all the hoops everybody was making her jump through. He thought it was peculiar. The new plan, the quieter plan, was to just drive everybody out of business, and that plus the re-zoning, well, wow, that would get everybody what they wanted, just a little bit slower than buying them out up front."

I crumpled up my burger wrapper. Jessie the dog whined. She could see something was going on and she wasn't sure what it was but she didn't like it. That was just about how I felt.

"Did Dave really ask your help installing Lisa's security system? Or did you find out about Lisa's problem and my candidacy *from* Dave and show up at the club because of your interest in the questionable activities of councilmen and their friends and maybe even people now running for council?"

"The latter," Chuck admitted, looking a little uncomfortable. "You're smart," he added.

I wasn't sure if he thought that was good or bad at the moment.

"I think that whole need-to-know thing is coming up," I said. "For example, I need to know if you want to protect me, if you want to *move in* with me, to get yourself a real inside track on this campaign stuff."

There. I'd done it. Kind of in a roundabout way, but still I'd done it. I'd brought up the moving-in thing.

"Honestly, Jessie. You act like you don't even know me," Chuck said.

The truth was I didn't really know him that well, did I? It just felt like I did, which wasn't the same thing at all.

"Of course I want to just be with you and protect you. But sure, sure it helps to be right here, where the action very well could be, where it was already proven last night some action was—and you were glad I was here then. At least I think you were. I think you should be."

I narrowed my eyes. There he went again. I
should be?

"Ah," I said.

Nature abhors a vacuum, so after a moment,
Chuck went on.

"Naturally, when Dave mentioned Lisa's club and
your campaign, I jumped to get a look. I didn't
know you were you. I told you that. And obviously I
had no idea you were running for city council when
we—when we had that—that cataclysmic moment."

I softened. Nope, I melted. Boy, I was easy. "It was
kinda cataclysmic, wasn't it?"

Chuck seemed to breathe out for the very first
time. "It always is with you," he said, leaning forward and taking my hand. "Yeah, I'm conducting
an unofficial, unsanctioned investigation into just
who wants to win this election badly enough to
force old Drew Bartlett out in the first place. Just
because he won't call it that, I know he didn't walk
away without a push. I want to know who's threatening Lisa, and you. And now I want to know if
Conway Marcus's death was accidental. Just because
something sounds right doesn't mean it is right."

That had certainly been my experience when it
came to men.

"Are you going to move out, as soon as this whole
campaign thing is over?" I asked.

"Do you want me to?"

"I want an answer from *you*. You're the one on
the stand, buddy."

He laughed. "I am, huh?"

"And you can't take the Fifth."

"I don't want to," he said. "No, I'm not planning
on moving out when I get my case. I was thinking
we're both gonna have to move. Get a bigger place.

This is bigger than my studio, sure, but that kitchen isn't anywhere decent to cook in, and I like to cook, when there's there's any food around and there's someone to cook for. I really don't mind being the one who makes the salads. And if you're going to have any privacy to write your songs or listen to some weird hip new crap like the Red Hot Chili Peppers—"

"They're not that hip anymore. They were never weird. And they certainly aren't new. Smog is new." I was just babbling, trying to keep myself from hyperventilating.

Here I was trying to make sure Chuck and I weren't rushing things, reassure myself that he really did want to be with me, and he was already so sure we were meant to be together, he was scoping out larger apartments.

Chuck shrugged his acquiescence. "Anyway, I think you need some private space, so that's a second bedroom. It would be great if we could get a place with a garage I could make into a gym—you know, just some weights, a bench."

He looked at what had to be amazement on my face and he just laughed. "So, no, I wasn't planning on moving out on you. I think you only get this chance to literally crash into somebody like we did, once in a lifetime, like in that Dave Matthews song. I am sure you know it—they are or they were hip and pretty weird too if you ever saw them live in concert. They're like so into their own trip."

"Wow," I said.

"Because I know the Dave Matthews Band or because I know you're gonna need that second bedroom?"

"Because you're really serious here."

"And you're not?"

"Wow," I said again. "It's really all or nothing with you, huh?"

He ran his fingers through his hair and made it all stand on end again. This time I didn't fight the urge to smooth it down again; I smoothed. I liked smoothing his hair. I liked just being with him, on the sofa, here in our apartment. I liked thinking of this place, or some bigger place, as ours. But did I like letting him call all the shots? Was I really ready not just to let him move in but move out, to a place that was really, written on the lease legitimately ours?

"You're getting awfully quiet on me. Are you going to kick *me* out when this campaign's all over?" he asked, clasping my fingers in his own.

I drew my hand out of his hair, out of his grasp. "What if this doesn't work out and we can't stand each other? I mean, Chuck, this is just so fast and—"

He tried to hide it, but his face sort of lost its usual cocky self-confidence. He gave his half smile. He nodded.

"Well, I guess we won't know until we give it a try," he said. "Right now, we'd better get moving again. Work to do." He stood up and headed for the door. "I'll catch up with you here before the meeting." He had one hand on the knob.

"Wait," I said. It was one of those times that I was glad my sofa was practically in my hall and that my hall was only like three feet long. He was right; my apartment was small.

I caught up with him fast. I took his hand off the knob. "I'm not sure you're getting what I'm trying to say here."

"I'm getting it," he said.

"No," I said, "you're not. I'm not planning to kick you out. I'm not planning for this *not* to work out. I'm not planning anything, because when I plan something, when I count on something, that's when it seems like it absolutely doesn't happen. So when you start making plans, that kind of scares me. It's like you're coming right out and telling me it's hopeless."

"You were absolutely right to enter politics. You're twisting everything I've said."

"I guess the bottom line is I keep finding reasons not to believe that you and I—that something this—" I fumbled for the right word. Crazy, impossible, strangely right, wonderful?

"This cataclysmic," he said. "Come on, I know you liked it when I used that word before. You can borrow it."

I laughed. "All right, I will. It's hard to believe something this cataclysmic could be real."

"You don't think this is real because you've looked for the real thing for so long and you haven't found it. And then just when you've stopped looking, I turn up and sweep you off your feet. Is that about right?"

"More like almost knock me off my feet, but that's about right, yeah," I admitted.

"You can't win if you don't play," he said.

"That's an ad for some Indian casino near Palm Springs, isn't it?"

"Maybe it's a line from a new song by The Killers." He shrugged. "Lousy name for a group, in my opinion, but maybe that just goes with the profession."

He got that cocky look again and he leaned forward and he kissed me. The kiss was really nice and it was really nice to kiss him back. It was maybe too nice, considering the fact that we really hadn't exactly resolved our whole living-together thing, or maybe it was just *my* living-together thing; and there was a bad guy out there who broke into my apartment and left me a stupid, creepy note, and was possibly going to try to kill me or assault me at the special candidates' meeting this afternoon. Of course, that threat-of-death thing had a certain defiant sexual cache to it, it was a little bit of a turn-on, or maybe that was just my excuse for keeping the whole kissing thing going.

"You are so—you're just so very—" he said between kisses. "So you."

That was one of the nicest things anyone had ever said to me.

It was pouring rain again, driving so hard against my porch that the motion sensors kicked in and my porch light came on. Or maybe what kicked the light into gear was Chuck pulling me back against the door so that it rattled, pushing my little sweater off my shoulders, kissing my neck, my arms, unfastening my bra with dexterity. He really was a fast learner.

He had my camisole pushed down and my breasts cupped in his hands and I had my mouth on his again, and we couldn't seem to get enough of each other into our hands, our lips.

He unzipped my jeans, pushed them down, and fumbled on my sneakers. I bent down and got one off but not the other before he lifted me up and wrapped my legs around his hips and we slammed back against that door again, his jeans and mine tangled down around our calves, me grabbing his back, pressing him hard against me and inside me.

"Oh, God," I said, "this is good."

"This is good. Oh, God, yeah," he replied. "That feel good? Or is this better?"

"Both—better—yeah."

That was about as coherent as we got. The door was really shaking now, and we were all gasps and moans, and I thought of course we were going to live together, of course we had to live together, of course it was right, he was right, we were right, we had to keep doing this every day of our lives.

And then we heard somebody's gravelly voice shouting, "Hey. Hey, is anybody home?"

So it wasn't just us that triggered the motion sensor or made the door rattle. Okay, well, whoever it was just had to wait a minute, wait a long minute while I arced against Chuck and he pressed himself deep into me and both our hearts were pounding louder than whoever's fist was hammering at the door.

"I know you're screwing around in there," the voice said.

Yeah, well that was one way to put it, I guess.

Chuck lowered me gently to the floor. He pulled up his jeans and tugged his shirt down. Although his face was still flushed from our exertions, a kind of cold "I'm a cop, don't mess with me" mask had dropped down over his features.

I hopped down the hall into my room as Chuck plucked a .38 from an ankle holster I didn't even know he was wearing. Only after it was firmly in his right hand, did he open my front door with his left.

"Can I help you?" Chuck asked, his voice gone as cold as his face now.

"I sure as hell hope so," Royal Garritty growled.

Chapter Thirteen

I threw myself back together as fast as I could, ran a comb through my hair, and joined the other Jessie in staring warily at Royal in my living room.

Royal was sweating profusely, the rolls of fat along his thick neck glistening with perspiration. Chuck had ushered him over to the sofa and was picking our burger wrappers off the coffee table with one hand. The gun, I saw, was still gripped in the other.

"Mr. Garrity claims he has something to talk to us about," Chuck said.

"How can we assist you?" I asked pleasantly.

"Oh, cut the crap," Royal said. "That reporter Harrigan called me. Mentioned the two of you were together, trying to get a reaction out of me. I didn't bite, of course." The veins were standing out in Royal's forehead, all tangled up like the cloverleaf connection to the 101, 5, and 110 freeways downtown. "So of course you know what I want to talk about." He glared.

I didn't, but maybe Chuck did.

"Maybe you should spell it out for us anyway, Royal," Chuck said in a hard, even tone.

"Jesus," said Royal, and he flopped down on my sofa, making the springs groan, "I can't believe you won't help me." He put his head in his hands, and when he looked up again, he was crying. The tears were kind of spurting out of his eyes and running back behind his ears, like a lawn sprinkler run amuck. I'd never seen anything quite like that before, and I couldn't help staring.

He waved his pudgy hand in my general direction. "Don't look at me like that, acting so high and mighty, came clear out of nowhere and here you are, just another goddamn thorn in my side."

There was something menacing in his tone and I didn't like it much, but then Chuck didn't like it much either. He leaned close to me and whispered, "His voice sound familiar? Phone familiar?"

I shook my head. Royal was growly but his voice didn't have the same so-deep-it-almost-sounded-fake register as my caller.

Chuck relaxed just a little, but didn't clue Royal in.

"Get a grip," he said. "Or you can have whatever tête-à-tête you envisioned through the bars of a holding cell."

Royal glared at him, Chuck glared at Royal. Royal was a better glarer, but Chuck was deeply unfazed. Besides, he had that gun.

"Tête-à-tête," Royal grumbled. "Yeah, like you really think I swing that way."

I stifled a laugh.

"We're waiting," said Chuck. "But we were planning on leaving here sometime within, say, the next twenty-four hours."

Royal rubbed at his eyes viciously, making them redder still.

"Tell me something first," Royal said. "She just a

plant? Just like a joke candidate thrown into the mix, see what she can stir up?"

"I'm no joke," I said, and I was kind of annoyed now.

Chuck cut his eyes at me, but only really briefly, like he didn't trust Royal enough to take his eyes off him.

"Jessie," he said in that same hard, even tone, but I realized he was not talking to me. He was talking to my alter ego thumping her tail on the floor, teeth bared in a snarl, ready—I was just sure she was ready—to fly at Royal with a moment's notice. It would be nice if I could get Sally to react like that. Maybe I could train her to go pee on people she didn't like. Of course if I could train her to do that, I might be able to train her to use her litter box, too.

"She's not a plant," Chuck said. "Are *you*?"

"I'm as real as it gets," Royal bragged. "I know there's some people think I'm not as slick as Ned, not as friendly as Benni, not as refined as Ida, don't have a chance. But they're wrong. I've got plenty of money, plenty of clout."

He cracked his enormous knuckles, doubtlessly attempting with that one gesture to prove he was slick, friendly, and refined.

"And the greatest interest in rezoning."

"No greater than Ned's interest. Mine are just a little more specific. A little more focused. A little better," Royal insisted. "So some people who invest in my company aren't maybe as perfect as you think you are. It doesn't mean I'm a bad guy. It doesn't even mean *they're* bad guys. And even if they were and you can prove it, you can't prove anything on me."

"So that's why you've come here to invade Ms.

Adams's personal space, to tell me I can't prove anything on you?" Chuck muttered.

Without warning, Royal began to sob again. "Oh, man," he said. "That's not why. I'm going off track here. You gotta help me."

"How exactly?" Chuck tucked his gun into the waistband of his jeans as if he didn't care anymore if Royal saw it or not. He sat down across from Royal. I sat down next to Chuck.

"She'd better help too," said Royal, throwing me a menacing glance. It occurred to me that maybe he didn't really mean to be menacing—that was just who he was—like Sally probably didn't really mean anything by peeing on the rug every single morning. That was just who she was. Although sometimes I really think she has Machiavellian impulses.

"I've only met you once, and you're my campaign rival. Why would I help you?" I blurted, leaving out the other reasons that I wouldn't help him, like I didn't like him, and he'd more or less already admitted he was wrapped up with the dirty money guys Chuck was after.

"Well, for one thing it might just keep you alive, missy," Royal sneered.

Chuck went rigid next to me, but he didn't say anything, he just fixed Royal with that cop stare and it seemed to get Royal to blabber an apology without Chuck having to lower himself by asking for one. It was an interesting technique. I wondered if I could perfect such a stare and get people to . . . say, give me money.

"All I meant from that comment was we should work together here, help each other out," Royal

explained hastily. "Here's the thing. I have had some
threats. Some serious, big-time threats on my person."

He went from bluster to eyes overflowing again
in like three seconds flat. "I've been getting some
phone calls the last coupla days. But I kinda ignored 'em. Thought it was somebody Marcus put
up to it. Be honest with you, he and I've had some
issues. Maybe even Pinckney's hubby. I foreclosed
on her kid's house like twenty years ago and the
family hasn't forgiven me since. But these calls got
more specific. Stuff neither one of them could
know anything about. Hey I even thought maybe it
was you, Detective, trying to get me to bow out.
Knowing what you *think* you know and all."

"Sorry to disabuse you of that notion," Chuck
said. "I don't threaten people. I don't have to."

I could see the word *disabuse* threw Royal, but he
went on anyway.

"Anyways, it was upsetting more than scary, these
phone calls. Somebody *impugning*"—he paused
and looked at Chuck, like see, I know a word maybe
you don't know—"impugning my character. Like
you did with that freakin' e-mail got sent out."

A slight flush rose up high in Chuck's cheekbones. If I were Royal, I wouldn't have mentioned
the reporter's faux pas around Chuck.

Royal saw Chuck get that flushed, not-too-pleased
look and he hurried on. If a squat, thuglike, sweaty
guy can be envisioned as skating on thin ice, well,
that's what was happening, and he knew it.

"But now, now it's getting heavy. Today I get a call
saying that I'm next. That I'm going to get blown
right out of the campaign, and I should take it literally. Guy spoke in this trippy, low voice. And he
goes, 'I know what you're after in this election, and

you could die for it!' Just like that. Who would say something like that? I'm a nice guy. I really am." He wagged a fat finger at me for emphasis.

"I can't imagine everyone is happy with what you do. Maybe, there are a lot of people as annoyed with you as the Pinckney family," I said.

Royal didn't take offense. He sort of shrugged, like maybe.

Chuck got into it. "And of course there's the fact that your money does come from some sources that are a little bit unsavory. I mean we can just lay our cards on the table here, right? I mean you don't have to admit that the names I named in that infamous e-mail are the right ones, but your resources don't stem from Mr. Clean and friends. Maybe one of your business partners is dissatisfied with you. Maybe one of them has a different candidate to support."

"You mean Ned," Royal said bluntly. "He has everyone's support, he's everyone's friend, even my friends' friend?"

"Could be," Chuck said.

Royal thought about it for a minute. "Sure, except he doesn't need to threaten people to win the election. Him with so many friends and all. He thinks he has me beat cold anyway. Why try to drum me out? And hey, how come you're not on his bandwagon? Why are you on hers?"

"I'm not a particularly political guy at all, Garritty. My friendship with Ms. Adams has very little to do with this campaign."

"Ha," said Royal, like he didn't believe it.

Chuck actually laughed. "Now you said you wanted some kind of help here." He looked at his watch. "From both myself and Ms. Adams. Maybe you could kind of cut to the chase."

"Well, since I've assured myself here that you don't appear to be the guy doing the threatening, I want you to catch whoever it is trying to interfere in the electoral process. You're always looking for evildoers. Find this particular evildoer guy. And I want her"—another wave of the finger—"to open her eyes. Saving her friend's little club isn't what this is all about."

"What is it about?" I asked him.

"Getting elected is just a stepping stone. To a lot of big rocks. To being king of the mountain."

"Or queen," I interjected.

He floundered. "What's the joke, the idea of me swinging that way?"

"I meant a woman could win as well as a man," I said.

"Whatever. Point is, there could be someone out there doesn't want *any* of us to win, for reasons of their own accord."

His eyes glazed with self-pity, but he shook it off and stood. He shook Chuck's hand, all his bluster gone now. "I appreciate any help you could give me. I mean I know you're probably an upright guy. We don't have to like each other for you to protect the citizenry, right?"

"Sure. You want a tap put on your phone, I can arrange that," Chuck offered.

Royal laughed. "I don't think so."

"Then I'll look into the information you gave me. Best I can." He pressed his card into Royal's palm. "In case you've lost my number. Somebody threatens you again, something on your mind, call me."

He led Royal to the door. "I don't want to see you coming around our apartment again," he added.

The word *our* was not lost on Royal or I.

And then Royal was out the door, and my door with all its security features shut behind him.

Chuck went into the kitchen and washed his hands. "I don't know why, but shaking hands with that guy always brings out the Howard Hughes in me."

I took a bottle of water from the fridge and drank deeply.

"I guess I'm not the only one getting funny phone calls."

It could be he's the perp," Chuck said. "He could be making up his own worries, throw off the scent."

"All that blubbering, though. He doesn't strike me as a very good actor."

"Me either. And I suppose it would be too easy. Nailing a guy I've been wanting to nail."

"I thought you liked things easy."

"Liking them and having them that way are two different things." He grinned. He gave me a quick kiss. "But not all the time, I hope."

"We kind of got interrupted before. But to rejoin the program already in progress—"

"You want to actually go into the bedroom this time, or should we take on the kitchen." Chuck rubbed my hips playfully.

"I mean the talking part. About us living together and how fast we're moving and everything."

He lifted his hands from my hips. "I figured that was what you meant. I was just sort of hoping you didn't. I do like things easy. So, we can keep things light if you want. I know I have a tendency to just go for broke. We don't have to do that. We can sort things out later. After the election. I don't mind light. I really don't. We can do that."

"No. I don't want to do that," I protested. "I'm going to do something I've never ever done before. I'm going to just plunge on in. And to make it a real first, I'm going to say I'm wrong, and you're right. Even if you are kind of pushy about it. I'm just going to have to train you to finesse me better than you do."

"Okay. I'll put up with a certain amount of training. I'm not that old a dog. I can learn new tricks."

Chuck put his arms around me and held me. The rain was spattering against the window, on what was altogether a dismal, gray-skied, thunder-rumbling afternoon. But it didn't feel dismal right there in my kitchen, it didn't feel that way at all. It felt like somewhere just on me, the sun was shining, or even if it wasn't, strangely enough, that was fine. Like I told Chuck, like Chuck pointed out to me, I was fine. Strangest of all, *we* were fine. The universe, or at least my universe, was at that moment completely and perfectly in balance.

Chapter Fourteen

Cozy, content, and balanced as I felt, we had to break it up and go out on the rainy street again and knock on doors.

Chuck did a better job at his doors than I did at mine. He went knocking for information and came up with a full description of the vehicle that tried to run us down. According to the resident, it was an olive-green hybrid Element, and according to the resident two blocks down whose house it had idled beside, one person got out of the car, and the other drove away, so now there were two bad guys out there. The one who got out of the car could only be described as fairly tall and wearing a sweat jacket with a hood hanging low over his face.

I went knocking for votes, but what I came up with was nada. I figured I'd get points for braving the weather, but of the few people who opened their doors, only one seemed to think it was noble of me to campaign, and he wasn't a registered voter. The others looked at me like I was crazy; one even asked me if I *was* crazy to come out in that kind of weather; and the last potential voter I contacted asked me if I knew I was abusing my dog for taking her out in the downpour, and threatened to call the ASPCA. Absolutely no one agreed to put my posters in their windows.

On top of all that, I couldn't stop looking over my shoulder in case someone was sneaking up behind, ready to slug me; I couldn't stop wondering if one of these less-than-enthusiastic residents was my archenemy, and why.

"Damn it, I want to win," I said. Jessie gave an agreeable bark, but I seriously doubted she was a registered voter.

I called it a day and went back to my apartment and double bolted the door.

As soon as we came in, Squeak and Sally snuggled up next to Jessie and licked the rain off her fur. It was really the dearest thing to watch, if not to smell. There is nothing like the combination of old Sally pee and wet dog in a small apartment.

Just before the candidates' meeting at five, Chuck came in, told me what he'd learned, and noticed we were getting late.

"I could still bag the meeting," I said hopefully.

"No way," he said. "Who knows what'll happen there?"

That was kind of my point. "Maybe I should wear a bulletproof vest," I joked, but I wasn't really joking.

By the time I reapplied my makeup and Chuck got me out the door, it was five on the nose, and he threw a portable flashing light on top of his brown sedan car.

We made record time, pulling into a loading-zone-only space behind city hall five minutes later.

City clerk Susan Birch was already speaking

behind a wooden podium when we slipped inside the council chambers. She was pontificating over the loss of Conway. "He was a unique citizen with a history of volunteerism in the community."

Benni Cardell, seated in the front row near the podium, gave a large and derisive snort.

Sue raised an eyebrow at Benni and then went on. "It is a great loss, coming on the heels of the sudden retirement of our dear, multiterm councilman Drew Bartlett. I am hoping that you will all join together in this hour of loss and put to rest any base rumors that are circulating about Mr. Marcus having substance abuse issues. It shocks me that such stories are being repeated."

The council chambers were moderately full. Conway wasn't there of course, but a tiny, birdlike woman who was apparently his widow sat off to the side of the podium wiping at her eyes.

Tad was in a wheelchair in the aisle. He had a cut on his cheek and a leg in a cast. He looked smug and somehow pleased with himself. There were a couple of guys who looked like the Allman Brothers hanging out around him.

Salome was across the room with a bevy of hangers-on, the same people I'd seen out with her signs, thin and pretty women with large breasts, rather fey-looking guys. She had a bandage fetchingly placed on one side of her forehead, like a little white beret, but appeared otherwise perfectly coiffed.

Everyone in the room kept glancing at Tad and Salome uneasily, so I glanced at them uneasily too. Maybe the writer of scary notes had already attacked while Chuck and I were looking for a parking space.

Royal and his many thick-necked **sons**, son-in-laws, and possible grandsons were all sitting with their arms crossed in the back of the room, and Royal most pointedly did not acknowledge us.

Ned was there in a neatly striped rep tie and a dark suit and a concerned expression that appeared to have been painted on, as it did not vary from moment to moment. By his side was apparently his wife or someone he had superimposed next to him to pose as his wife. She had short, dark hair in a Jackie O style and a Burberry-type trench coat.

Ida was holding hands with a younger woman who looked enough like her to be her daughter, and had the same kind of powdery pale complexion but without the actual powder. Ida's lips were pressed together as if she were holding back from saying something. Occasionally, her daughter glanced over at Royal and his boys and shook her head.

Benni had the largest contingent. Filling the entire front and second row were Boy and Girl Scout troops, about twenty-four kids in all. Several thick-in-the-middle women of indeterminate middle age were also in the mix, including the symphony lady from debate night. They all had the kind of square jawline and determined squint of the fourth grade teacher who once told me if I didn't learn my multiplication tables I would end up in prison. I confess I was relieved to see my station manager wasn't still hanging out with Benni, eating a pie or something. Hopefully he'd returned from whatever sojourn he had with the dark side without spilling too much water cooler gossip about me.

Although I'd brought Chuck with me, I thought it was really kind of odd that so many of the other candidates had also brought significant others.

Maybe the city clerk had asked everyone to bring their friends and family but had not bothered to tell me because she didn't think I had any.

"I realize," Susan the clerk went on, "that all of you are feeling the strain already. Of Conway's passing. The base rumors. The pressure of the swiftness of this campaign. And for some of you, the threats you've reported."

Chuck and I exchanged the briefest of glances.

"If we can draw together to—"

"My truck was messed with. That's more than just a threat," Tad burst out, as if he couldn't contain himself any longer. He spun his wheelchair to face the rest of us. "That's the God's honest truth."

He was playing mostly to the very back of the room where Brian Harrigan had slipped inside the entrance with his notepad out, his freckles dark against his skin. Next to Brian there was a guy in a Tribune Broadcasting windbreaker with a video camera and a mike on a pole. And next to him was the guy in the turtleneck, still in the turtleneck, who videotaped such exciting venues as this for cable access. Wow, this meeting was big time. No wonder the candidates wanted to show up with their support groups.

"The gang's all here," Chuck remarked, when the chamber doors opened again and an officious, round-faced man entered. He had a bad haircut and a bad suit, and he was flanked by two uniformed police officers, one of whom I was pretty sure had given me my last "rolling stop" at a stop sign ticket two years ago.

"That's Chief Martin Little," Chuck whispered about the guy in the suit. "My boss."

"Oh. The asshole," I returned, and naturally

Susan chose that moment to stop speaking and my voice carried a little bit.

Chuck was looking away from me like he didn't know me, his hand over his face. I felt his body shaking beside me and I looked at him carefully. He was shaking with laughter.

"Did you hear me?" Tad tried to stand up but then remembered he was in a wheelchair. "I said my truck was messed with. I was giving my fellow candidate Ms. Finch a ride home. We stop for a cup of coffee, and it was then, I know it was then, when someone caused our so-called unaccidental accident. Someone observed us together, and took it upon himself to try to end our campaigns! Two stones for one bird."

"Someone tried to end our very beings' existence on this gentle planet," Salome added.

An uproar of sorts filled the chambers. Susan Birch pleaded, "Quiet, please!"

Now Chuck was no longer shielding his face. He was staring at Salome like he couldn't keep his eyes off her. I confess, I was pissed. He was really taking her in—the tall, perfect body, the curves in all the right places, the beautifully made-up face.

I elbowed him, but this time made sure my voice was just a whisper in his ear. "You'd better not be thinking you selected the wrong candidate to get close to," I hissed.

Chuck frowned, puzzled, but he still didn't take his eyes off Salome.

She was giving him an almost insolent look in return, like how dare he check her out that way. Yeah, how dare he.

"I didn't select the wrong one," he said absently.

I elbowed him again, hard enough that it made him jump.

He looked at me this time. "What did I do?" he asked.

"The way you're looking at her! I know she's beautiful and all that but she's—" I stopped, at a loss from what was really wrong with her. She was vacuous and given to platitudes? Tad drooled over her and now Chuck showed all indications of getting ready to drool?

He was giving her a knowing look. And Salome gave him a genuine appraising once-over.

And then he smiled, but it wasn't a very pleasant smile. He mimed taking a photograph.

She paled beneath her makeup.

"What's going on?" I asked. "Why did you just pretend to take her picture?"

"Because one of these days I'm going to capture her in more extenuating circumstances than I've managed so far."

Now it was my turn to frown at Salome. "Extenuating circumstances? I don't get it."

"The call girl ring I told you about staking out? I've seen her talking with the ladies of that house. Not at the house, but they sometimes meet for lunch or a drink, and they all defer to her. If I had to guess, she's the off-site madam."

"The madam? She used to be a showgirl in Vegas, but that doesn't mean she—"

"I bet she was more than just a showgirl in Vegas."

"But if she's engaged in uh, that kind of uh, enterprise, why would she want to run for city council? Why would she do something that might, well, expose her? Expose her in a different way than she's used to exposing herself, I mean."

"That's what's blowing my mind."

"At least it's just your mind," I joked.

But he was too preoccupied to be amused. "Maybe she thinks she can legalize it."

Susan clapped her hands over and over again and the rumblings and catcalls and muttering voices gradually diminished.

"Ms. Finch is right," Tad went on. "Our lives were in danger. Someone's out not to just stop our campaigns but to stop *us*. But let me tell you, that's not going to happen. We are unstoppable. We're both going to win—"

"You can't both win," Ida Pinckney pointed out in a surprisingly resonant voice. "That isn't possible. And your lack of civic knowledge is frankly disreputable."

"Ms. Pinckney," Salome chided gently, "Tad only means the best. That was what brought us together. The both of us meaning the best for this community."

Chuck cast a quick glance at his superior officer. The guy was nodding approvingly at Salome with a positively salacious gleam in his eye.

"If she did make it on the council, and she had certain friends in other branches of government, say the law enforcement branch, well, maybe she thinks she'd be untouchable," Chuck said to me.

"In other words, you might not be the only policeman on the force who doesn't support Ned Rutkin?"

"Who says I don't support Ned?" Chuck joked.

He got another elbow in his ribs.

"I know who did this," Tad said. "Someone in this room."

"In this room? You think you know, spell it out, son," Benni Cardell demanded.

"I'd like to know that myself, Tad," Ida put in. "It's unfair of you to make such a leading statement without the facts to support them."

"I do have the facts. There were business cards left in my truck," Tad said smugly. "You know, the truck with the cut brake line? A whole passel of cards, in a box, the kind that comes straight from the printer. And the cards read Royal Garritty, our so-called dream merchant."

Chamber-wide murmuring was about to erupt again, but Royal stood up, punching his fist into his hand.

"You accusing me? That's a laugh! I've been threatened myself," Royal said. "I've even gone to the police about it. On top of my life being in jeopardy, I will not tolerate being blamed for your car accident. You probably drove into a tree, couldn't read which way was the left turn—there *are* left turn signs ya know, Tad, not tfel signs."

"You're a son of a bitch," Tad said. "The sign of that's like tattooed on your forehead." The Allman Brother guys nodded their heads vigorously behind curtains of long, blond hair.

Salome waved her hand. "Please! Peaceful goodwill here!"

Susan started clapping her hands again. "I need everyone to be quiet, now! Mr. Garritty, if you have something legitimate to say—"

"Sure I do. If someone did cause Tad's little accident, then that someone is trying to pin it on me," Royal said, his voice vibrating like the bass turned up all the way on the radio in a low rider, "Someone must've lifted a box of my cards—my cards!—like nothing is sacred."

I didn't think his cards were, that's for sure.

"But it doesn't really matter what you all want to accuse me of. I came here, with the support of my loving family, to announce my withdrawal from this race." Royal paused, as if waiting for someone to stop him, or at least act disappointed.

"Go ahead," Benni said. "A bad apple spoils the best apple pie."

"Her and those pies," I muttered.

Susan cleared her throat. "Let's not do anything hasty here. We need to make a concerted effort, together, to get to the bottom of these shenanigans . . . and to show the public at large that we are united in our support of Mr. Marcus."

"None of them, with the exception of our dear friend Ida, supported Conway in life. Why would they support him after it?" Mrs. Marcus asked.

"This is getting ugly," Chuck said to me, his eyes gleaming with interest.

"At least nobody's trying to kill me at the moment," I said. I was actually starting to feel pretty chipper. It wasn't, after all, just me singled out for persecution.

"Nobody yet," Chuck agreed.

My eyes flicked around the room again, in case I'd missed anybody wielding a weapon.

Brian was scribbling away on his pad. The cable access guy was swinging his camera wildly back and forth, back and forth across the floor. The Tribune Broadcasting guy finally turned his camera on.

No one looked particularly threatening, at least, as Chuck pointed out, at the moment. So it was time for me to get brave, to stand up and sound like a real candidate instead of another petty squabbler.

I played to the cameras in the back of the room. "Maybe we should all focus on the issues in this community instead of our own differences, or real or imagined harassment," I said. "I'm sure the police will get to the bottom of anything untoward that's going on. At least I have every confidence. For those of you who don't know me, I'm Jessie Adams."

No one applauded me or anything but no one booed me either.

Royal boomed out like I hadn't even spoken, and the cameras swung toward his raging bulk. "You're all getting a lucky break from me, because there's no changing my mind now. I am making a formal announcement here. I'm gonna withdraw from the race. Nobody can persuade me otherwise. Of course me withdrawing doesn't mean the rest of you have a snowball's chance in hell of winning, but still."

"Some of us have to win!" Tad shouted.

"One of us," Ida chided.

"Why are you withdrawing?" Chuck and I both shouted out.

Royal grimaced like he was witnessing something that disgusted him, and that was most definitely the two of us, even though just a few hours earlier he was asking for our help.

Still grimacing, Royal went on. "My business partners have suggested to me that the benefits gained by having an intelligent, developmental point of view like mine on the city council are kinda outweighed by the fact that dying isn't part of my game plan."

Tad shouted, "Good riddance."

"I would almost be inclined to agree," Salome voiced.

Royal continued, his forehead drawn into deep wrinkles, and something, tears or sweat I wasn't sure

which, was leaking down his cheeks. "Anyways, I
imagine my bowing out will end the threats against
me, and the need for whoever is trying to smear my
name to smear it. At least I certainly hope so."

He stood up and edged his way from the room,
waving his square-headed squat minions ahead of
him.

"Quitter," Tad jeered.

"Loser," Royal turned and spat out, standing livid
in the doorway.

Ned stood up and spoke for the first time. "This is
becoming quite a travesty. I call upon our esteemed
chief of police"—he nodded toward Chuck's boss,
who was smiling tightly—"and his staff." He inclined
his head toward Chuck, who smiled not at all. "I call
upon our community to get to the bottom of things
here immediately, before any more of our colleagues
leave this campaign."

"Ned, you'd like nothing better than for all of us
to leave," Royal said, red-faced, still framed by the
exit. "Gotta be the people's choice, even if most
people don't choose ya." Royal stalked out.

Chuck's boss strode down the aisle to the front of
the room, lifting the microphone right out of the
city clerk's hands.

"Now let me reassure all of you. We will do everything in our power to protect you from harm. From
harassment. We want to keep you all a part of our
great Democratic process. Now if Mr. Garritty
chooses to resign, that is unfortunate, but nothing
we can control. Just as, sadly, we could not prevent
the untimely passing of Mr. Marcus. A great asset to
our community."

"Yeah, right," said Conway's widow. Though
pretty much everyone else, even Chuck, had shut

up and were listening to the chief of police, she seemed eager to take him on. "You thought he was an alcoholic fool. And he was. But he was mine!"

And then she was weeping, and Ida was comforting her, and in that moment of sorrow, Chief Little saw fit to point a finger at Chuck, and then jerk that finger toward the door.

"I'll be outside," Chuck said to me. "Have to talk to Little."

"I'll be fine," I said, reassuring myself, although you never could tell, somebody scary could burst through the chamber doors at any minute. Ned's wife could have a bomb tucked inside her expensive raincoat.

"I'll keep an eye on the door, make sure nobody comes in this room," Chuck promised. He took his time about leaving, passing as he did so directly in front of Salome. She averted her eyes. She whispered something to one of her glammed-up supporters, who looked surprised.

The meeting went on for what seemed like an interminable amount of time but was actually only about fifteen more minutes. The two videographers and Brian left, Chief Little returned the mike to Susan and followed the media out of the room. The discussion became one of reassuring the public, of confirming our belief in each other as candidates. Susan reminded us that we had the opportunity to participate in another televised debate tomorrow night, and how important it was to reach out to the community through it.

I slipped out of the room, steeling myself for ninjas wielding machetes in the lobby, but found only Chuck and his boss, arguing in low voices.

Chuck looked tense and his hair was standing on end again.

"She's the same girl," I heard Chuck say, a note of fury in his voice.

"You haven't proved conclusively—" Little began.

"You shouldn't have put me on the case if you didn't want me to resolve it," Chuck said hotly.

"You came to this meeting to accuse a friend—"

"You have so many friends, I didn't know I was accusing *another* one," Chuck said.

Little turned his gaze solidly on Chuck and they regarded each other with plain dislike.

Chuck got a grip first. "You want to put this aside for now, I'll play. But what if there's a connection between her possible supplementary income and this so-called car accident she was involved in? And could that tie in to the threats some candidates have received? The fact is, sir, you have to take a closer look at some of the people involved in this race."

"I've heard you're already doing that," Little said.

I colored, and looked away, busying myself rummaging through my purse.

"My friend is not the one *you* need to look at, no matter how much you want to kick my butt personally," Chuck said.

Little cleared his throat. "We've both been on the edge lately, Jackson. And we truly need to back away, don't you think?"

Chuck nodded, but barely.

"Now this is what you can do to get me off the edge and yourself safely away from a very dark abyss. Get a fucking grip and stop alienating police supporters, stop upsetting the city council and the mayor and the very political process with your ridiculous and insistent investigating about nothing. Despite our proximity to metropolitan L.A., this is a small town. I scoff at the idea of drug money and hookers being a part of this election. You're suffering from paranoid delusions."

"Paranoid delusions—" Chuck's fists were clenched.

Little put his hand on Chuck's shoulder. "I'm going to suggest something very strongly in regard to smoothing our working relationship. In fact it's more than a suggestion. It's an order. Take a few days off. A week off. Unpaid but no disciplinary action. Nothing on the permanent record. Fair enough, I think." His tone brooked no argument otherwise. "And when you come back, say a week from Monday—come back with a handle on things."

Little dropped his hand and Chuck stepped back at exactly the same time as if they were squaring off for a fight. And maybe they were, but before they had a chance to take a swing at one another, Salome, pushing Tad in his wheelchair, shoved through the chamber doors and right past them both.

Little looked at her with clear admiration, and Chuck's gaze followed, but there was nothing like admiration in it. Salome did not look at either of them.

Tad seemed like he was about ready to fall out of the wheelchair, Salome was walking so fast, but there was no stopping her in her headlong pursuit of the city clerk. "Susan!" she called out, and the clerk stopped walking and turned back to Salome with a smile.

Salome rushed up to her. "I must talk to you immediately," she said.

There was a brief huddle between Salome, Susan, and Tad, straining up from his chair.

When the huddle broke, Chuck was standing

next to me, Little was gone, and Susan's smile was equally absent.

Susan nodded once, then twice, and left.

Salome waved to her entourage and they scurried around her. She gave a squeeze to Tad's shoulder, leaned down, and kissed his cheek. Then, surrounded by her followers, she left.

Tad spun his wheelchair forlornly to us. "It's not only Royal withdrawing from the race. Salome's stepping out, too. And you know what, so am I. And you know what? All your fault," he said to Chuck. "I think she should file sexual harassment charges against you, you peeping cop. Watching her with binoculars and taking pictures!"

"Interesting that you would know I was doing that," Chuck said. "Do you know *why* I was doing that?"

"You got the wrong idea, that's why. She gives parties sometimes. It's not against the law to give parties," Tad said.

"Certain kinds"—Chuck shrugged—"it actually is."

"I was invited just once," Tad said with surprising political glibness. "And I never partook. I just watched. And what I was watching was private, legal, and . . . bottom line, she is a great lady. The accident scared her but it didn't prevent her from telling me, 'Tad, we're fine, your injuries are minor.' A great lady. And I only, I repeat, only, went to one party."

"Then I may not even have you on film," Chuck allowed.

"Didn't think you were a narc," Tad said to me, narrowing his eyes.

"I'm not a narc."

"An informer, then! A police-state suck-up! I'm the one told you Salome was a showgirl. And I guess you told your pal here, which was enough to make him think his evil thoughts."

"I had Ms. Finch under surveillance long before I knew she was a candidate, or even her name, much less her employment history," Chuck said. "Unfortunately, not under close enough surveillance that anyone observed your accident. If we could get back to that—"

"Yeah, why don't you investigate *that*," Tad interrupted vehemently, "instead of some little indiscretions? Everybody has a past. Some of us have a future, too."

"Why doesn't yours include running for city council anymore?" I threw in. "I mean, you haven't done anything wrong. You just went to a party one time, right?"

Tad scowled at me. "I don't wanna end up like Marcus. While the po-lice are too busy exhibiting extreme jealousy that the hottest chick isn't dating them to give a crap. And tell you the truth, without Salome at my side, it'd be a empty victory."

He wheeled himself away, out of the building, into the rain. We could hear cars skidding in the wet street and Tad himself make a kind of kung-fu "eee iii" sound, as he evidently wheeled himself right into traffic.

"I suppose he'll find Mr. Garritty's cards in the spokes of his wheelchair wheels, too," Ida Pinckney said, gliding up at my side.

"You don't think Royal's involved?" I asked.

Ida shrugged.

"I saw him with you at the Java Hut. He was yelling at you, shaking his fist."

Ida smiled. "Always pick a public place for confronting your nemesis. Then they can't really hurt you. Someone is always watching."

"Did he threaten you in some way?" Chuck questioned her.

"Oh, he's always threatening someone about something," Ida said, blithely. "I pay it no mind. I pay him no mind at all, actually, because he hasn't one."

I laughed.

"I have absolutely no love lost for the man who stole my son-in-law's home when he was experiencing pecuniary difficulties," Ida went on, ticking off a list on her fingers. "And I do believe that his so-called fears for his own safety are all trumped up, an excuse to get him out of the race before publicity shines too bright a light on certain of his business partners. You're aware of some of his unsavory business partners?" she asked both Chuck and I. I just nodded, having become only newly acquainted, but Chuck jumped right in.

"More than aware. Have been following their activities long before they plugged into Playa Vista. And if there's anything you can give me on Royal—"

"Nothing I'm sure you don't already know," Ida interrupted. "Royal is a big barker whose bite is only hurtful when sanctioned by his partners. Whom I really doubt appreciated Royal's entry into this race, which is the real reason Royal has stepped out of the fray, in my opinion. Too much attention."

I was surprised at her perception, but Chuck seemed to regard her speculatively.

"Do you think Royal was involved in Tad and Salome's little wreck?" he asked her.

"I don't think anything about that. For all I know, Tad cut his own brakes to play rescuer or victim or perhaps even persecutor—you know the drama cycle, or you should, it's a common psychological game people play all the time, I'm sure understanding it would come in handy in your line of work."

Chuck studied her a moment. "Have you had any funny phone calls, received any notes or letters, experienced any of the type of harassment Royal and Tad describe?"

"No. But then no one really considers me a serious contender in this race. I'm more of a moral conscience. I can't really expect to win, all that."

"Unless everyone but you was eliminated from the race," Chuck pointed out.

"I guess you consider me a suspect in some evil plot," Ida said.

"Not really," Chuck said mildly.

"I rather wish I could take responsibility for Royal stepping out, but poor Conway, he was, as I told you, a friend. And his heart, if not his head, was always in the right place. I won't be painted a villain in that regard."

Ida smiled and turned her attention to me. "And I do admire you for stepping up to the plate. We need more concerned citizens like you. In fact, you make me wish I could be as ignorant as Tad and suggest we both deserve to win." She laughed lightly. "But at least we both deserve to win more than the rest of our competition."

"Tad and Salome have dropped out of the race just like Royal," I told her.

"Have they?" Ida didn't seem particularly surprised. "Well, you never know then, do you? The less fragmented the playing field, the better. Perhaps a good guy will win after all."

She folded her hands in front of her as if trying

to prevent herself from still counting things off on her fingers. She shook her head.

"A shame they're all listed in the candidates' statements—mailed yesterday morning. People will still vote for all of them, you know. Possibly vote more for them than for me. I'm a low-profile candidate. No paid statement, no signs or banners." She patted my arm. "At least you have signs up, my dear. And an officer of the law at your side. And youth." She shook her head again. "Well, I mustn't be maudlin. That's not going to get me any votes. As my daughter keeps telling me, most likely nothing will."

And she was off, leaving a faint scent of patchouli and hair spray and an aura of discontent behind her.

It occurred to me that maybe whoever wrote the note in my morning paper was getting what he wanted. People were indeed dropping out of the race by the five o'clock hour, just as he'd strongly suggested I should do or else. But he hadn't gotten rid of me. And he wasn't going to, either. Maybe I could win. I did have my signs. Maybe the ghost of JFK would haunt Ned Rutkin into resigning, too.

I gave the city council lobby a once-over, just in case someone, not a ghost, was lurking with a wooden club or an SUV, but Ida, Chuck, and I were the only people still hanging around.

Outside though, about to climb inside a minivan already crammed with Girl Scouts, I saw Benni in a ridiculous plaid rain poncho. She gave me her tight-lipped smile.

"Things are getting interesting," she said.

"You could say that."

"Well, I could, but I don't have to." She sounded very defensive.

"Have you been experiencing any harassment, Ms. Cardell?" Chuck asked her.

"You know, I always look at the bright side. One person's harassment is another person's reaching out and touching someone in maybe not the most perfect way."

"Has someone reached out and touched you imperfectly?" I asked.

"Goodness, what a thing to say." She swung her legs inside the minivan.

As the van pulled away, I realized this race was now down to me, Ida, Benni, and Ned. And of course, a bunch of candidates who were no longer running. Really, what it came down to was Ned's shiny brochures and plastic rainproof signs against my runny-inked ones, Benni's pies, and Ida's genteel manner. Or maybe what it came down to was not who would win the election, but who would survive the campaign.

Chapter Fifteen

"I'm a little disappointed," Chuck said as we ducked around the back of City Hall Plaza, splashing through the ankle-deep water rushing down the gutter.

"About what?"

"Those five o'clock shadows fell and there was no shoot-out, no tear gas in the council chambers, not even any real verbal fireworks."

"And still people are dropping out of this race like flies. I really might win, you know."

"You really might," he said. "If Ned Rutkin bows out next."

"Why are you so sure he'll win?" I demanded.

"Life's not fair and then you die," Chuck said cheerfully. "And speaking of not fair, I'm taking some enforced time off, at the request of my superior officer."

"I heard," I said.

We reached Chuck's car. He pulled a wet parking ticket from his window, crumpled it into a sodden ball, and hurled it into the back seat with Jessie's other toys. "Just like the late Rodney Dangerfield," he said. "I don't get no respect."

We climbed in his car, out of the rain. The lights of City Hall Plaza clicked off, and even though it wasn't quite seven o'clock, it felt much later. It had been a long day following a long, if mostly pleasant, except for almost being run over, night. I was beat. But as Chuck noted, at least the shadows of five o'clock had fallen and nothing bad had happened to me. I was definitely still alive, even if sitting through all the bickering, accusations, and banal remarks—including my own—inside city council chambers had rendered me a little bit brain-dead.

Chuck squeezed my leg. He was trying very hard to seem playful, but his heart wasn't in it. He looked as tired as I felt.

"You don't like taking the time off, I know," I said. "This being told what to do, take a step back, mind your own business. Not to mention lose a week's pay."

"Nope. I don't like any of it. But I like being with you," he added, like he was afraid I'd get the wrong idea.

I took his hand in mine. I liked being with him, too. This relationship thing really was pretty simple, when you didn't fight it or question it or worry about it or think it through or figure in your past experiences or what the future might bring.

"But there's something really not cool going on around here," Chuck said.

He put the key in the ignition but he didn't turn on the engine, and we just sat there and watched the rain stream down the windshield.

My cell phone rang, and for once, since I wasn't

at home or inside any building or behind a hill or on a hill, I could actually answer it.

"It's Sandy" was the reply to my hello. "I thought I'd just get your voice mail, as usual." He sounded like he wished he had.

"What's up?" I asked. Since he was my boss, and he sounded so out of sorts, I almost expected him to tell *me* to take an unpaid vacation for a week.

But it was more or less the opposite. "Need a favor," he said curtly. "I know politics and rock and roll don't go that well together most of the time, and you're all busy with this"—he hesitated—"this election stuff. But anyway. Still need the favor."

"Um. Okay. You have to tell me what it is first, though."

"Need you to sub for me tomorrow. I know it's Sunday, I'll sub for you sometime. I hope. I will, I mean."

"Is there something wrong?"

Chuck looked at me like what's up, but I shook my head.

"No, nothing's wrong. Just need you to cover the Brunch Beat. Nothing wrong with that, right? I'm just—I'm taking a few days off."

"There's a lot of that going around," I said.

"Ha, well, whatever."

"You feeling okay though?"

He sounded both kind of down and kind of pissed off. Sandy wasn't maybe my favorite person in the entire world, as in he never gave me a raise period, or an advance without me begging for it, and he kept all the best free CDs for himself, but he was more or less fair and more or less left me alone except for the occasional request that I play something by the Knitters, the female member of which he had the hots for. Besides, I just had this feeling there was something going on and I should at least make the effort to politely inquire.

"I'm fine!" He was practically biting my head off. "You ever just need some time alone, or with someone you really care for?"

"Um, yeah, yeah of course."

He didn't sound like he cared for anyone or anything at all except for making me shut up.

So I did. There was only his breathing and my breathing.

"So tomorrow's show, ten to two, you'll do it?"

"Sure," I said. Although why he didn't call Theodore or Samantha or the new kid who called himself Punk Idol, none of whom were involved in a political campaign peopled with quitting, dying, threatened candidates, I wasn't sure. Still, at this point it seemed weird to ask him to try someone else.

"Great then. Fucking great," he said. He hung up.

"I have to work tomorrow," I told Chuck. "The oldies show."

"Then I'll go to work right alongside you," he said. "I won't have anything else to do."

"Don't sound so down about it," I said. "Maybe it'll be fun, just the two of us, alone in the studio on a Sunday afternoon."

"It's just the two us now, alone in my car," he pointed out. He squeezed my leg again, and put a little more juice into it this time.

"Maybe we can make this fun, too." I turned my face to his for a kiss.

It didn't take much. Chuck grinned and his hand moved higher up my leg.

"Insatiable, aren't you?" I teased him.

"You don't know the half of it," he said.

He stroked my thigh and pushed up my skirt, and I slung one leg, and then I wriggled the other over his lap.

He reached below the seat and slid it back so I could fit behind the wheel comfortably, and there I was on top of him, unbuttoning his shirt while he was lifting mine, right there behind the city hall council chambers.

"Maybe . . . we should go on home. . . ." I said, but I was still kissing him and he was still kissing me and touching me, and the lights were out in the plaza. And who was going to catch us anyway, who would be crazy enough to go out walking down the dark street behind city hall in the now-pouring rain?

His lips moved along my collarbone and then he dipped his head down so that he was veiled by my shirt, unseen, doing all sorts of nice little things with his tongue against my nipples and breasts.

We were so busy steaming up the windows that I only caught the faintest glimpse of Benni Cardell inside her unattractive plaid rain poncho, pausing in a very brisk walk down the street to peer in at us. What was she doing back at the council chambers?

It was definitely her though. I saw her big horsey face looking in the car. How much she could see through the fog of our breath, I wasn't sure. I could only hope, that unlike Chuck, she was not surveying some call girl ring and hoping to implicate me.

I pushed Chuck away, but before I could do more than that, she was gone, heels clicking noisily and rapidly away on the wet sidewalk.

"What?" said Chuck, but his voice was muffled, he buried his face against my chest again. I just sighed.

What could Benni do anyway, except be jealous?

Announce at the next candidate debate that she'd caught me making out in an unmarked police car?

And it felt so good to be doing just that, I more or less forgot all about Benni again within thirty seconds. There's something so irreverent, so deliciously stupid about doing it in a parked car in a public place. It was one of those things like visiting the Great Wall of China that was on my list to do, but I'd never had a chance to do before. Maybe someday Chuck and I could visit the Great Wall and do it there, too.

In the meantime I was busy unbuckling Chuck's belt.

"Let's climb in the back seat," he suggested.

And we actually did that, Chuck going over first, pulling me on top of him, both of us laughing like idiots as we fell into the back seat, landing on a variety of squeaking balls and rubber bones. Chuck pushed the toys onto the floor while the rain pummeled down, a kind of primal drumbeat against the roof, rapidly punctuated by our own kind of primal rhythm.

Already damp and disheveled, we made a run from Chuck's car to my place, sloshing through the puddles and up the slippery stairs. We were greeted before I even had my key in the lock by the sound of canine Jessie barking joyfully.

Naturally, she jumped on me, but I was already getting used to her spontaneous, enthusiastic greeting, just as I was already getting used to having Chuck to more or less spontaneously jump on myself.

Squeak and Sally were sitting up on the kitchen counter eyeing the commotion, Jessie licking my face, Chuck with my bra dangling from his jacket pocket. It looked like they were saying Hello, this is the way it is now I guess—crazy.

I was getting used to that, too. I was liking it. I was liking it a lot.

Jessie the dog turned her affection on Chuck, and I petted Squeak til he purred and Sally until she growled, and then I turned to the day's mail, delivered late, and lying on the floor beneath my mail slot. Amazingly enough Sally had not christened it, although when I picked up the stack, rain off my own hair made the paper wet.

There were a couple of bills, and Ned Rutkin's shiny mailer, which unlike his hand-out flyer didn't place him on a PT boat. Nope, this one had him standing on the steps of the Capitol smiling at Martin Luther King. I tossed Ned in the trash and reluctantly retained the bills. Then I flipped open a thin, gray newsprint magazine with stars and stripes on the cover: the candidates' statements.

I flopped down on the couch to read it. The candidates' names were randomly ordered, as they would be on the ballot. On the first page was Salome's, full of peace, love and understanding and ending with an actual peace symbol and a smiley face. Ida was probably right; it didn't matter that Salome had left the race. People would vote for her just because of her cloying, easy-to-understand sentiment, and the fact that she was at the top of the ballot.

The next page was Ned's. His was a real eye-catcher, because somehow he'd managed to include a color photo of himself grinning and shaking hands with the mayor.

He must've spent a small fortune getting a picture included in the mailer. The surprise was why he didn't use a photo of himself being embraced by Clint Eastwood and Mahatma Gandhi. If only *Ned* would resign from the race for being a ho. He basically was; he was just even less honest about it than Salome.

Since Ida hadn't paid for a statement, her page listed only her name. I could almost sense her soft-spoken negativity rising from the blank sheet.

Next came my page. I skimmed my copy. I thought it read very well if anyone read anymore as opposed to just looking at photo ops and computer icons. At least it read well until it got to the last sentence. Which I had not written.

All of a sudden the flush of love making left my cheeks and the damp night gave me a chill.

"Chuck," I said. "Read this."

He had Jessie's leash in his hand, ready to take her for a walk, and Jessie was circling him eagerly, so it took him a moment to reach me, and by that time I was out and out shivering.

"What's wrong?" he asked me.

I thrust the candidate statement into his hands. He took it and began to read out loud. "'Jessie Adams, thirty, professional comm—'"

"The last sentence. Read the last sentence!" My voice sounded hysterically overwrought even to me. Jessie stopped circling Chuck and flopped down, whining.

"'Ms. Adams thinks she knows a lot but really knows nothing at all. She's not as smart as she thinks she is. She's a dying breed.' What the hell . . . ?" Chuck asked.

"Indeed," I said.

"Who wrote that?"

"Not me."

"How did it get printed?"

"I sure don't have a clue."

"Someone does."

Chuck reached for my phone and punched in some numbers. A recorded voice came on the line; he waited for the beep and spoke, sounding brusque and official. "I know this is after hours for the city clerk," he said, "but if you check these messages this weekend, which you undoubtedly will considering all the changes in the candidate lineup for this special election, will you please call me, Detective Chuck Jackson, on my cell—" He gave his number. "You should've proofed the candidate statements before they were mailed," he added, and hung up.

Then we just sat there on the sofa and looked at each other.

"I don't know who else to call," Chuck said.

"Will people think I wrote that, and think I'm nuts and not vote for me?" I asked.

"I don't know." Chuck shook his head. "Maybe that's all it's intended to do—damage your chances of winning."

"That's not fair. That's not right. I want to win this thing. I'm going to win this thing for—" I had almost forgotten why I wanted to win it. Why I wanted to be in the race in the first place. Why I kept somewhat obliquely getting my life threatened. "For Lisa," I remembered at last. And for my own hubris. And oh yeah, the good of my community, sure.

"No, it's not fair or right. But I'm less concerned with political fallout than I am with the fact that I consider this to be another threat on you."

"To make me drop out of the race," I said.

Even though I most definitely didn't want to

make the campaign another of my lost causes, I admit, there was almost kinda sort of a part of me that wanted to drop out. I wanted to be one of a "dying breed" even less than I wanted to be one of a losing breed.

"I hope that's all it is," Chuck said grimly. "But that doesn't cover the assaults. On you, on Lisa, on both of us. You trust me, we'll get to the bottom of this," he vowed. He snapped Jessie's leash against his hand, hard, and Jessie looked up at him, hopeful.

I changed into my sweats again, and we both walked her down the shiny wet streets.

"Must get an umbrella," I said, ducking my head against the drizzle.

"We can use these," Chuck suggested, as we approached a corner packed with campaign signs, my own among them. He yanked the stakes of Royal and Salome's signs out of the ground and handed me one to hold over my head.

"This is probably illegal," I said.

"Yeah," Chuck agreed.

"At least you're not one of those cops who's a stickler for rules."

"I'm not even officially a cop at the moment. I'm an 'on vacation without pay' cop." Chuck sighed.

"You're gaga over him, aren't you," Lisa asked me on the phone in the morning.

"Gaga? Kind of high school."

"You're talking to someone who just got her first set of Mickey ears," Lisa bubbled. "We both wore them, Dave and I, at the club last night. You should've seen the looks. It was hilarious."

I laughed as appreciatively as I could, but Lisa knew something was up.

"You *are* gaga, right?"

I could hear Chuck singing in the shower. Sinatra. He was singing Sinatra and not well. Just hearing him made me smile.

"Yeah. I guess I am," I admitted.

"Dave tells me Chuck doesn't do things like this every day."

"Well, that's good to know. That he doesn't move in with every girl he crashes into on the street." I was still smiling.

"More than that, though. Chuck's acting all solid and settled. And apparently, after his marriage broke up, he was completely anti-commitment. And he's committing to you after just a couple of days! So you better be gaga. 'Cause we think he is."

"Solid, settled, and gaga, okay," I said. I noticed the "we" part.

Moving away from romance to political intrigue, Lisa was pretty concerned when she heard about the candidate statement.

"So that's why you sound edgy. Maybe you should just step out of the race. I mean everybody else is. Maybe there won't be anyone left to fill the council seat, so they can't have the zoning vote anyway. But even if they do vote, and they vote against me, I mean you're more important than this election. The club isn't worth it," she added, although in that last part she sounded unsure.

"If some stupid paragraph in a mailing is the worst someone can do to me, then I'm not going to worry about it."

I was assuring myself of course, as much as her.

"But it *isn't* the worst! Someone broke into your apartment and—"

"Look, I'm not worried. I have virtual full-time police protection," I assured her. Gaga police protection, I thought proudly.

Besides, it wasn't just that I'd promised Lisa I'd do this. I promised myself I would too, so crazy or not, I was doing it.

Just once I really, truly, absolutely wanted to stick with a stupid cause and make it work for me. I could win if I put my mind to it and stuck enough signs with runny ink into the ground and hung out at the grocery store and shook everybody's hand. I knew I could.

Besides, if I dropped out of the race, lost interest in the whole election thing, wasn't there just the teeniest, slightest, possible chance that Chuck would lose interest in me? My smile slipped a little.

But anyway, I was not going to just give up, walk away, and lick my wounds. I didn't even have any real wounds yet.

Chuck and Jessie-with-a-tail both came to the station with me. I got the definite "I'm protecting you" vibe, and I was going to protest, on principal if nothing else. I could take care of myself and all that.

But what was the point? I liked the company, and if the company was couched in a little bit of macho bodyguard, that was okay, given recent circumstances. It was even okay that I kind of enjoyed the macho bodyguard part, too. I was glad it wasn't just me and my pepper spray against the world.

Sandy's regular show followed an A.M. gospel live

cast from The House of Blues, so we would be alone in the studio, and there was no one to see me being a dependant female or whatever I was afraid of being seen as anyway.

With the station all Sunday-quiet, it would've been kind of eerie, honestly, being there alone, knowing there was somebody out there who knew where I worked, who kept trying to scare me, who had tried to attack me.

Chuck cased out the station as soon as I'd unlocked the doors. Gun in hand, he looked under desks and behind the CD shelves. He wouldn't let me enter the studio until he'd finished "scoping it out," which meant we had almost ten seconds of dead air, which I was sure Sandy would dress me down about when he returned.

"Welcome to Sandy's brunch beat. Jessie here, subbing on this rainy-as-usual afternoon. This is KCAS L.A. and the OC, but the weather is more Seattle, so let's get a little grunge on." I slipped in some Pearl Jam.

Chuck's cell phone rang. He mouthed at me, "It's Susan—the city clerk." And then, because the reception was lousy in the studio, he took it out to the lobby.

He was out there through the Doors' "Rainy Day Woman" and a commercial break, and meanwhile my request line was lighting up like those trick candles you can't blow out on birthday cakes. You answer one, the next button lights up.

I didn't mind subbing for any other jock, but subbing for Sandy was a hassle. The show was all-request and all-oldies, and so after I squeezed in these first weather-thematic songs, not only would I not get to play what *I* wanted, a lot of the callers in discovering me as the sub were insisting I play the several different versions of "MacArthur Park," right in a row.

So I was already feeling a little bit of trepidation when I answered yet another call.

"Indie rock KCAS, all-request Brunch Beat," I said. I thought maybe if I left off identifying myself, the "MacArthur Park" requests would stop, too.

But this caller didn't seem interested in making a request at all.

"Why'd you pick that pissy yellow color for your signs?" he asked.

It was the same guy who'd called before, but he was whispering, making some sort of an effort to change his voice.

"I like yellow," I said, playing along. I hit record on the tape delay we had hooked up to the studio phone. We often record callers so we can play back requests on the air, or the excited shouts of listeners who've scored a couple of tickets to see Arcade Fire, or bleep out any obscenities. Of course usually we tell people they're being taped and ask if they mind first. I didn't feel inclined to ask this time.

The guy just stayed on the phone, heavy breathing. I was afraid he'd hear the faint whir of the tape and hang up before I could get anything good on him, whatever it was I hoped to get.

I could hear Chuck still talking on his cell phone out in the lobby, faintly. I wanted to summon him but I didn't know how. The request line was an old-fashioned cord phone with not much play in the cord.

"So you'd prefer I'd used a different color?" I asked, to keep things going.

"Sure, almost any. Yellow. Color of cowardice.

Gives people the wrong idea, like *you* are a coward. Makes people think, push comes to shove, you'd run before you'd fight."

"I wouldn't count on that," I said.

"No?"

"No. Are you threatening me?"

"No. I'm a big fan. I'm just saying you shouldn't have picked the color yellow."

"I'll bear that in mind," I said, trying to sound cheerful. "I appreciate the advice, actually, really."

"You do, really?" There was a faintly familiar tone of contentiousness in the caller's raspy voice, but I couldn't place it.

"I try to do the right thing," I said.

"Really? Helping out friends, getting intimate with the police, things like that?"

"Sure, things like that," I said, absolutely desperate for Chuck to come back in the studio. I had a weird feeling crawling up my spine that this guy was nearby and watching me. I glanced out the studio window. Well, he wasn't out there hanging from the ledge or anything, anyway.

"You could be a good girl if you tried," the guy continued. The breathing got a little farther away and I got the feeling that he was about to hang up.

"Say," I said, "were you the one who put a little advice in print? In the candidates' statement that got mailed out?"

There was a beat, and then the voice said, "Not as smart as you think you are."

The phone buzzed in my hand.

I thrust Coldplay's "Yellow" into the CD player and opened the mike just long enough to lie that "This song was a request by my last caller. Hope he's still out there listening."

And I hoped maybe he'd call back on the strength of what he'd perceive as my insane misinterpretation, and maybe incriminate himself.

But for once not a single phone line lit up.

I opened the studio door. Chuck was still on his cell, taking notes, just listening and murmuring, "Uh-huh."

"I have to talk to you," I said.

He waved his hand at me.

"This is important," I said.

"Hold on," Chuck told whoever he was talking to. "Just a second, just a second."

He pressed a button on the cell phone and looked at me expectantly. "Please don't tell me we're going to go over the living together thing again."

"No! We're not. Not now anyway. The guy called again. The threatening-my-life guy. I taped him. I'm hoping he'll call back. Could you maybe actually *be* with me and listen if he does, please, instead of saying 'Uh-huh' over and over into your cell phone!"

I could hear my voice going to shrill. I was just overloaded all of a sudden. In fact, I really would've been happy, all of a sudden, to let Chuck indulge his inclination to tell me what to do. Preferably he would tell me to do something like just relax.

But he didn't. He looked concerned, and got up to put an arm around me. A silly tear rolled down my cheek.

The guy never called back, but I did have plenty more "MacArthur Park" requests. I played whatever anybody asked for, numbly and with no real sense of segueing the songs together. If it was old Beatles followed by old Rolling Stones, great. If it was Bob Marley followed by the Moody Blues, okeydoke.

Meanwhile, Chuck listened to the taped caller. "Inadmissable in court, but good for trying to pin this guy down."

He felt, as I did, that the voice was disguised, maybe run through a filter or something. "And there's an edge to the voice that definitely indicates instability."

"Wow, that's some insight," I said, but I was still too shaken to stay sarcastic.

"I'll drop the tape off at the lab. See if they can filter the voice." He didn't sound very optimistic. "Of course I'm still waiting for analysis on the note in your paper yesterday morning, so we won't hold our breath. But there's other ways we're gonna get this guy. Don't worry."

He tried to trace the call, but the guy wasn't on the phone long enough, and the station's automatic call log only showed the number was "private."

Chuck filled me in about his own phone conversations. The city clerk said she was already "on it," as far as the "printing error" went. She said she had left several "intense" phone messages with the printing service, because that was where the problem had to occur. She claimed she did not consider the extra sentences to be a threat, just "typographical error." She stonewalled any of Chuck's questions about other threats, regarding Tad, Salome, or Royal. She said she knew that Chuck was on "temporary vacation" and suggested that he use his relaxation time "more wisely."

Chuck seemed happy about all this.

"She's dissing you and you're grinning," I pointed out.

"Sure I am. She's confirming—and doesn't even know she's confirming—that she's concerned about this. That she knows something is up and she's working hard to spin it. She's confirming that Chief Little knows there's something seriously up here, too. He's informed her of my status. He doesn't want her to talk to me. He doesn't want her to admit what's going on."

"And this is good because?"

"Because, baby, I'm convinced my boss is at least somewhat inside whatever development schemes and scams I'm close to uncovering. He's helping keep the lid on, anyway. And even if the lunatic threatening you isn't in on the scam, I can use his craziness somehow, I know I can, to blow the whole scene wide open. And Little must know that, too. That's what I'm figuring."

"Well, swell," I said. "But that doesn't make it any less, you know, scary for me."

Chuck's enthusiasm dimmed a little. "I know. I'm sorry. But look, we really are getting there. I talked to the printer, too."

"And let me guess. He lays out the candidate statements with the help of a Ouija board."

"Might as well. He has no idea," Chuck said, "how the strange text showed up on your page. But yours was the only statement not computer typed and transmitted via e-mail or diskette. Yours was faxed to him. You fax it yourself?"

"No. I just left it on the clerk's desk. And she wasn't around when I left it, so someone could've lifted it off her desk."

"And added whatever they wanted to. Off-duty or not, come Monday, I'm gonna park in Sue's office until she finds that fax. Promise."

Chuck patted his jacket pocket. "That last phone call was from Puhalu Motors in Honolulu. And he just gave me a list of purchasers of vehicles like the one that tried to run us down behind the Java Hut the other night. A list!"

"Anyone we know on it?"

"Not as yet. A coupla corporations. A few more phone calls, even on a Sunday, and I bet I can get the names behind the corporations. Of real actual people." He picked up the studio line. "You're sick of requests anyway, right? I keep you company in here that should make things a little less scary."

It should've, but the scariest thing of all maybe was realizing how much I really did just want to be near him. How I was more or less depending on him. And not just because some crazy guy was out there, stalking me.

Suzee Cue, the Sunday afternoon jazz-and-blues aficionado, had already played her first seven cuts by the time Chuck got off the phone a second time.

"Your buddy gonna be in here like forever?" she asked me. "I mean maybe you enjoy the endless phone drone behind you, but it's cramping my style."

Chuck cut his last call short and managed to win her over by praising her jazz selections, and chatting her up about the history of the historic Lighthouse jazz club in the South Bay, his "neck of the woods." Soon he was laundry-listing his favorite jazz musicians and why.

Her ire retreated, but I was getting annoyed. He was talking intimately with someone else about the one kind of music I knew absolutely nothing about. It was like dating a Frenchman and not speaking French and he runs into some French wine connoisseur or something.

"Nice guy," Suzee told me. "Less neurotic than the guys you usually date."

"Thanks," I said. "How do you know we're dating?"

"You're not? Can I ask him out then? He knows Chet Baker's life story! How many guys can you meet who know Chet—"

"I'm not dating him. I'm living with him, in fact," I blurted out.

"Oh. Cool. For you. Spends too much time on the phone anyway," she said.

"You didn't tell me how great *my* selections were," I noted when Chuck and I were outside the studio, Jessie leashed up and happy, twisting around our legs.

"You played "MacArthur Park" eight times," Chuck said. "The people may have requested it, but still."

"I'm surprised you even noticed. You were on the phone the whole show."

"Yeah, and it was time well spent, too. I've got something now, all right."

He started humming to himself, I think it was Sinatra again.

"So?" I said, as we skipped around the puddles in the dripping parking garage to Chuck's car. "At least give me a hint of what you got."

"Atlantis Development. Or at least I almost have them."

"What are they doing—building a lost city?"

"Building stuff using lost money is more like it," Chuck said. "Drug money, well-laundered, fostering not only development but the political growth of dirty politicians who are only interested in supporting their friends' personal interests."

"Watch what you're saying about a friend's personal interests," I said.

"I didn't mean you. I meant grubby-handed louts like Royal Garritty, who is a partner in Atlantis, and in this particular case, one of the members of the board of directors of a company that Atlantis is a subsidiary of—and that's not Royal, nope, it's squeaky-clean police-supported Playa Vista dude Ned Rutkin."

"They work together," I said to Chuck, "and yet they're running against each other for city council?"

"Were running against. Some business associate told Royal to drop out, right?" Chuck noted. "Maybe it wasn't some illegal substance entrepreneur afraid of the light shining on him. Maybe it was Ned, competitor for the throne and corporate associate."

"What, like Donald Trump and Martha Stewart are on the same episode of *The Apprentice* and they duke it out for who gets the air time?"

"Right. You know, why can't it be Christina Milian and Jessica Biel on the same episode and they mud-wrestle for—"

I socked him on the arm.

"Anyway, what's weird is not Royal and Ned both jockeying for an official position. What's weird is that in all my digging around during my LAPD days, I didn't see any connection between them whatsoever. I didn't have Ned on the radar screen at all. Although I suppose they could have joined forces for the first time in the South Bay. Their mutual home turf."

"It makes more sense that Rob tried to run us down than Ned," I said, although the guy who'd raced down my front stairs had not a passing resemblance to either of them. "But that wasn't Royal running down my stairs, and it wasn't his voice on the phone, either."

"An accomplice. Probably an employee. We'll get him and we'll get him to rat Royal out, or Royal to rat him out, and Ned," Chuck said. "You eat an elephant one bite at a time."

"As long as the elephant isn't Royal and I don't really have to eat him."

Chuck waggled his eyebrows at me.

"I was not inferring anything sexual," I said with as much dignity as I could muster. I changed the subject. "So what's Ned doing with a Hawaiian corporation, anyway?"

"Company is actually in Delaware," Chuck said. "Has some developments going in Oahu as well as here. And that's why someone who works for that company bought a car to drive around the island. And maybe that car was used for more than just scoping out the site of an upscale shopping mall people are protesting will ruin a pristine North Shore snorkeling spot. Maybe that car isn't even *in* Hawaii now, if you get my drift."

"How do we find out?"

"DMV records based on the vehicle identification number. Monday I'll get the lab results on your newspaper note, the blood work on Marcus, whatever we can off this taped call of yours then, too. Although I'll have to take it a little easy on the lab stuff, supposedly being on vacation and all."

"But in the meantime, today, there's nothing we can do, right?"

"Not a lot," Chuck agreed.

I sucked it up. "Okay. So I'll just put this all out of my mind and go around knocking on doors, and hope nobody tries to knock me out of the race again."

"I dunno," Chuck said. "I can think of other better things you could do today."

I laughed, waiting for a playful proposition, but Chuck looked very serious and thoughtful, and it never came.

We were standing in the fetid garage alongside Chuck's car. Still looking very wrapped up in his own thoughts, Chuck unlocked the passenger door and opened it. Jessie the dog jumped in, eager to take her usual spot in the back seat.

Chuck turned the key in his ignition. He drove around the three dark levels of the garage up from the basement to the entrance and out into the splattery street to a stoplight before he spoke again.

"Here's my idea, Jessie—" he began. And then he stopped, and he kind of laughed, and he kissed me.

"Not a bad idea," I said. "Except I kind of promised Lisa we'd come over for a late lunch and then she and I would campaign some before tonight's debate." I glanced at my watch. "But I guess we could just make it an early dinner, and do a little less campaigning. No harm in that. . . ." I kissed him back. The kiss lasted a long time.

The light changed and someone tapped a horn behind us. Chuck made an impolite gesture with his middle finger and took off down the rain-slicked street, his eyes on the road now, not on me, and his voice suddenly so low I had to lean in close to hear him over Jessie the dog's steady, eager panting.

"We should just do it," he said.

He threw me one of his endearing, vulnerable little half smiles. He dropped one hand on my knee, and I thought about what we'd done in the back seat the night before. I wasn't adverse to a repeat, except with canine Jessie aboard there wasn't really enough room.

"Sure," I said, "but this time, maybe we really should drive on home first. Where there's a bed or even the sofa. Or hey, like you suggested yesterday. The kitchen table."

"I don't mean let's do *that*. I mean let's get married."

"What?"

"Sure, I know we'll have to pick up a license to make it official but if we drive to Vegas there's no blood tests or anything and—"

"Get married? I just thought you wanted to have sex," I finished, feebly.

"I do want to have sex. I didn't think getting married and having sex were mutually exclusive activities." He laughed. "You think it sounds crazy, don't you?"

"Well, yeah, I guess I do, honestly I—"

"Come on. Just look into my eyes awhile and I'll look into yours and we'll be great. We will."

He landed another red light, and there was only the sound of his panting dog, and the sloshing back and forth of the windshield wipers, and the light rain ticking against the glass.

I bit my lip and he went on slowly, his gaze melting into mine. Some of the craziness did, I have to admit, dissipate under that joined gaze.

"If I were to think about it, it'd sound crazy, too, I know. But sometimes you just *can't* think, you have to just—just feel. And you know this feels right. Don't you? Besides, it's raining again, it'll be a lousy day for campaigning, I can't do any of my own leg-work 'til tomorrow, I'm officially off the clock.

I mean come on, we might as well accomplish something today."

There he lost me. "You want to get married to accomplish something?" I don't think he picked up on the negativity that was part and parcel of my incredulity.

"Sure," he said. "I mean why not? I mean I know my track record on marriage hasn't been so good, but then your track record with guys in general hasn't been so great, I mean that Jack guy, if he's any indication—well, in comparison, I'm a prize, lady, so you'd better grab me. Point is, your apartment's too small, we've already agreed on that one, and why pay rent? We should just buy a house. A house with a yard for my dog. And we should be married if we're going to buy a house."

"You want to buy a house."

"Yeah, absolutely. I break this case, I might get a raise. I break this case, there might be a lot more affordable housing available in Playa Vista, too, ha. Or if not, we can move someplace else."

I must've looked astonished.

"I know," Chuck said. "Move where? I haven't figured that part out yet."

"It seems like you've figured out everything else," I managed.

"Who knows? Maybe we'll move to Hawaii." The light changed, Chuck drove. "So how about it? Even with this lousy weather, we can make Vegas in five hours. Want to hit it?"

"So," I said, "you really want to marry me?"

"Let me be the first to say it," he declared. "I do."

He looked at me. I looked at him.

Truly, I wanted to go for it, I did. I could almost hear myself saying something like what I'd said in my kitchen Saturday afternoon, that for once I won't hold back.

I wanted to feel his lips on mine, his hands on me and then, yeah, his hand *in* mine. Forever and ever, right? But forever—wow, this was too fast. This was too furious.

"I don't know." I struggled. "I just don't know. This sort of feels like the consolation prize for not being able to solve the 'case of the crooked candidate' this afternoon. Doesn't it? Would the idea have even occurred to you if you could've talked to somebody at the DMV today? Come on. Convince me that it would."

"I have to convince you to marry me?" He looked deeply disappointed.

"Well. Yeah, honestly, you do. Or else you just have to wait until you're really ready."

"I am really ready. You're the one saying no."

"I am not saying no. I'm saying—not this afternoon. Not right this second. I mean I have a debate tonight. I mean—we really need to think about this—" I protested.

"Oh, God. The thinking again." He sighed. "Okay. Not today. We'll think. You'll think."

"We've hardly even lived together yet," I reminded him. "You haven't even made me a single organic salad."

I thought he'd laugh, but he didn't.

I wanted to tell him I liked the idea of getting married. Of marrying him. Of our cataclysmic meeting cataclysming right into Happy Ever After. I did like the idea. If he'd just try to convince me a little harder, maybe I would just plunge on in.

We were right by the on-ramp for Interstate 10. He could take it straight through downtown out to

San Berdoo and Highway 15, zoom on to Vegas. I could get married in a jeans skirt and a black lace cap-sleeved blouse, assuming I took off my U-2 sweatshirt and my battered leather jacket that I was wearing to keep dry. Because of the rain I was also wearing sneakers with my black tights. Was this any way to get married? Was my attire really going to stop me?

Or Chuck could by pass the freeway and just slide on down Lincoln to Sepulveda to PCH to home again, which seemed kind of boring all of a sudden, even if I wasn't dressed just right for a wedding.

"Chuck," I began, but he lifted his hand off my leg and gripped the steering wheel in both fists.

"It's okay," he said. "You're probably right."

Chapter Sixteen

Lisa fed us with leftover chili from my fund-raiser, coupled with a stylish radicchio, endive, pine nut, and basil salad, baked potatoes with cream cheese, cheddar, and chives, and a stunningly good chocolate creme pie for desert.

Chuck and Dave were watching the Lakers on TV, and musing about the amazing Royal and Ned connection; Lisa and I were rolling campaign posters into neat little cylinders and binding them with rubber bands. We could've been in Vegas.

Dave got up from the sofa and went back to the dining room table and cut another slice of pie.

"This stuff is good," he said. "It's a shame where it came from."

"Where it came from?" I asked, distractedly.

Lisa rolled her eyes.

"You haven't told her yet," Dave realized, shrugging his shoulders in my direction. "Well, guess you will now." He called into the living room. "Shall we walk your dog, Chuck?"

"It's perfectly good pie even if it was baked by one of your rivals," Lisa began.

I groaned. "Benni Cardell brought you a pie! And you're eating it. Traitor."

"We're all traitors," Dave said, rubbing his stomach. "She brought a cherry one, too."

"Let me explain?" Lisa asked.

"I'm not stopping you," I said huffily.

"She came into the club with the pies last night, and told me, 'All politics aside, I defy you not to enjoy my cooking.' And then she just left again."

"Does she think you're going to vote for her?"

"I think she's hoping I'll stock her pies at the club. I mean if I even still have a club after the election."

"I woulda thrown one in her face," I muttered. "I bet she doesn't even bake her own. I bet she buys them someplace and puts them in those homemade-*looking* tins."

"Someone's feeling crabby," Lisa murmured. "Come on. I'll lend you a respectable-looking raincoat and we'll hand these posters out until you're cheerful again."

I thought that might take a while, but I didn't disagree.

"There's something wrong," Lisa said wisely, in between meeting and greeting customers by the front entrance to Albertson's market.

"I think people are being pretty nice, overall. I know Ned Rutkin's supposedly guaranteed a win, but—"

"I don't mean with the election. Chuck hardly said a word to Dave or I at lunch, and you hardly said a word to him and—"

"He asked me to marry him."

"What?"

"Yeah, that was kind of my reaction, too."

"And you said?"

"I said it was too rushed. I didn't say no. I might want to marry him. I don't know. I mean I have an election to win before I can even think about something like getting married."

"Well. This is all kind of fast. But you turned him down because of the *election?*"

I got very defensive. "The election I promised you I'd win to save your club."

"It's not that I don't want you to do just that," Lisa said gently, squeezing my hand, "but like I told you this morning, if you feel even the slightest bit at risk, you have my blessing, my encouragement, to get out of the race. And if this interferes with things between you and Chuck, then it's not worth it, either. You can't give up your life for local politics."

"The funny thing is, I didn't have anything to give up before local politics." I sighed. "Look, Chuck's proposal wasn't even a real proposal, I don't think. Today's a slow day. He's on a forced work hiatus and he can't get any more info on the guy who tried to run us over until tomorrow. He said getting married to me would at least be *accomplishing* something. It didn't seem very well thought out."

"No, I guess not."

"And it wasn't very romantic, either. He'd have a lot better chance getting a 'yes' if he hadn't mixed things all up with politics and police work."

A little old lady pulling her own two-wheeled grocery cart almost slipped past us. "I'm running for city council," I told her, offering my hand. "Jessie Adams. I'd really like your vote."

She smiled at me and shook my hand gingerly. "Well, dear. That's very nice."

"Let me tell you a little bit about myself. I'm against rezoning and in favor of—"

"Good, good. I'm voting for that nice Ned Rutkin," she told me.

"Ned's a slime bag who uses drug money to fund some of his corporate operations," I told her.

She walked away. "Best of luck to you."

"He's a Satanist," I called after her.

"It's not that I want you to rush into anything," Lisa went on when we were alone again, "but I do realize that sometimes things just . . . happen."

She started smoothing the folds of her skirt, and I knew she meant Dave. I said so. She smiled.

"Things happen," she went on, "that defy any reasonable expectation."

"So you guys are like—together?"

"We're getting there," she said. "But this isn't about us, or how fast or slow relationships progress. This is about you. You're pretty conservative for a scruffy musician type—"

"Scruffy!" I objected, even though I was wearing Lisa's raincoat, her rose-colored turtleneck, and her black leather pumps, which were a half size too large and kept slipping up and down on my heels, all definitely more candidatelike attire than black lace, sweat jacket, tights, and sneakers.

"My point is you think life should be played in a major key, with a good solid chorus line."

"Well, sure. Everybody likes The Beatles. You don't hear a lot of people humming say, Stravinsky."

"I love Stravinsky," a thin blond woman carrying a bag of oranges enthused. She plucked a poster out of my hands. "I'll put this up over my piano."

"The thing is," Lisa said, "sometimes life is, well,

a little atonal. Good or bad, it doesn't always turn out the way you expect. Or even when you expect."

"Yeah, just wait 'til that lady sees my name instead of Stravinsky's hanging over her piano," I agreed.

We stayed at the grocery store until I'd handed out every single rolled poster, and at least a few people I handed them to both knew what they were and wanted them. A few more said they'd definitely vote for me, even if they didn't take a poster, and a few others promised to watch the debate that evening. All in all, I'd really accomplished something standing in the grocery that afternoon. Maybe not as much as I would've accomplished if, say, I'd gotten married, but still.

And then it was time to hurry down to the council chambers for my next great debate. I was all hyped up but I had nowhere to go. There was a sleepy feel to the proceedings, or more accurately, a comatose one.

There was no sign of Brian representing the *Daily Sail*, no cameraman in a Tribune Broadcasting windbreaker, no ponytailed cable access cameraman in a turtleneck shooting the flourescent lights. There was hardly anyone at all around, maybe ten people in the audience, including Chuck, but not Lisa and Dave who were at the club. The entire audience, even Chuck, seemed most interested in the free pie and punch that the League of Women Voters had seen fit to offer this time around.

The debate itself was pretty anticlimactic, maybe because only Ida and I showed up. Benni was down with a cold and sent her regrets and the pies in the back of the room. Ned was traveling on important business. Royal and Salome and Tad and deceased Conway were of course no longer in the race.

Ida and I found we were pretty much in agreement about everything. Even Lisa's club, which she praised as a "landmark institution." I was the more dynamic speaker, to be sure, and certainly I'd wager that I looked hotter than Ida in, say, a bathing suit, but all in all we were, as she told Brian Harrigan when he finally showed up after the debate, "like-minded."

Brian apologized for missing the proceedings. He'd had to cover a school board meeting in another South Bay town.

"They're talking about resurfacing all the playgrounds with rubber cushioned mat things, which sounds good, but apparently there's a substance in the rubber that can cause allergic reactions in some kids. Big important controversy," he said. "That's why no cable access over here tonight. With so many candidates dropping out of this race, the interest level in tonight's debate was deemed low in comparison with the playground resurfacing. I mean I deemed it low."

Brian was clearly antsy to be off, but if I was going to win this election, I had to curry the press's favor, even if its representative was apparently the dork Chuck said he was.

"Well, since you missed us up there on the stage, we're happy to answer any questions you have now," I suggested.

He might've begged off, but he glanced over at Chuck, pouring himself a cup of coffee but still able to cast an intimidating look in Brian's direction.

So Brian asked Ida and I both cursory questions about our views on rezoning—neither of us were in favor of it—and got us to go on record again with our sympathies for Conway Marcus's widow. I brought up the "typo" in my candidate statement, but all Brian did was yawn.

"I don't think that'll make a difference to the voters. I'm not sure anything will. The League of Women Voters' poll will be in tomorrow's paper, and it shows Ned winning in a landslide if the election were held today, in part because he's the only candidate with any real name recognition in the community."

"When was that poll taken? I was out introducing myself to local residents all afternoon," I protested, but Ida just shook her head.

"We don't have people in every precinct working the phones for us, we don't have postage-paid mailers reaching every registered voter in town," she noted. "All we can do is present an alternate viewpoint, really, and open up the avenues of discussion. We can't possibly hope to take on Ned Rutkin successfully."

Ida really did have a negative streak, I thought.

"I don't agree. We just have to get out there and reach people," I said with a lot more enthusiasm than I felt.

"You have your work cut out for you," Brian said. "And some company. That's what Benni Cardell is doing. Not taking no for an answer, that woman."

I could hear the admiration in his voice.

"She's holding nightly bake sales in front of the pier, and people are lining up for her baked goods. Lining up! Great PR. I've been over twice myself. She dropped off the refreshments for the debate tonight, you know, even with a head cold."

"Hope she didn't drop off the virus, too."

Ida gave a genteel chuckle.

Brian scribbled the word *echinacea* in his notebook.

"Any idea how the dropout candidates are doing?" I asked him. "I expected to see Royal heckling from the audience."

"Mr. Garritty is always busy with his work," Brian said.

"Many houses to foreclose, so little time," Ida remarked drily.

"This was a real blow to him—to his pride anyway, stepping down," Brian told us.

"That, and the weeping in public," Ida threw out.

"How about Tad and Salome?"

"Both out of town," Brian said. "A little bird told me they're together."

"Ah. A little bird named Ned I bet." I smiled.

Tad and Salome were probably getting married and moving to Hawaii.

Brian stopped short of giving up the information both Ida and I were most interested in hearing— which candidate his paper was going to endorse.

"That's up to our editor," Brian said, to Ida's question, suddenly less gossipy. "I wouldn't even know, much less be able to tell you, his decision at this point."

"Well, I hope you'll put in a good word for me," I said as Brian headed off to make his deadline and avoid more eye contact with Chuck.

For some reason my request made Brian nervous. "Please tell your uh—Detective Jackson—that I'll do my best. That I certainly won't say anything *against* you."

Well, that was comforting.

"Not that the *Sail*'s recommendation guarantees a win by any means," Ida murmured, "I mean especially today when so few people even read that newspaper except for the surf report, but it is a definite *asset*, and if they recommend Ned, we're both completely washed up."

Despite Ida's powdery, friendly embrace, secretly I thought *No, only you are washed up. All that negativity, that's your problem right there.*

I was determined to stay positive. After all, I had signs! I had youth on my side; Ida had said so herself. I had Lisa passing out my posters at the club tonight, not to mention handing them out with me at the grocery store all afternoon.

And of course as Ida had also pointed out earlier, I had a certified officer of the law on my side. At least I hoped I still had Chuck on my side. He congratulated me on my debating prowess, but I could tell his heart wasn't in it. He had Thelonius Monk in his CD player and we listened to the music in silence as he drove us home. I felt as negative as Ida by the time we got there. I was ready for Chuck to tell me that he'd realized I was so right about the marriage thing that he was moving out.

But he didn't say anything like that; he didn't say anything about anything about us.

Instead, he pointed out that Sally seemed at least temporarily cured of peeing on the rug, because whenever she tried it, Jessie barked, and the barking seemed to upset her more than just giving up and using the litter box.

Then he told me that the bad weather had driven the police lab analyst back to work, and he'd spoken to Chuck and Dave while Lisa and I were out shaking hands with prospective voters.

The analyst hadn't found a single print or identifying mark on the threatening note I'd received a seeming lifetime ago; and Conway Marcus's remains had tested positive for massive alcohol consumption, combined with the slightly less massive consumption of tranquilizers, the prescription kind. The prescription was in Conway's name and in his pocket, which wasn't indicative of foul play.

Chuck left the crank caller's audiotape and a six-pack of Bud at the lab, and received in return a promise that he would hear a remix in a day or two.

"Best I can ask for, me being persona non grata around the department this week." Chuck sighed.

I was feeling pretty persona non grata myself. I felt like even though Chuck was talking to me, he was looking right through me.

Before I could comment, Chuck laid the zinger on me. "I won't have to hit the DMV tomorrow," he said. "Puhalo Motors called back. They knew exactly where the car was."

"Where?" I asked.

"Sitting on their lot. Atlantis bought it, but they never took delivery. Sales manager was told the North Shore development gig went bust, keep the car, resell it. But Atlantis never turned the title over, and there it sits, lost in the shuffle. He wanted to know if I had any phone numbers, anybody they could contact at Atlantis here. Do you believe that? I get a link between Ned and Royal and then I find out they're not the assholes who tried to run us over? Man, this has been a lousy day."

If it was lousy for any other reason, Chuck didn't say, and then the pizza he'd ordered arrived, fortunately not delivered by my downstairs neighbor; and shortly after we'd consumed it, we fell into an extra-cheese-induced sleep with two cats and a dog lying between us.

Chapter Seventeen

In the morning, Chuck left the apartment before I was awake. There was a note on the night table.

> *Gotta hit the Harbor Freeway early. I'm gonna rummage through Los Angeles county building permits—anything connecting Rob and Ned, anything suspicious for Atlantis. Rest assured—I'm still gonna nail them.*

I would've been more assured if he'd nailed *me* before he went after them.

I walked Jessie and then I went to work early, shocking Theo, who almost fell out of his chair.

"An hour early? If Sandy was around you'd give him a heart attack," Theo said with his usual scowl.

"Where is Sandy, anyway?" I asked, plucking CDs from the New Releases shelf.

"MIA's all I know. He was supposed to have a meet about the station sponsoring a bunch of concerts over at the El Rey this morning, and he didn't show. *I* took the meeting. Just like I do everything around here. We might as well just become another

one of those stupid iPod stations playing all automated schlock rock and I can be the one who flicks
the switch, leans back, lets it all roll."

"It's not like Sandy to miss a meeting. He likes
meetings. He gets to act important."

"He called in an hour later to say he just plain got
tied up and everybody deserves a little downtime
and he's taking it, won't be in today. I think he's
losing it over some girl, if you ask me. He'll come
back married or something."

"Is that all people do these days?" I snapped. "Get
married?"

Theo shook his head. "New fella not working
out?"

Before I even had the chance to reply, Jack
walked into the studio.

"Jack?" I said, like it wasn't obvious who he was.

Theo gave me a knowing smile. "Back to the old
fella, huh?"

"No," I said irritably.

Theo just laughed knowingly. "You're here early,
you might as well start early—make up for all the
times you've been late."

He slipped out of the studio, leaving Jack and I to
contemplate the musty carpet and listen to the
steady dripping of roof rain into the gallon trash
can, which now seemed like a permanent accessory
in the studio.

And then of course, we contemplated each other.
Jack was wearing black leather pants, a black
leather vest, and a semi-sheer Indian cotton shirt.
His hair, was of course, like the late Warren Zevon's
"Werewolf in London," perfect.

I heard Lisa's accusation that I was "scruffy" echo

in my head, and I could see it reflected in Jack's eyes, too.

Because of the rain, and walking Jessie the dog, and not seeing Chuck, and not messing around with Chuck, and not talking to Chuck, and being just a tiny bit well, depressed about that, I was wearing the same rock-and-roll T-shirt I'd slept in, over a sports bra and a pair of jeans that had either seen better days or would soon be available in Abercrombie & Fitch and described as professionally distressed, cost hundreds of dollars, and need to be dry-cleaned only.

"What are you doing here?" I asked Jack sullenly.

He smiled his soft gentle smile that usually preceded asking for a handout of some kind—monetary favors or sexual favors or at least a free beer.

If he thought the smile would move me, he was wrong. The only smile that would get to me was Chuck's. That half smile, that hopeful look, that self-deprecating, I'm-just-the-guy-who-wants-to-marry-you smile. I sighed.

"What do you *think* I'm doing here?" Jack asked.

The Roots cut Theo put on was about to end in dead air. I sat down at the console without answering Jack, flipped a switch, and talked into the mike.

"It's Jessie at the board, giving Theo a little much-needed time to explore all the new rock and roll filling our shelves. Not seeing too much sunshine again today, but I hear from the National Weather Service that just three more days—on top of our past three weeks of rain—and we'll be having blue skies. Instead of just clicking my heels together or saying abracadabra to make it so, today I'm only playing songs that bring to mind the warm and dry, in the hopes that some little bit of magic will come into our gray, dreary, soggy, miserable lives."

It was a little intense as a lead-in to The Temptations' "My Girl," but too bad. I also had stacked up beside me The Beatles' "Good Day Sunshine," The Georgia Peaches' "Sunny Day," even Shawn Colvin's not quite apropos "When Sunny Comes Home."

Jack scooted his chair next to mine. He touched my shoulder. "I had to come see you. Since you called Saturday night, all I've been doing is thinking of you."

"Uh, right," I said, swiveling my chair to face him. "That would certainly be a first."

"Oh, Jessie, come on. I know I was a little self-involved. Couldn't handle the long-distance thing, let a few momentary attractions get in the way."

"Yeah, just a few, I bet."

I stuck the next CD in the changer ready to go. I made a big show out of shuffling papers, my commercial copy, the weather forecast, a candy wrapper of Theo's.

"What do you really want, Jack?"

"You. Unless you're too wrapped up with the so-called new boyfriend."

I narrowed my eyes. He widened his own, made a dimple appear in his left cheek. He thought he was so perfect, but he only had one dimple, not two.

"Oh, I get it," I said. "Suddenly somebody else wants me, so now I'm desirable."

At least I thought Chuck still wanted me. I knew I still wanted Chuck. Even if I wasn't ready to marry him. Or at least to admit that I wanted to marry him. But I had said no. Or not exactly no, just, later.

"You've always been desirable," Jack said, and he sounded undeniably sexy as he leaned close and

whispered in my ear. His lips actually brushed my
ear in fact, and my cheek, and made their way to
my lips, at which point I shoved him away with my
feet and all the impact of a chair on wheels.

"Ow," he said. "You almost got me in the balls."

"'Almost' only counts in hand grenades," I said.
Jack was not amused.

I was not interested, and I said so. "Jack, I am so
over you."

"You are? So fast? Then why'd you call me? Why'd
you call me late at night with that stupid story about
your key—"

"The key," I said.

Maybe Jack being here was all a front to disguise
how he'd given my key to Royal Garritty or someone like him to use.

"Yeah, what about that key exactly?" He rubbed
at his thighs where the chair and I had attacked
him. "What's the big deal? And don't give me the
bullshit about the boyfriend, who is probably just a
fantasy anyway."

I sucked in my breath sharply. I tried to sound
polite. To wheedle just a little. I could always kick
him in the balls for real later.

"You're right. It's not about my boyfriend," I said.
"It's about another guy. Who broke into my apartment and tried to attack us. My very real, actual
boyfriend and I. This attacker, he had a key. On a
Playa Vista mayoral candidate key ring. Just like the
one I gave you."

Jack looked blank. "What?" he said.

"I'm not accusing you," I said reassuringly. "I
mean you just left it by my front door, right? Under
the mat or something? And anybody coulda just

taken it then. But maybe you saw somebody or talked to somebody or—"

"You really think I'm a loser," he said, as if surprised by the revelation. "You don't really want me back."

"No," I said, "I don't. But I would really appreciate it, fondly, deeply, and kindly if you would tell me what happened with that key—"

"I didn't want to drop it by your place, because I didn't want to run into you and have another fight. I am not big on confrontations—you oughta know that. I was really horrified, Jessie, at the way you just got on the bus and left me standing out there on the corner that day. Just 'cause I sort of broke up with you. I mean just because I'm not looking for a commitment or something, I thought we'd always be—well, intimate friends."

His hand touched my cheek gently. "I prefer having things quiet and simple," he said. "No unnecessary harshness. There's no need for discord. You don't always have to tell it just like you see it—"

"Yes, I know. You're very evolved," I agreed.

I realized Chuck was not that evolved, and really, neither was I. We did tell it like we saw it. Even if we ran the risk of offending someone, like each other.

I pushed Jack's hand away. "The key?"

"So I didn't drop it off at your place. And I didn't lose it or give it away or some stupid thing, either. I put it in an envelope with a very nice note, I must say, and I left it for you right here at the station."

"Here?" I said. "When?"

"Same day you called me. I was on my way to that party and I thought it was bad form to go to a party with my ex-girl's key still in my pocket."

"I never got the key."

"Well, don't blame me. You'd left early."

"I don't leave early. I am always here. Oh. That's right. I left for my fund-raiser," I said, realizing.

"Oh, so you *admit* you weren't in. You gonna admit this boyfriend of yours is all made up, too?"

"No. Now go on."

Jack gave up. "The station manager guy, the one who wears aloha shirts, he was here. So I left it with him. He said he was gonna see you later anyway."

"Ah," I said, remembering. "He did say he had something to give me."

"Say, he isn't the new boyfriend, is he?"

"No!" I said.

"Okay." Jack shrugged, leering a little with the shrug, to let me know he didn't believe me. "If he *isn't* the new boyfriend and he *doesn't* already have the key, then maybe it's still sitting on his desk," Jack said. "That's where he left my envelope, somewhere in that clutter."

"You'd better not be lying," I said.

Jack smoothed his in no-need-of-smoothing blond hair, wearily. "You're always giving me these ultimatums. Call you, meet you, don't lie. It's pretty hard-nosed, honestly."

I didn't bother to contest it.

I went out to reception and I asked Heather to come in and sit behind the console while I looked for something. "Play list's all laid out for an hour. Just plug the CDs in the slot."

"You gonna pay me for doing your so-called job?"

"I'll give you twenty," I said. "Which is more than I get an hour and this won't take an hour."

"What about the phones?" she objected, but then she saw Jack, slouching in the studio doorway, turning his smile on her, since I was not going to succumb to his charm.

"Hi," she said.

"Well, hello. I'm Jack Crawford. Lead singer of Jack's Back . . ."

"Oh," she breathed, and the studio door clicked shut behind them, Heather's concern for the phones forgotten.

I made for Sandy's office. It was locked, as usual. Unless he was actually sitting in his office, and even sometimes then, he kept the door closed and locked.

What Jack dismissed as clutter was Sandy's precious memorabilia, primarily related to the Beach Boys and the Rolling Stones, but also including stuff like Dodgers game bobble head baseball dolls and rubber pancakes with legs, smiles, and names nabbed from International House of Pancakes kids' meals.

Sandy didn't trust the cleaning staff, or really, any of us around this collection. He came into the studio to talk to us, or called us into the miniature conference room. His office was his private kingdom. I don't think I'd been inside since he hired me four years ago.

I went back to reception and snagged a key ring from Heather's top desk drawer, and on the third try I opened Sandy's office door.

The place smelled mustier than the studio because the ceiling had a leak in there, too. With Sandy out and the cleaning staff not allowed in, the rainwater had, over the course of the last few days, slowly dripped over the top of the trash bucket used to contain it, and soaked into the carpet.

That is the part of the carpet visible from beneath

stacks and towering stacks of outdated *Billboard* and *Rolling Stone* magazines now mildewing.

My eyes darted around the room, walls crowded with posters of Mick Jagger shaking it, and the Beach Boys posing by the Hermosa Beach pier; original, framed, limited-edition *Smile* album cover artwork, a ukelele, a kukui nut lei, a poster for Maui potato chips with some beach boy who was not Brian Wilson holding the bag. Hawaii. I allowed myself a moment of longing, for Chuck and I married and moved there, looking off a balcony at the blue-green sea.

Then I edged my way deeper into Sandy's office and began rummaging around his desk. His chair was covered with an aloha-print fabric. Coconut shells held pencils. Plastic leis were strung along the edge of his desk. Maybe Sandy should move to Hawaii, not me. I knew full well how much he reveled in the Beach Boys, but I thought his longing to be a surf bum was focused on Southern California shores.

On the edge of his desk, almost hidden behind a towering stack of CDs, there was an envelope with my name written on it, and inside was a note that said, "Here's your key. All good wishes, Jack—of Jack's Back." So that was the alleged nice note. Like I wouldn't know who Jack was or I should be impressed by the name of his band. What there wasn't was an actual key.

So possibly Sandy had brought my key to the fund-raiser, but instead of returning it to me, he'd given it to someone else, who'd then used it to break into my apartment. The question was who.

Since Sandy told Theo he was staying home, I

decided I'd walk over to his place and ask him point-blank about the fate of my key.

He lived only a block away, and I'd been to his apartment—the outside of the building at least—several times, having given him a ride home back in the days when I had a car that ran. Sandy never drove himself; he was too cheap to pay for parking. Of course I couldn't leave Heather ensconced with Jack unsupervised while I went off to potentially harass Sandy. So I hit the record library, and sure enough, Theo was still there.

"What's up?" he asked.

"I need you to step back in for me."

"Jesus. I've been stepping in for you all week. I thought you were here now for once. I mean you look here. You look to be here in the corporeal flesh and all, unless you're just like a hologram—"

"Heather's sitting at the console right now with my ex-boyfriend and I have to go over to Sandy's," I said, making it sound as if Sandy had requested that I do so.

"Oh. Great. He need somebody to bring him a 'Cheeseburger in Paradise' or something? Jimmy Buffet, the Beach Boys, that's all he likes. For him the scene is all SoCal, Key West, and Oahu."

"Oahu," I said.

"Bless you," Theo said, pontificating relentlessly. "He doesn't know New York exists. He probably never heard the expression 'Detroit Sound' or 'Seattle grunge.' Do you know he never even heard of The Meat Puppets till I introduced him?"

"I won't be that long," I said.

"I'm not going to keep playing sunshine-theme songs or whatever it is you think you're doing. You love that theme crap, don't you? 'Born to Be Wild,'

'Born to Run,' 'Born with a Gun in My Hand' . . .
And if it is sunshine theme stuff today, why aren't
you playing 'Sunshine Superman,' which is actually
like a classic? You know I heard Mighty Mouse is
going to do a cover version of that?"

"Play it. Play tons of your weird obscure stuff, I
don't care. I've probably lost all my listeners anyway
by refusing to play 'MacArthur Park' today."

I could've just waited until my shift was over to hit
Sandy's place. I realized that heading to Sandy's in
and of itself was very likely a fool's errand. Knowing
Sandy, seeing Sandy's office, I could only imagine
what his apartment was like, and I could only imagine
that it would be a very rare female companion indeed
who would want to hang there instead of at her place.

Still, I had to give it a shot. And I couldn't wait
until my shift was over. I couldn't wait another
second. All at once everything just came together,
I had a major, earth-shaking epiphany, or at least I
thought I did.

I ran out of the station, forgetting my jacket, not
even noticing the rain was a lot more intense now
and soaking through my T-shirt and jeans. I
rounded the corner at a dead run, and then I
couldn't remember if Sandy lived at 730 or 720
Stoner Avenue, no jokes tolerated on the street
name.

Both buildings were pretty damn identical,
fronted by a blue mosaic on top of faded blue
stucco. They looked more motel than apartment,
and had palms that more than likely had rats leaning over their gated, underground garages.

I went over to the front entrance of 720. Sure
enough, Sandy's name was on the tenant dial-up
list. I dialed his access code, but all I got was his

phone answering machine. I said, "Sandy, it's Jessie, I need to talk to you," but nobody picked up.

I saw the gated garage was hanging open, so I ducked inside. Partly I ducked in to get out of the rain, and partly I wanted to see what I just felt sure I was going to see, if Sandy was in fact at home and just not answering his phone.

And, oh my God, there it was. I mean the rest of the garage was empty, except for a bicycle and a puddle of oily water off to one side. But there stood what had to be Sandy's car, a slate-gray rather than olive-green Element, an easy mistake to have made in the dark, with a license plate holder that read PAHALU MOTORS, containing no rear license plate.

"God," I said. I reached for my purse, for my cell phone, to call Chuck, but my purse, like my cell phone, like my jacket, were back at the station.

"Stupid," I said out loud. My own voice echoing off the parking garage wall could not quite conceal the sound of someone's boots clattering through that oily puddle behind me.

I only just started to turn when I was struck on the back of my head with something that felt like a club, and then I was facedown against the dirty wet cement, struggling to get upright again.

I opened my mouth to scream but I got hit again, and then the cold cement passed into blackness.

Chapter Eighteen

"I drove up to the station to apologize. For pressuring you. I was just too damn distracted with the whole Atlantis thing last night to think it all through. But this morning, downtown, I realized there was this whole big rift opening between us, all because as usual, I wanted to hurry things up. I like conclusions. I like the case solved. I do not like to wait. When I really want something I just get this kind of tunnel vision. I want it and I have to have it." He took a deep breath. "So, I'm sorry."

"You're forgiven," I said, thinking this was maybe not the time for an explanation, but Chuck went on.

"So, there I am, ready to come to you contrite, and who do I run into at the station—Jack. Of course I knew it was Jack, even though we were never formally introduced, because he was definitely the guy I'd seen you sing with at Lisa's place two years ago. The only difference was today, he wasn't hanging all over you—"

"Obviously not," I reminded him, but even that did not dissuade Chuck from continuing his monologue.

"He was hanging all over the chick from the front desk, but still. I said I was looking for you and the chick says you went out. Over to Sandy's place, be back soon, although soon was already half an hour earlier, and some idiot was playing a song that sounded like the guy had swallowed razor blades, and it was blasting on the speakers. And Jack starts singing along, I admit he has a much better voice than whoever it was who was actually singing, and then they both started laughing, and I didn't like it. So I make the girl give me Sandy's address, 'cause I didn't feel like waiting around and listening to Jack laugh. Not sure what you saw in him. Pretty boy. Can't throw a punch."

"He threw a punch?"

"Self-defense, I'm sure you'd call it technically, because I pushed him up against the wall and was, just for the heck of it, and the mood I was in, ready to cold-cock the son of a bitch. I asked what he was doing there at the station and then he started babbling on about how oh now he knew why you wanted the key so bad, the new boyfriend, that was me, right, the tough guy?

"And then the girl at the front desk, she gave me the address, so I let old Jack go, and as I'm walking off straightening my shirt, I hear her say, 'You believe, that's the guy rumor has it Jessie's in love with?'

"Felt pretty good, I must say, walking over here—until I pressed Sandy's buzzer, no answer, thought I heard a moan down in the garage, and found you all tied up like this."

At last he had me completely untied; I was no longer a captive audience. I'd had a rope tied around my feet, wound between my legs to the front tying my hands, wound back around in a kind of noose around my neck. It was lucky I hadn't been strangled, and maybe I would've been, except whoever it was that had me tied up, and stuffed me unconscious in the back of Sandy's Element, had left me like that upon hearing Chuck walk into the garage.

I had rope burns and pressure marks on my wrists and I knew it could be a lot worse, so I wasn't complaining, even if my head hurt in two places.

"I'm so glad to see you," I said, and I threw my arms around Chuck now that they were free, because I was glad to be alive as well as to see him, and because I realized that if I wasn't still alive I would never have been able to say, "I do love you, very much."

"That's good, that's very good," Chuck said, and beamed at me. "Because I love you, too. I think I fell in love with you the first minute I held you in my arms, no matter how crazy that sounds."

"I felt that way, too, and I thought I was crazy—"

"Maybe we both are," Chuck admitted. "But it's because I love you so damn much that I wanted to drive to Las Vegas yesterday and marry you."

"And I just didn't believe—"

"That I really felt the things I feel for you. Yeah I know, I can see how that could be, if the last guy you were serious about was Jack who's not back. Stupid name for a band. I heard them once too, at Toe's Tavern down in San Pedro. Used to like to watch the container ships come in and then go have a beer. That band single-handedly turned me off that pursuit."

"I used to watch the ships come in myself," I said.

"When the band got too awful, I started walking down to the docks. In fact, I found my cat Squeak there."

Chuck helped me down from the back of the Element and brushed some of the garage floor detritus off my jeans. He tried to rub a spot of oil off my cheek, but it streaked. He didn't seem to care. He leaned in and kissed my lips tenderly. I kissed him back.

"I love you," we both said at once.

"You know, some people make that kind of declaration over candlelight, champagne, and roses," I said. "In some place like Paris."

"But not us," Chuck said, kissing me longer, deeper this time. "We'll always have this parking garage."

I managed a laugh in spite of my throbbing head.

Chuck stroked my hair gently. "Did you get even a glimpse of whoever nailed you?" he asked.

"No. Except I don't think it could be Sandy. I know this is his car and all but—the attack was sudden. Sandy lumbers, he doesn't spring. I heard a footstep—and then wham."

"Whoever it was went out through the laundry room," Chuck said, surveying the garage.

He crossed to the laundry room and kicked the door open, gun in hand. I followed behind him, warily. A single light bulb burned from the ceiling, and the washer and dryer were both running. Chuck opened them both, like he thought somebody or something could be hiding inside, other than some grubby-looking towels, scary-looking Speedos, and a pair of bunny slippers.

Behind the dryer there was a window, high up. The window was open and rain was spattering in.

"Sandy would be too big to fit through that window, too," Chuck noted. "Still, we'll start with him. I'd call in some more of the cavalry, but since technically I'm still on vacation, I think we'll handle this ourselves."

"Okay," I said, but I felt wobbly, and I leaned back against the dryer.

Chuck looked me over, concerned. "You don't look so good."

I knew that. I tried to run my fingers through my totally tangled hair, but it wasn't working. And now I wished I'd at least put on a decent T-shirt that morning.

"Maybe we should get a paramedic to look you over."

"I'm not leaving you," I said. "And I don't need a paramedic, I need a trip to a hair salon. So quit faking it, buddy. Besides, you might need someone to watch your back."

"The way you could've used me watching yours?" he asked.

As a response I put my arms around his neck and kissed him again. That seemed to satisfy him.

Then Chuck walked us out of the garage and around the back of the building, to the alley that abutted the laundry room and the knocked-over trash can on the street onto which my assailant apparently jumped. No cars, no shadows, no footprints, just rain and a soggy box that once contained pull-up diapers.

We left the alley and circled to the front of the building again. Conveniently for us, a withered-looking man in a yellow rain slicker was just coming out of the building, and Chuck pushed his way inside the courtyard after him.

"Hey," the guy said.

"Police," Chuck said, and sort of the way he said

it would have brooked no argument even if he hadn't been flashing his badge.

"Know which apartment is Sandy's?" Chuck asked me.

I shook my head. He had to go back out front, me holding the door so we wouldn't get locked out, and look for Sandy's name on the mailbox slots.

Then Chuck led me around the U-shaped court-yard, landscaped with bedraggled birds of paradise, to a back-corner apartment more or less right over that laundry room.

And Chuck didn't even bother to knock. He just kicked in the flimsy door, on which was flapping a tiny plastic surfboard secured to a nail. "Police," he shouted out by way of introduction.

Inside, the lights were off, and the living room into which the front door slammed open was dim and still and almost as musty as Sandy's office, with-out the leak.

Like the office, it showed its owner's predilection for recording industry accoutrements and tropical beach kitsch, pack-rat division.

A surfboard hung, sort of arty, from the ceiling, a surfboard-shaped throw rug was in front of the sofa. Cheap carved tikis from thumbnail to arm size crowded Ikea shelves on one wall. Magazines, CDs, tapes, and old LPs were stacked on the floor. Some were on the floor but not stacked. To be charitable, it could've been that someone had ransacked the place.

Behind the sofa, covered with what looked like two big beach towels, the dining room table held the congealed remains of a meal, and half of a pie on a serving plate.

In the kitchenette, there was a pie still in a box—

a red, white, and blue box with Benni Cardell's campaign flyer taped to the cover. There was also a mess of flour and water congealing in a metal mixing bowl, a bunch of broken eggshells piled in the sink.

More shocking than anything that had transpired so far today was the possibility that Benni was baking in my program director's kitchen.

Last but not least we hit the bedroom. Here, behind a closed door, the apartment's gloom became full dark. Here, the stacks of records and magazines and newspapers formed towering columns, almost obscuring a view of the bed. Here, on the bed, eyes wide, Hawaiian shirt bunched up around his chest, was Sandy. He was trussed just like I'd been trussed, only more trussed than that, and his hands were handcuffed over his head to the headboard, his mouth gagged firmly. All he could do was make his eyes wider and thrash around a little bit, making his shirt crawl up even higher.

Chuck snatched a knife from the kitchen and I found a pair of scissors in the bathroom, and we got to work on the knots and ropes. With the gag out of his mouth, Sandy wouldn't shut up.

"I have to pee so fucking bad," he said. "Will you please hurry it the hell up because she was only allowing me to get up once in the morning and once at night and it is what, two P.M. now and she gave me a beer with breakfast, I think it was part of the torture, the unrelenting torture. Did you really think I'd bail on a meeting? No way! And I heard, she put the radio on, I heard what a hash you made of my show, Jessie."

"Hey," I said, still sawing at his bonds.

"Okay, I should be glad you're here I guess, we can critique your on-air performance another time, but—hurry up!"

Chuck got Sandy unbound enough at last that he could offer a kind of ersatz chamber pot, a.k.a. a Tupperware container, and I discreetly looked away.

"Ahh. Better but not perfect," Sandy opined.

Chuck carefully disposed of the Tupperware container's contents in the bathroom.

We finished with the rope removal, but we couldn't do anything about the cuffs, which still held Sandy fast to the headboard.

"Best I can do for now," said Chuck.

"Only *she* has the key," Sandy said. "That horrible witch!"

"Who're we talking about," Chuck asked, "before I call the local cops and a locksmith?"

"Your friend." Sandy waved a hand in my direction. "She's nuts, you know."

"Lisa?" Because Lisa was my only friend, except for Chuck, my cats, and his dog.

"Benni!" Sandy said. "You are dim! That is why I cannot trust you to handle an all-requests show. Were you this dim when I hired you?"

"Benni Cardell isn't my friend," I said, ignoring the usual Sandy tirade.

Chuck didn't ignore Sandy's bluster. "You aware that you're still manacled to your own bed, bubba?"

Sandy managed to tone it down a notch. "Well, Benni *said* you were her friend, and I believed her. I mean, why else, if she was also your competition for public office, would she come to your fundraiser? I mean why else, unless she was nuts, which she is," he amended. "But I didn't know that. She seemed perfectly nice, and if not exactly the super hottie of the month. Well I'm not exactly all that myself, and I liked that she seemed to think I was. She said I couldn't come to her place because of her children. Grown-up and moved away or not, her kids keep an eye on her, and besides, the neighbors might see us, and it would play hell with her reputation. As a nut, I guess. So anyway, I brought her here. I thought, hell, why not, could be lust at first sight, at least on her part."

Chuck and I exchanged a brief smile. The smile made my head throb again and it turned into more of a wince.

Sandy was silent, brooding. "It was fun at first, I'll admit."

"What was?" Chuck prompted him.

"Well, she fed me pie, and she kind of seduced me more or less. And then I kinda passed out, I think there was something in the pie. That was not just a sugar rush I was experiencing."

"No?" Chuck prodded.

"I've been out of it, I don't know, days? Last Friday I met her. This is what?"

"Monday," I said.

"—She'd disappear, I'd be asleep. She'd come back she'd—well, seduce me all over again and feed me, and let me take a shower, and it was all like I was sleepwalking, and then she'd tie me back up again! I was like powerless against her. Oh, man, it got weird sometimes. I mean she did some kinky stuff."

"Well," I said, clearing my throat, hoping to preempt any further discussion of the kinky stuff.

"But you liked this—er—relationship at first?" Chuck asked him.

"Let's be real, man," Sandy went on. "The pies and the drugs and all the kinky stuff, it *was* fun. Or it was before I realized the time going past and the way she'd just leave me alone all tied up, and then she makes me, *makes* me call in and cancel my own show! Makes me call *you* of all people. No offense, your eclectic taste is not my eclectic taste!"

"How did she make you?" I asked. "She withhold a BJ from her favorite DJ?"

Chuck raised an eyebrow at me, but I just wasn't buying that big Sandy couldn't have bested medium-size Benni in four days. No matter how adept she was at hog-tying and hitting somebody over the head from behind and drugging pies.

Sandy ducked his head, a little embarrassed, although nothing else seemed to have embarrassed him up until that point. "She threatened to torch my signed Brian Wilson poster. And—and smash my LPs, and some of them are real collectors' items, and I believed her. She would've just used that big rolling pin of hers, same one she used to beat up on me."

"A rolling pin," Chuck and I said together. Not true Vulcan mind-meld stuff, since we'd both been smacked with a heretofore unidentified clublike weapon.

"I couldn't let her mess with my collection, man. And I couldn't see what harm there was really in letting you sub for me, either. She said she just wanted me all to herself." He frowned at me and his voice rose a notch, involuntarily. "You have no respect for classic rock, do you?"

"There was a lot of harm in going along with this woman," Chuck told Sandy. "As in 'aiding and abetting' harm."

"Aiding and abetting her in what? In some S-and-

M flavored goings-on in my bedroom? Puh-leeze. Even at the most threatened, I had every reason to believe she'd just stop fooling around and we'd get on with our lives. Until last night, anyway."

"What happened last night?" I asked him.

"She came back here in a real bad mood, 'cause she'd missed the debate and didn't even want to do me"—he coughed, but I was already looking away— "do me up a blueberry pie. I don't know how to explain our relationship. But the pies—I'm gonna miss those pies."

Sandy admitted easily that he'd waited for Benni in his Element the night of the fund raiser behind the coffee place on 190th Street.

"She was coming home with me. I mean the girl I brought—twenty-three, great bod—to Jessie's so-called event, it bored her so much, she left."

"My *event* bored her. Yeah, that must be why she left," I muttered under my breath.

"So why were you waiting for Benni by the Java Hut?" Chuck asked.

"She wanted to pick up some stuff at home, so I dropped her off nearby and she told me to wait for her in the parking lot. Like I already said, she didn't want her kids, or any of the neighbors, or as she put it, "campaign spies," seeing her, a soon-to-be-public servant, a mother of four, a ten-year-term PTA president, going off with a 'raffish young music industry executive.' You can see how when she put it that way it really worked for me," he said.

"But she didn't pick up something at her house. She broke into mine," I said. "Or really she didn't break in. She had my key. The key Jack gave you to give to me."

"Oh yeah, the key," Sandy groaned. "I guess she kept it, huh?"

"I guess so," Chuck said. "But how did she get it in the first place?" Chuck was looking like he wished he'd withheld that Tupperware container.

"From me." Sandy groaned even louder. "You *are* going to hold me liable or something, aren't you?"

"Depends how she got it from you," Chuck said.

"Well, your stupid key fell out of my pocket, and Benni picked it up. That's all, folks. Really."

"You just let her keep my key."

"Oh, for God's sake. Benni asked me about it, was all interested 'cause the key ring had the name of your local small-town mayor dude or whatever, and she wondered if I knew him. I told her I had no idea who the guy was, it was your key. You were up on that stage giving some kind of speech and I wanted to leave already. So Benni said she knew how forgetful men could be, and she'd take it on herself to give it back to you, seeing as you were practically neighbors and best friends and all. Okay, so she was lying, she was nuts, but how did I know that?" Sandy asked irritably.

I believed him. Besides, how mad could I be at Sandy anyway? He was still my boss, and he was still manacled to his own bed.

"Okay, so that's the key story," Chuck said. "And you've told us why you were waiting for Benni, but that doesn't explain why you almost ran me over that night."

Sandy sighed. "She came running in my car, like exhilarated about something, and she said 'Let me drive, big boy,' so I did. And she tore out of that parking lot I will admit like the proverbial bat out of hell, but I also have to admit that I admired her recklessness. And her weirdness. She said she had to get out of Dodge fast, before her grown-up children and her grown-up children's friends all saw her behaving so irresponsibly. I didn't think she was actually trying to hit you. She was just driving a little fast for a wet night. I made her slow down after a while. I know it was sort of dangerous."

"Especially for us," I pointed out.

"She was fun." Sandy sighed. "She really was. More fun than any of the younger, hotter, saner women I've had, and I have had plenty," he assured us.

Chuck rolled his eyes. "One last question. That license plate holder of yours. Where'd you get it?"

"Off eBay. I wanted one that read 'Down in Kokomo,' but that already sold. Thought this one was pretty cool though. People would think I bought my rig on the islands. Damn thing never did fit the car quite right though. Rear plate fell out of the holder, DMV wants a couple hundred bucks to replace it.

"Still. You know what else I got off eBay? Every single one of those Tiki heads on my living room wall. Benni liked them. I think she genuinely liked them. Genuinely liked me, too. Just nuts, that's all. I don't want to file charges or anything against her, and what would I file exactly, that this woman terrorized me with a rolling pin? Forced me to take drugs and eat pie? But it would be a mistake to let her come near me again. Maybe I could take out a restraining order or something? Even if I will miss . . . certain things," he finished wistfully.

"I bet she's already on her way out of town," I told Chuck, when Santa Monica PD arrived and took over for us with Sandy.

"I bet she isn't," Chuck said. "So she had a close escape today. It's not her first hasty exit. We didn't actually catch her in any of these acts. You had no idea who attacked you. And now it's just her word against that of a guy who lives in an apartment filled with termite-chewed Rolling Stones and Tiki heads."

"But we've seen her—we saw—" I stopped.

"A guy. In a hoodie. That's how your downstairs neighbor would describe her, too."

"She wielded a rolling pin."

"We think she did."

"Well, if we're right, I bet there's DNA evidence on that."

"If we can find the right rolling pin," Chuck said. "Just think how great it'll look if I confiscate a whole bunch of rolling pins with nothing on them but flour."

"So you're telling me we can't nail her?"

"We'll nail her. I just don't think we're ready to nail her today. I'll have to do a little surveillance first. But I'm good at that. Even if Benni isn't quite as pleasing to the eye as your average call girl ring."

Chuck was, I could tell, a little bit disappointed that it wasn't Ned and Royal he could nail after all, but he'd settle for Benni. Especially as she was the one who tried to kill us and everything.

We drove over to Lisa's club to fill her in and find Dave, who wasn't answering his cell phone. When we arrived, the door was open, wide open, like Lisa was giving the place a good airing-out.

I stepped right inside, but Chuck put a hand on my shoulder and I knew enough to step in behind him this time. He had his gun out again, and I saw that was a good idea when I got a look at the bar.

It was covered with pies.

* * *

Chuck proceeded me around the bar, behind the stage, into the kitchen, scene of happier times with a whipped cream container. And then, following the murmur of voices, we entered Lisa's office.

There, Lisa, Dave, and Benni were seated around Lisa's desk chatting pleasantly. There were a couple more pies on Lisa's desk, which had slices cut out of them. I'd never thought seeing a slice of lemon meringue would leave a cold jab of fear in my heart.

Chuck dropped his gun to his side but didn't put it away.

All three evinced surprise to see us.

"Well, hello there," Benni said unctuously, a vision in a pink flowered shirt and matching hot pink stretch pants. "I guess you caught us in the act."

She gave me a meaningful look, meaningful enough that I actually blushed. I blushed over my own make-out session in a parked car with Chuck, as if I were the guilty one here, not the kidnapper and attempted murderer, or, depending on what really happened to Conway Marcus, the actual murderer.

She laughed her raspy laugh and smiled her tight-lipped smile. "Yes, ma'am, caught us in the act of tasting, ha."

Dave stifled a belch.

"It's not what it looks like," Lisa said, springing up hastily. "I've told Ms. Cardell that no matter how many delicious samples she drops off, until the election is over I can't stock her pies."

"I was against keeping this place in business," Benni said, still smiling, "but I have to say that I realize that was a counterproductive, counterintuitive

way to go. I mean this is a perfect venue for my
baked goods. And why, when I would be so much
better equipped to serve the community than you,
continue to encourage your presence in this race,
Miss Jessie, by acting against the only institution
you have any interest in whatsoever. Even if I do
support rezoning, I could always issue this club a
variance."

"So you're saying you'll support Lisa's club if I
slip out of the race and leave you to win," I said.

"I'd even put it in writing. Let me tell you, I know
people in local high places. I could get this place its
obviously well justified landmark plaque, and no
one will go after it again. Not even me, ha ha. Assuming of course Lisa here will be kind enough to
admit I have the best baked goods on the planet."

Benni was looking past my shoulder at Chuck,
and clearly his presence and that of the gun in his
hand made her nervous. "Why is your—uh—
weapon—unsheathed there, Detective?"

Chuck made no response.

"I've told Be—Ms. Cardell—that there is no way
you'll be withdrawing from the race. Despite all the
nastiness that's been going on," Lisa said, but I
could tell from her voice that she actually thought
it might not be that bad of an idea.

I scowled at Benni. "Of course there's no guarantee you'd win even if I did withdraw," I pointed out.

"Well there's a *practical* guarantee," Dave said.
"According to Ms. Cardell here, our polished pro
Ned Rutkin has something to hide."

"Really?" I asked innocently. "What could that
be?"

Benni turned opaque eyes to me, but I got the
feeling she was more interested in the effect her

words were having on Chuck and his big manly weapon than on me.

"Well, your friend here knows a lot of it. He's dug up dirt same way I have. About Mr. Garritty and Mr. Rutkin and their various business associates. And I know how to use that information to get them out of the game, so to speak. Which is the same thing your friend wants, I believe. Only I come to the fray with a spirit of community building rather than a tearing down. I think it's a male-female difference, don't you?"

"Maybe so," I said.

"Mr. Rutkin is very professional about his business relationships, and any closely held corporations are held by other less close corporations, so he is a slippery little devil, and then he has all those PR firms working for him and Century City legal types. But amusingly enough, the one connection you can make quite easily, even though he acts as if he is so high and mighty in comparison, is between Neddy and Mr. Garritty, through their mutual interest in one or two business ventures. A business stickier in its own way than any a honey toffee fluffer nutter pie. That's marshmallow, toffees, honey all crumbled together with graham crackers. It's very good." She smoothed her hair behind her ears. "Honestly, the only candidate around here, and I mean no offense to you, but you're not really very political, are you, Jessie? The only *real* candidate around here with a clean slate is myself, unless you count poor little feeble Ida, and no one can count on her for anything other than being depressing."

"You have a clean slate?" I widened my eyes as if with surprise. "Despite your habit of leveling threats at people?"

"Threats? Now who have I threatened? You mean because I bake such good pies, that threatens somebody?"

"Well, there's Royal Garritty for one," I said. "You threatened him."

Not even a shadow of doubt crossed her face. "I would never threaten him," she insisted.

Chuck gave a tight smile. "I imagine you researched some of the same data I did and discovered Royal has some unsavory business partners who might not have known about Royal's political aspirations."

"Speculation killed the cat." Benni laughed. "Isn't that how it goes?"

"And they didn't like having any light shown upon them, and so ultimately, the big threat came from Royal's partners, not you," Chuck went on, as if she hadn't even spoken.

Benni laughed again. "I would so surmise that's why he stepped out of the race. I mean when you lift up a stone and worms come crawling out, well, goodness. You've summed up rather well, I suppose," Benni said. "But you make it sound so hard of me. And I'm not that way at all. I only want the best for people. Franklin D. Roosevelt wanted a chicken in every pot? Well I just want a good pie in everybody's oven."

"What about Royal's business cards? Should they be in everybody's car?"

"Why, Royal left a whole box of those cards on Tad's check-out counter. I saw them there when I delivered my promotional pies. If some of those cards ended up in Tad's car, well, anyone could have dropped a handful on the seat. Tad himself."

"Of course," I intervened. "You'd never do

something like that. We know there isn't a hard, mean bone in your body. If people say something mean, after all, it's like ripping a hole in a feather pillow and all the feathers come out and you can't stuff them back in. You told me that when we met, the night of the first debate."

"Well, yes I did," Benni beamed. "One of my favorite sayings. A wise man said that to me—"

"Was it Sandy?" I asked.

She looked blank.

"You know, the dashing young music executive you were too busy trussing up to attend the last debate?"

Benni leaned forward in her chair. Her eyes lost that opaque quality and became hot and wide. I had the feeling that it never occurred to her before that Sandy might not be completely in her thrall. "What sort of slander are you spewing about a private relationship?"

"You wanted to truss me up as well," I said, undeterred, "Sunday afternoon, right? When you thought I'd be alone at the studio. Unfortunately for you I wasn't alone then, but today you got lucky." I stretched out my wrists, which were rubbed red and raw.

"Oh, what happened?" Lisa cried.

Now Dave had a weapon in his hand, too.

Chuck gave him an almost imperceptible nod, and then Dave was out of his chair and he had one of Benni's arms in his large, capable left hand, and Chuck had Benni's right arm.

"You're under arrest," Chuck said, and began with the Miranda. "You have the right to—"

"What in the world am I under arrest for?" Benni

asked, and she began to struggle, somewhat effectively, to break their grasp on her.

Chuck cuffed her, and you could almost see the feathers flying out of Benni's virtual pillow then.

Benni was flabbergasted. "How dare you! You've never seen me do a single thing wrong!"

"But we've all heard you," I said. "Those threatening phone calls. I admit, up until just this minute, I thought it was a guy making those calls."

"And now you think I called you and threatened you in some way? Why do you think that? Do I speak in a man's voice?" Benni balled her handcuffed fists.

"At the station we have all sorts of cool little things we can do through our mixing board. Sound effects, echo effects, voice distortions. Some of those things are pretty simple. The kinds of things you can do with, say, just a cheap Karaoke set. Which you actually *told* me you owned, and would love to bring down here to Lisa's club."

"Prove it," Benni snapped, and for the first time I noticed the reason for her tight-lipped smile. Behind it were rather large, wolfish teeth, the kind Mrs. Palazo, former dental hygenist, noticed on the guy who broke into my apartment.

"We will," Chuck said, sharply. "The police lab is already analyzing a recording of your voice. And we're not just talking about threats, or even assault and attempted assault. Conway Marcus is dead. And according to Jessie's boss, you seem to know how to drug a piece of pie pretty well. I wouldn't mind getting a glimpse inside your medicine cabinet. And comparing whatever I find there to what the medical examiner found in Mr. Marcus's blood sample."

Benni's mouth opened and closed again.

Chuck shrugged. "Now, let me finish with the Mirandizing, Ms. Cardell."

She let him finish with the boilerplate, and then she spoke, wrathfully.

"I'm a martyr," she said, "to this town. I sacrificed myself for this community! I had all the tools I needed to win this campaign, and then you show up. Jessie the political naif. You were the straw in the straw poll that broke this camel's back. You forced me into action! I've always had the very best intentions. I still do. And people will know that, no matter what you have to say against me. People know me and they love me and I make a damn good pie, too. You'll never take that away from me."

Chapter Nineteen

"Apologies, Jackson," Chief Little said. He said it stiffly, and he certainly wasn't ready to hug Chuck or even clap him on the back or anything, but still. "Not that I'm condoning your recent attempt to use the press to put pressure on this department. Not that I am condoning your disrespect to a superior officer. I could have you removed from your position for both of these offenses. Twice over."

The apology part was getting lost in the shuffle.

"But, grudgingly, I must admit you had insight. To see my friend and the mayor's, Mr. Rutkin, involved in a business relationship with Mr. Garritty that is in part funded by associates of the so-called new drug mafia, here in our own pleasant little town, why, it's shocking. To see such things is to be grateful for a watchdog such as yourself, however insubordinate."

"Okay," said Chuck, who apparently really believed that brevity was the soul of wit, because then he laughed. "Our streets are safe again," he said, "for now. For someone else to gentrify up the a—"

The Dublin Five struck up an echoing chord

and what Chuck was about to say was lost in the rush of music.

We were all gathered in Lisa's club for a post-election party for the winning candidate.

It was an easy win. Benni was after all incarcerated while awaiting her mental health evaluation, which would not, I thought, be rosy. The drugged dessert she presented to Conway Marcus had, she confessed, been intended only to humiliate him into leaving the race during perceived public drunkenness, but intended or not, combined with his own alcohol intake, he'd died because of her. Tad, Royal, and Salome all had their own less lethal attacks perpetrated on them by Benni, and then there were the assaults she'd made on Chuck, Lisa, and I. Sandy refused to press charges, but willing or not, he'd be called as a witness. There was also a tampering charge against Benni.

It seemed she stopped by the city clerk's office to chat just after the filing deadline when she'd come across my campaign statement on Susan's desk, and took the opportunity to add her own verbiage to mine. That one was particularly easy to prove, as unlike her care in concealing her phone voice, she hadn't changed her handwriting in the slightest.

Ned, tainted along with Royal by the information Chuck uncovered about their financial backers and development schemes, was busily seeking legal counsel, too busily to involve himself in local politics after all.

Ironically, if Royal and Ned hadn't competed against each other for city council, it was a fair guess that their connection through Atlantis Development would never have been known. Pride had definitely come before their fall, and Benni's—maybe it was even civic pride.

With Salome and Tad withdrawn from the race, and reportedly working on a plan to bring convenience stores into a cooperative effort with legal call girl services in Nevada—a whole new level of convenience—it all came down to Ida versus me.

I waited until the band finished, and then I took a deep breath, flashed a big smile, and stepped up on Lisa's stage.

"Here she is," I said, "your new city councilwoman!"

There was tepid applause, and one lout who shouted, "Let the damn band play."

"Thank you for turning things over to me," Ida said, as I handed her the mike. "I know very well that without your concession I would not be serving this town."

"You'll be great at it, though," I said.

She put her hand over the mike and studied me, her gentle eyes suddenly intense. "You're certain you don't mind not winning?"

"I already have won," I said.

And I had. When your life depends on surviving both love and a political campaign, I've decided winning is only half the battle. Maybe conceding to love can be the sweetest victory of all.

The *Daily Sail,* by the way, had endorsed Benni. But they retracted their endorsement.

Lisa and I planned to use all my leftover yellow-and-black signs and posters to promote a concert at her club, with me as a headliner, not the emcee or a spur-of-the-moment opening act. I mean why not go for it, at least on the local level? The cable access guy was even willing to tape my performance, or at least my feet and my boobs.

And at last, the rain finally stopped. The sea grew more blue than gray, and we could go jogging on the Strand, right past Chuck's old apartment. Roofs stopped leaking, you could buy an umbrella for two bucks at Big Lots again, instead of paying premium prices at a department store. L.A. would never be the Islands, but it really wasn't so bad. We did have our palm trees and fish taco stands and the speedboat cruise around the harbor, which thankfully would not be turned into either a swamp or a mega-port. Nobody asked me to play "MacArthur Park" anymore, which was a good thing, because Theo melted both CDs in the conference room microwave.

There were jacaranda trees in bloom, littering the ground with their beautiful but sticky confetti. Under their purple canopy one afternoon, Chuck even fixed my car.

He was under the hood with a can of Bud on the engine block and Muddy Waters spilling out of the cassette player in my dash. Oh, well, so he hadn't been listening to my show. I'd just come home from the station, and I slipped up to him from behind and kissed the back of his neck.

"Thank God you're not Benni," he said without looking up from the engine. "You'd have me hog-tied on the ground by now."

"You know, I can almost understand how Benni entertained Sandy there for a weekend. I mean I sorta like the idea of using those handcuffs of yours and my bed and a dessert item or two. We never have gotten to dessert."

Chuck laughed, but he was still studying the

engine. I moved in beside him and took a hit of his beer.

"Sandy still not able to look you in the eye?" Chuck asked, adjusting something with a wrench.

"Not only that, he gave me a raise," I said, "and a paid week's vacation time. Paid!"

"I have another week coming myself," Chuck said. "Nonpunitive time off."

"There you go with those big words again that turn me on," I said. "Punitive. Very sexy. Anyway. Maybe we should use our vacation time and go to, I don't know, Hawaii," I suggested.

Chuck stepped out from under the hood and wiped his hands on a shop rag. "Get in the front seat and turn the key when I tell you, will you?"

"What's wrong with it anyway?"

"Wires were damp, you needed an oil change desperately, but the biggest problem was that some fool disconnected the distributor cap."

Jack, of course. Jack who'd been part of a life I had quite a long time ago, a month that might as well have been years.

I slid into my dusty front seat. "Waiting instructions," I said.

"Oh, wow. You are? You're not telling me not to tell you what to do?" Chuck was laughing now.

"I'm on hiatus," I explained.

"Turn the key now."

I did. The engine turned over.

"Hit the gas."

I did, and there was a pleasant zooming sound, like if I slipped the car into drive, it would actually go somewhere.

"Test drive time," said Chuck, grabbing his beer

and slamming the hood in one long swoop. He threw open the passenger door and climbed inside.

"Put her in gear," he said. "Let's go."

I did. Considering the age, previous lack of maintenance, and basic overall cheapness of my vehicle, the car practically flew down the street.

"Man, I thought this car was a lost cause," I said.

"Just needed a little lovin'," Chuck replied.

And it struck me that maybe I was done with the whole lost cause thing. Maybe all I needed was a little loving, too.

"You're good," I said.

"I know," said Chuck, pleased. He finished his beer and crumpled up the can. "Gotta hide the evidence. In case the po-lice stop you for speeding."

Speaking of police, I actually had one in the car. So I actually *stopped* at the stop sign, instead of pausing and gliding on through, as was my usual inclination. I stopped a little late and a little abruptly, so that Chuck slid forward in the seat.

"Get a grip, girl," he said, and he lifted one of my hands off the steering wheel. "Maybe even on me, later?"

I laughed.

He raised my hand to his lips, and he kissed my palm, and then the fingers, one at a time. I loved it when he did that.

"There's only one thing wrong with you kissing that hand," I said.

"Yeah? What?"

"There's no ring on my fourth finger."

He looked at me. His lips slipped from my pinkie.

"What are you saying?"

"I'm saying the next time you ask me to marry you, you should have a ring."

"You want me to ask again?"

I hesitated, but only for a second. "No. Actually I don't."

A frown creased his brow, and I hurried on. "Because right now I want to ask you. Will you marry me? Ring or no ring? Do you still want to?"

He didn't say a word, but I got my answer just the same. He kissed my lips and I kissed his, and it was a perfect kiss, like our lips were just absolutely made to melt together, and maybe they were. It was a perfect example of one of those times when the universe was utterly in balance.

So we drove back to my place still kissing, even as we parked my car and walked up the stairs. And Chuck opened our apartment door, and once our dog and our cats were fed, we went on into the bedroom and continued with the kissing and moved on into the necking and undressing, and then with the rest of it, the rest of our lives.

Say Yes! To Sizzling Romance by
Lori Foster

__Too Much Temptation

0-7582-0431-0   **$6.99**US/**$9.99**CAN

Grace Jenkins feels too awkward and insecure to free the passionate woman inside her. But that hasn't stopped her from dreaming about Noah Harper. Gorgeous, strong and sexy, his rough edge beneath the polish promises no mercy in the bedroom. When Grace learns Noah's engagement has ended in scandal, she shyly offers him her support and her friendship. But Noah's looking for something extra . . .

__Never Too Much

0-7582-0087-0   **$6.99**US/**$9.99**CAN

A confirmed bachelor, Ben Badwin has had his share of women, and he likes them as wild and uninhibited as his desires. Nothing at all like the brash, wholesomely cute woman who just strutted into his diner. But something about Sierra Murphy's independent attitude makes Ben's fantasies run wild. He'd love to dazzle her with his sensual skills . . . to make her want him as badly as he suddenly wants her . . .

__Say No to Joe?

0-8217-7512-X   **$6.99**US/**$9.99**CAN

Joe Winston can have any woman—except the one he really wants. Secretly, Luna Clark may lust after Joe, but she's made it clear that she's too smart to fall for him. He can just keep holding his breath, thank you very much. But now, Luna's inherited two kids who need more than she alone can give in a small town that seems hell-bent on driving them away. She needs someone to help out . . . someone who can't be intimidated . . . someone just like Joe.

__When Bruce Met Cyn

0-8217-7513-8   **$6.99**US/**$9.99**CAN

Compassionate and kind, Bruce Kelly understands that everyone makes mistakes, even if he's never actually done anything but color inside the lines. Nobody's perfect, but Bruce is about to meet a woman who's perfect for him. He's determined to show her that he can be trusted. And if that means proving it by being the absolute gentleman at all times, then so be it. No matter how many cold showers it takes . . .

Available Wherever Books Are Sold!

Visit our website at **www.kensingtonbooks.com**.